"In this profoundly beautiful and exquisitely ambiguous novel, Jon Raymond questions the opposition between the terrestrial and the celestial—between desire and virtue—while showing how we may hope to bridge them through love, friendship, and art. It is hard to stop reading *God and Sex* once you start. And it is impossible to stop thinking about the dilemmas it presents after turning the last page."

—Hernan Diaz, author of the Pulitzer Prize–winning novel *Trust*

ALSO BY JON RAYMOND

BOOKS

Denial

Freebird

The Community: Writings About Art In and Around Portland, 1997–2016

Rain Dragon

Livability

The Half-Life

SCREENPLAYS (WITH KELLY REICHARDT)

Showing Up

First Cow

Night Moves

Meek's Cutoff

Wendy and Lucy

Old Joy

God and Sex

Jon Raymond

Simon & Schuster
NEW YORK   AMSTERDAM/ANTWERP   LONDON
TORONTO   SYDNEY/MELBOURNE   NEW DELHI

Simon & Schuster
1230 Avenue of the Americas
New York, NY 10020

For more than 100 years, Simon & Schuster has championed authors and the stories they create. By respecting the copyright of an author's intellectual property, you enable Simon & Schuster and the author to continue publishing exceptional books for years to come. We thank you for supporting the author's copyright by purchasing an authorized edition of this book.

No amount of this book may be reproduced or stored in any format, nor may it be uploaded to any website, database, language-learning model, or other repository, retrieval, or artificial intelligence system without express permission. All rights reserved. Inquiries may be directed to Simon & Schuster, 1230 Avenue of the Americas, New York, NY 10020 or permissions@simonandschuster.com.

This book is a work of fiction. Any references to historical events, real people, or real places are used fictitiously. Other names, characters, places, and events are products of the author's imagination, and any resemblance to actual events or places or persons, living or dead, is entirely coincidental.

Copyright © 2025 by Jon Raymond

All rights reserved, including the right to reproduce this book or portions thereof in any form whatsoever. For information, address Simon & Schuster Subsidiary Rights Department, 1230 Avenue of the Americas, New York, NY 10020.

First Simon & Schuster hardcover edition August 2025

SIMON & SCHUSTER and colophon are registered trademarks of Simon & Schuster, LLC.

Simon & Schuster strongly believes in freedom of expression and stands against censorship in all its forms. For more information, visit BooksBelong.com.

For information about special discounts for bulk purchases, please contact Simon & Schuster Special Sales at 1-866-506-1949 or business@simonandschuster.com.

The Simon & Schuster Speakers Bureau can bring authors to your live event. For more information or to book an event, contact the Simon & Schuster Speakers Bureau at 1-866-248-3049 or visit our website at www.simonspeakers.com.

Book text design by Paul Dippolito

Manufactured in the United States of America

1 3 5 7 9 10 8 6 4 2

Library of Congress Cataloging-in-Publication Data has been applied for.

ISBN 978-1-6680-8491-5
ISBN 978-1-6680-8493-9 (ebook)

For Emily, again, always

It is just as when one looks straight at the sun. Afterward, everything has the image of the sun in it. If this is lacking, if you are not looking for God and expecting Him everywhere, and in everything, you lack the birth.

—Meister Eckhart

1

A book is round.

To a reader, it unscrolls in a single line, left to right, snaking down the page, wrapping onto the next, but to a writer, it turns more like a wheel. It rolls out of darkness and catches you up, trapping you inside its circle for a year or ten years, however long it takes. You move around inside it, back and forth, until finally it releases you, although it never really does, not entirely. You could say a book eats a writer many times. You could say it eats itself. In any case, to a writer, the idea of a beginning or an ending is absurd.

I don't know where this book is supposed to begin. It could be deep in the action or back in the prehistory, at the river or on the mountaintop; any of them would probably do. Many times, I've opened with the first moment I saw Sarah—cast from many angles, using many tones—and the last moment I saw her, but none have worked out. I've tried starting with dialogue, with the weather, and with quotations, but everything was too tight, or too ponderous, or too forced. All those beginnings felt like they were coming from up in my throat, not down in my body, where the better writing is born. Maybe in another writer's hands they could have become something, but for me, they all felt like carving into petrified wood.

Most writers would have given up by now, but I've kept on seeking. As a writer, I think that's what you do. You keep peeling back, you keep whittling. Eventually, maybe, you find the right phrasing. And then you move on to the next sentence and do it again. The next sentence often changes something in the sentence before, and you have to go back and start all over. Problem after problem, you try to solve it. What is writing but the solving of impossible problems?

Or like Suzuki said: Nirvana is to see a thing through to the end.

The next beginning I'll try is the day I met Phil. Phil, my teacher, my victim. Phil, my good friend. It's not the most dramatic moment in the story, but it's the one I have left, and that must mean something. Looking back, I can even see where it might be the true beginning after all. Maybe this was the moment the universe began talking to me, when the veil tore and the signs began coming through. Maybe it was the moment when God or the devil or whatever it was peered into my world and began laying its traps. Maybe this very intuition is a message from that entity. We'll see. I may not ever know for certain, but this time, at last, I'll obey.

It was the Tree Book that brought me to Phil. The Tree Book was my last book, the book following the Light Book, and, in a way, it was Phil's book, too. I can't think of the Tree Book without thinking of Phil and all the contributions he made. The Tree Book encloses our entire time together. So to understand how and why I met Phil, you have to begin there.

The Tree Book was a book I'd decided to write in the autumn I turned forty-one. I didn't know much about trees at the time, no more than anyone else, anyway, which might seem odd for a person on the verge of taking them as a book-length subject. But writing a book is never about what you already know. It's almost the opposite, in fact. It's about exploring what you want to know, what you suspect you might be unable to know. For many reasons, I'd decided I wanted to sit in a room for the next two or three years and contemplate the mystery of trees.

Most obviously, I felt like trees needed an advocate. Every year, humans destroy some eighteen million acres of them, or about thirty-six football fields' worth every minute. In a hundred years, that means we'll have no rain forests, nor most of the plants, animals, and birds who live therein. Everyone knows this already, but it seems important to say over and over again until the last tree is gone. The world is locked in a death spiral. Something must change.

The irony of writing a book in defense of trees didn't escape me, of course—a screed printed on their own, flayed skin—but as a writer of spirituality-cum-science texts, often with the aspiration of imparting some kind of deeper, mythopoetic worldview, I labor under the belief that even a small book has the power to change the pattern of humanity's consciousness. The way I saw it, the more the writers of the world could flood the collective mind with nurturing thoughts about trees, the more likely that we as a species could begin acting toward them in a nurturing manner. This faith in the power of written words to alter the shape of shared reality, and thus the path of history, is one of the premises of my creative life.

It helped that trees were becoming more popular in the marketplace of ideas. You could feel the tide of the book industry turning, exiting the long era of quantum spirituality books—all the tomes describing the wacky quarks and superstrings underlying the surface of everyday life—and moving into a more earthy discourse of trees and plants. People wanted books about the mycorrhizal network now, communication in the rhizome. They wanted books about the wisdom of the "mother tree" and the secret collaboration of mammals and insects with the vegetable kingdom. So there was a commercial impulse for writing a tree book, too. It was a way of attaching myself to the next conversation.

Most of all, though, I wanted to write a tree book because I believed trees had saved me. After the publication of my previous book, *Earth's Shadow*, the Light Book, I'd fallen into a serious depression. It was my fourth published work and the biggest failure thus far. Although the idea had seemed promising at the time—a compendium of theories about light through the ages, from the book of Genesis to Max Planck—and the writing had gone smoothly, if not joyfully, the reviews had been lukewarm at best. Not that there were many. And no invitations to read at festivals, or translations, or prize nominations, either. It's hard to express to most people the humiliation of a failed book, the pain appears so abstract and elective, but I can attest, it's very real. It plunges the writer into a cauldron of self-doubt, to the point where they no longer trust their own mind. You start hearing ghost conversations behind your friends' words and seeing cruel judgments in your absence from every podcast and year-end best-of list. You feel like you're walking around with your nerves exposed and dangling.

I ended up moving back to my hometown of Ashland, Oregon,

and taking up residence in my mother's house, under the assumption I'd never write another book again. My mom had moved away a year prior, heading to the East Coast to live nearer her gallery and collector pool, and the property needed a caretaker, so it was a beneficial arrangement for both of us. I'd always loved my childhood home. It was an elegant, cedar-shake ranch house, nestled among burly black walnut and oak, with big skylights and a lifetime's collection of art and books and funky tapestries on the walls. Off the back deck was an expansive view of the Rogue Valley, the ribbon of I-5 piping silent cars north and south, and the nearest neighbor was a hundred yards away. It was a house of great warmth, comfort, and privacy, and I could stay there rent-free as long as I liked.

Best of all, the property bordered a nature preserve stretching all the way to the Siskiyou Mountains. When I landed back home, I fell immediately into a new routine, waking up and making myself coffee every morning and heading directly into the forest of cedar and Douglas fir, maple and ponderosa pine, in hopes of getting as far away from myself as possible.

As soon as I got under the canopy, I felt more peaceful. The trees took me in. They didn't have any idea what a failure I was. They didn't know I hadn't earned out an advance in three books, or that my writing had never been anthologized, or that my publisher had sold off my paperback rights before the hardcover had even been printed. They just saw me as another animal walking in their shadows, sending out puffs of carbon dioxide to metabolize. I'd walk through the ghost fern, craning my neck at the branches above, watching the light filtering through the leaves, and for a few moments, forget the world of human ego and all its poisons. Under the boughs, breathing the musty scent of the Douglas fir and the sharp, tangy medicine of the sugar pine, I was able to remember, on the most basic level, that the universe was good.

I still remember the moment the idea for the Tree Book struck me. I was standing at the end of a trail, staring at a grove of cottonwoods shivering in the sun, the delicate triangles of the leaves swishing and spangling, and realized that I wanted to bring the trees inside me. I wanted to be a tree. What about a small, lyrical book in praise of trees?

I didn't tell anyone my idea at first. I was still too bruised from the Light Book to make that promise to the world. And besides, it wasn't anything yet, only the faintest, most formless intuition. But I started thinking about it on every walk I took. I thought about it quietly, tentatively, not wanting to scare it away. Was it something? I had no idea. It was too flimsy to withstand any pressure. Almost without acknowledging it to myself, I began reading books and essays that might relate to the subject and bookmarking occasional web pages. I started sketching the leaf shapes and the bark patterns of the trees I couldn't identify. I started thinking the word "tree" as I went around doing my errands.

Slowly, in silence, I was backing my way in. This went on for months. The thought came and went. I'd be raking leaves and start thinking about the decomposing litter sending its nitrogen into the earth. I'd be teaching a class at the local writing center and start staring at the branches of a red alder outside the window, wondering where the red came from and how it was concocted inside the alder's wooden veins. Always, I kept the idea of the book tucked in the back of my mind, like a seed warming in loam.

And then, one day, almost on a whim, I looked up the biology department at the local college, Klamath University. I was thinking

I might find an interesting syllabus, or news of an upcoming lecture, anything that might fertilize my ongoing rumination. I scrolled around the Environmental Science newsletter and tacked over to the faculty list, perusing their bios, until landing on the name Phil French. He was a forest ecologist, his paragraph read, with a few interesting-sounding publications to his name and some cool class titles. Genus and Genre sounded especially intriguing. It was cross-listed with the English department, which suggested some kind of literary bent. Without really thinking about it, I tossed off an email to him, saying I was a local writer considering a project about trees. Would he have any time to chat? He responded almost immediately, saying sure, swing by during office hours anytime.

And so it was, on a rain-soaked fall afternoon, that I found myself walking the carpeted hallway of the Klamath biology building, getting ready to share my secret idea with a stranger. I still wasn't sure it was a good idea, but time had already started doing its trick on me, and the anguish of the previous book's failure was gradually receding. The new idea was what I had now, and it was working insistently in my brain, filtering everything I perceived. I wasn't coming to him with any particular questions to ask, only the slimmest notion that he might be able to guide me somewhere interesting. He'd name an author or a text, and that would in turn lead somewhere else, and on it would go.

Most likely, I'd only end up exposing my own ignorance, but I didn't care. I didn't know this guy, Phil French. If he decided I was a fool, so what? Writing is a daily ego death. If you can't accept that, you probably shouldn't be trying.

I rapped on the door. From inside, a muffled voice came back, "Come on in!"

I pushed at the door and stepped into a long, narrow office space.

The walls were lined with books and a single, giant poster of a crosscut of a maple tree, with all the main parts labeled—xylem, phloem, cambium, crown. I couldn't read the finer labels because the lights in the office were off and the only illumination came from a big, rain-spattered window on the far side of the room. Watery light spilled onto a large metal desk piled with papers and yet more books. At the desk, sitting in the wan bubble, was Phil, grading papers.

I already knew he was a handsome man from his pictures on the web, but it turned out he was even better-looking in real life. He had broad shoulders and thick black hair, a hawkish nose, and high cheekbones. His skin was burnished from time spent outdoors, and his knuckles were fat and chapped from manual labor. In other words, he was nothing like the paunchy, balding, papery writer type who'd just walked into his office, with his soft palms and squinty eyes. In his crisp brown Pendleton shirt, Phil struck me a kind of modern lumberjack, but with the opposite purpose—a strong-jawed protector of the environment, a wide-chested Western Renaissance man, at home in the forest and the classroom alike. Already, he was smiling at me and sliding a pen behind his ear, generously waving me inside.

"Come in, come in," he said. "How can I help you?"

"I, uh, emailed a few days ago," I said. "I'm the local writer who was hoping for a little conversation . . ."

"Ah, yes, welcome!" he said. "Come on in. Great to meet you, Arthur. I'm glad you came by. Glad to talk."

I let my wet umbrella drop to the floor and hung my dripping coat on the rack. "I hope this is an okay time to visit?"

"This is an excellent time," Phil said. "My students are off doing labs. Next week will be busy. But today is great."

"What kind of labs are they doing?" I said, accepting the chair he offered across from his desk. Already, I was trying to make myself pliable, predicting his conversational cues. It was part of the job in the research-and-interview phase of a project. Before anything, you presented as nonthreatening. The more comfortable you could make a given expert, the more freely they would divulge.

"Nutrient cycling, nitrogen cycling," he said. "Basic stuff. They're out in the woods digging around right now. Perfect day for it. Nice and rainy and cold. They'll complain about it when we meet next week, but they actually love it."

"They have no idea how great they've got it," I said. "I wish I could go back to college sometimes. What a vacation that was."

"Free tuition for senior auditors," he said. "Once you're over sixty-five, you're welcome to join us."

"Something to look forward to," I said.

We politely chuckled at the non-joke. We were settling in, making each other feel at ease. We could already tell we were guys of about the same vintage and orientation, early forties, liberal, bookish. He was a lumberjack and I was a troll, but inside, we were on a similar wavelength. If we dug around a little, we might even find a few people and places in common. I knew he'd spent time in various California college towns; I'd spent some time in those places, too, adjuncting or prowling archives. I could guarantee we had similar opinions about the president.

To keep things rolling, I lobbed a few easy questions his way about his teaching load and sabbatical schedule, expressing as much wonder and delight at his answers as possible. I netted another little laugh or two, and when the vibration felt strong enough, not wanting to waste his time, I moved on to the business at hand, my still-forming book.

"So," I said, placing my palms on my knees to indicate a transition, "I got in touch with you for a reason, Professor French . . ."

"Please," he said. "Just Phil."

"Okay, Phil," I said. "Well, there's a project I'm thinking about starting that has something to do with trees. I'm still kind of feeling my way into it, but I'm wondering if I could maybe ask you a few questions, if that's all right."

"Of course," he said. "Whatever you like. I'll do my best."

"You'll have to bear with me, if that's okay," I said. "I'm still very early on in the process."

"I understand how things begin," he said. "Take your time."

I didn't have a particular plan of attack, but I assumed once we started we'd find our way. And sure enough, when I got going, I found myself almost overflowing with words. I opened by telling Phil a little about my previous books, which had all been essayistic, generally speaking, part memoir, part popular science, part polemic, part theology, a lot of things mixed together. The subjects had been elemental substances like water and light, or epiphenomena like rainbows, I said, and they usually got shelved in the spirituality section, although sometimes they ended up in other categories, too. They were spirituality, admittedly, but a little more sophisticated than the usual New Age pablum, I liked to think.

In this case, I said, I wanted to do something about trees. I wasn't sure exactly how it was going to work yet, but maybe each chapter would be about a different species. Or maybe profiles of people and their special relationships with trees. Or a census of trees in my neighborhood. I wasn't sure. I knew I wanted the book to be heavy on natural description, even lyrical at times. Not too academic, but not too commercial, either. I wanted it to feel relevant, but not too of-the-moment. I wanted people to walk away from it thinking about trees as fellow people in the world, with their own personalities, their own civil rights. That was my fantasy, to make people see trees in their full glory and magic and precarity. It was the first time I'd described the idea out loud to anyone, and it turned out I had a lot to say.

"It sounds wonderful," Phil said, after I'd started repeating myself. "It sounds like a book I'd like to read. I'm already sold."

"So right now," I said, sipping the peppermint tea he'd brought during my rambles, "I guess I'm just looking for source materials. Strange histories, odd treatises, obscure manifestos. Any out-of-the-way stories or images about trees that might add something to the mix. I thought you might be able to offer some guidance with that."

"That's a fun assignment," he said.

"I hope this isn't too vague," I said.

"No, no," he said, "just vague enough."

He tented his fingers and, for a moment, became almost performatively thoughtful. His thick eyebrows furrowed; his chin jutted. He nodded to himself a few times, parsing some initial ideas, discarding them, moving on.

Then he stood and drifted over to his bookshelf. He began browsing the spines. He was a graceful, well-formed man, but something about his bearing also seemed to neutralize that impression. It was the way he held himself, the excited foppishness of his gestures. His posture seemed to say: This handsomeness, let's not worry about it. Let's put it aside and talk like normal people do. Already, I was starting to like him.

"It sounds like what you're talking about is a florilegium," he said, caressing his chin.

"Am I?" I said.

"That's a collection of flowers," he said. "But also a collection of short writings around a given theme. The word 'anthology' comes from a similar root, *anthos*, or flower. It's interesting, isn't it? Flowers are somehow bound up with this kind of writing."

"See, that's exactly the kind of thing I'm looking for," I said. "That's already great. I might be able to use that." I had him spell the word for me and wrote it down in my little notebook.

"I don't have a ton to offer here in the office," he said, head tilted. "I have a lot more books at home. Mostly I keep the more nonscience stuff here. I try to impress these kids with the humanities angle. They're so uptight about their science degrees, so practical. I want to show them what the scope of environmental sciences can mean. But there are a few things I can suggest off the bat. Let's see, let's see..."

He reached up to a high shelf and came away with a thick orange paperback.

"There's always Yggdrasil," he said, blowing some dust off the top, "the tree of Norse mythology. Yggdrasil, the tree of creation. It's a cosmic ash holding nine worlds in its branches and roots. There's an eagle in it. And a dragon in the roots. It connects you to Asian cosmologies and shamanic traditions. There are a lot of ideas you can pull out of Yggdrasil. That's a tree with a personality."

"Interesting," I said, though I wasn't that interested. I knew Yggdrasil. Yggdrasil came up often in the current tree literature. It seemed a little played out.

"But maybe you don't want to write a book report on world religions," Phil said, detecting my lack of energy. He reshelved the book. "Or maybe you're looking for less-trod ground."

He went for another spine. "There's the story of St. Brendan. He discovered a tree where a flock of birds sings the liturgical hours in harmony. That's an interesting tree. But maybe too ecclesiastical for your purposes."

"I'm not huge on the major monotheisms," I said. "Unless it's the more apocryphal traditions."

"Ah, well, then this might be a good tree for you," he said, pulling another title. "More esoteric. The ympe-tree. This is a place where the human and fairy worlds overlap."

"Interesting," I said, and this time I meant it.

"It's the Eurydice story in Celtic drag," he said, riffling through the pages. "Orpheus becomes Orfeo. Hades becomes a fairy kingdom. In this telling, Heuodis—Eurydice—sleeps under an 'ympe-tre,' which is probably a cherry or apple tree. It's grafted, which means partly human-engineered, which is kind of interesting. The fairy king finds her lying there and drags her down to the fairy kingdom, where time stands still, and Orfeo has to descend and rescue her. He finds her sleeping under another ympe-tree in the underworld. So the ympe-tree is both the entrance into the fairy world and a tree inside the fairy world. A very bizarre mirroring. You could possibly do something with that."

"I've been thinking I'd like to write something about fairies," I said. "I'd love to read that book. What's the title?"

"Take it," he said, and handed me the book, *Premodern Ecology*. "I won't be using it any time soon. I had a feeling you might like that one. I just finished reading your last book, so I had a little head start on what you might be wanting."

It was always surprising when someone brought up one of my books, *Earth's Shadow* most especially. When they did, it was rarely in an unambiguously positive way. There was almost always some hidden knife in people's words. "I loved the cover." "The footnotes were quite well-done." Immediately, I was girding myself for the faint praise.

"I thought it was fantastic," he said without apparent guile. "I should've mentioned that as soon as you walked in, but I assume no one wants to hear a person's opinion about their book the second they meet them."

"If it's a nice opinion, they do," I said, which garnered another little chuckle from both of us.

"It was really fascinating," he said, returning to his desk. "And gracefully written. I was genuinely impressed. Such a fascinating premise, too. Light through the ages. I thought about light differently after I read it."

"That was the hope," I said.

"And the part about light as a living creature," he said. "What a beautiful thought. I hadn't really heard that idea before."

He was talking about the medieval chapter. Whenever anyone said anything complimentary about the book, it was usually about the medieval chapter. It turned out people loved the Middle Ages—anything involving secret illuminated manuscripts and flaming, stained glass, rosette windows, they ate up. I'd promised myself I'd always include medieval sources going forward.

"It was a pretty common concept in the ninth, tenth centuries," I said. "The solar mother, the solar nipple. Umbilical sunbeams. I mean, you know that; you read the book."

"It really got me for a second," he said. "I had to think about it. Is light alive? I mean, it doesn't excrete anything. It doesn't reproduce. And yet it gives life, so it must have some kind of life to give. I love that reasoning. It's very medieval, but it's hard to think around. I like to assign my classes Hildegard of Bingen every year. They're always amazed how relevant she is."

"Hildegard is great," I said.

"They call them Dark Ages," Phil said, "but they weren't really so dark."

"No darker than ours, I'd say."

We talked for another hour about the Middle Ages. It turned out Phil knew his Aquinas and his Augustine, his Scholasticism, and the full, wending path of the apophatic tradition. He could weigh in on the debates between Suger and St. Bernard regarding the relative divinity or blasphemy of stained glass windows. He wasn't a fan of Jan van Ruysbroeck, though he loved the title of his main extant writing, *The Sparkling Stone*, as I did. There weren't many people who could discourse on this level, which was fun, and the fact that he'd isolated the ultimate kernel of the Light Book, the very idea that I'd fallen in love with, the idea of light as a kind of amniotic fluid flooding the cosmos, seemed like an incredibly good sign. I'd stumbled on a certified forest ecologist who thought like a weirdo, mystical animist, like myself.

By the time his office hours ended, we'd agreed I'd come back for another visit. He'd already sent me a syllabus and a link to a documentary I might enjoy. We might have kept talking, but he had a faculty meeting to attend, and I accompanied him on the walk across campus. The rain was cold and pelting, pooling on the lawns, spitting from the gutters, rattling our umbrellas. As the administrative building approached, I started preparing to peel off and make myself dinner and possibly enjoy a celebratory bourbon with my night's bath.

"Thank you for all your time today, Phil," I said. "I usually wouldn't talk about a project this early at all, so thanks for letting me stumble through it. I really appreciate your patience."

"My pleasure," he said. "I don't get to talk about this stuff very often. And it's a good idea. An important idea. It's what everyone should be writing about all the time. Trees."

"I think so," I said.

"Actually, I have another little idea you can use," he said, "if you want it, anyway. It just occurred to me."

"Please," I said. "Lay it on me."

"I could never use this in an academic paper," he said. "That's the problem with peer-reviewed journals. All these ideas you can't use because there's no empirical evidence for them. So this is just a theory I have. It has to do with the lullaby 'Rock-a-bye Baby.'"

"Fantastic," I said.

"No one knows where the lyrics of that song come from," he said. "The tune starts to show up in sheet music in the eighteenth century, or thereabouts, but no one has any idea about the origin of the words. Some people think the Pilgrims wrote them when they first saw Indians attaching birchbark baby cradles to the limbs of trees. Other people think Davy Crockett's cousin Effie wrote them. Some people say they go all the way back to ancient Egypt and the baby is the god Horus. They can't find the source, no matter how far back they go.

"So here's my thought," he said, slowing his pace so our final destination was timed with his words. Up ahead, the safety lights of the main administration building blurred and spiked in the rainy gloaming. "What if it goes even further than that? What if it goes all the way back to our days in the trees? 'Rock-a-bye baby, in the treetops.' We spent our first six million years in trees. Trees were our original home. I like to imagine that lullaby as a remnant of our prehuman era. A memory of our monkey mothers in the branches."

"'Down will come baby...,'" I said. "Kind of dark."

"It's all dark that far back," he said.

"I love the thought," I said. "I bet I can find a place for it somewhere. I'll give you credit if I do."

"It's yours to have," he said.

Moments later, we parted ways, but not before I met Sarah. I barely remember the meeting, I was so blinded by my new source, so lost in thoughts about the Tree Book and all the hours of glorious labor ahead. If I plumb my memory, I can turn up the vaguest image—a shadowy figure in a raincoat, narrow wrists extending from too-short sleeves—but the picture might be a fabrication of retrospect. In any case, I'm told Sarah was standing at the door of the administration building, waiting for Phil. She'd misplaced a house key and needed to borrow his. They tell me that's the moment I first encountered Phil's wife.

2

That's one beginning, anyway. Every story has a thousand beginnings, a thousand places you might tip in. You could go all the way back to the beginning of the universe every time if you wanted to, map out all the branching realities that'd brought you to a given moment, but no reader wants that. Readers want beginnings with some kind of momentum built in and a few obvious clues as to where things might lead. They don't want every chicken and egg leading back to infinity.

In those days, I had no idea the story of Sarah and me was at its beginning. I assumed I was at the beginning of a completely different story, the story of the new book. That may not sound like much of a story to some, but to others of us, the writers, it's a story of major significance and suspense. It takes all a person's cunning and patience to write a book. In the beginning, you're trying to design a boat that won't capsize halfway across the ocean. You're laying in supplies for a yearslong voyage. It demands a kind of mental purification to make sure your motivations are correct.

The meeting with Phil was exactly what I'd needed to begin building my vessel at the water's edge. He'd thrown out a few stimulating ideas and suggested a few intriguing sources, but, most of all, he'd given me enthusiasm. The fact that a professional forest ecologist found my project interesting and even laudable was hugely encouraging. I was still far away from putting actual words on paper, but I felt like I was ready to start calling in my raw materials in earnest: buying more books, watching more online lectures, ordering the conceptual lumber that would eventually become my grand clipper ship of words.

I had a few more meetings with Phil over the next months, all of which were profitable sessions. We roamed freely and digressed easily. He wasn't above speculating at the edges of scientific reason, which I appreciated. I heard all about his theories of tree sentience, tree mind. The resemblance of the tree's bloom and root ball to the ganglia of the brain was not a coincidence, he thought. How could it be? The lobe, the branch, the whorl, they were the very signature of something or other. He taught me about the world of mosses and liverworts that had preceded our world of vascular plants, the giant mushrooms and fungi of the pre-tree era. He brought to the conversations the perfect balance of awe, logic, rage, and hope, I thought. Every time we talked, I came away with pages of scribbled notes and quotations.

"God loves a scale change," he said. That would go straight into the book.

I also wanted to find contemporary case studies to supplement the theoretical and historical materials, and Phil was helpful with that, too. I was looking for real-life examples of human/tree relationships, the kind of stories that would bring some living heat to the text. Phil suggested a bonsai master in Japan, the last of a centuries-long line, and a woman on a permanent pilgrimage around the American West who planted seedlings wherever she went. Both immediately became part of my store.

And then, as the winter started to taper and the first little minarets of the camellias began peeking into view, he emailed to invite me on a trip to the southern Cascades. He said he had a couple of friends doing regenerative work in a meadow on the north side of Mount Shasta; he thought I might be interested in checking out their program. They were working with trees, among other plants and shrubbery, and were fascinating, possibly visionary people. There might be something there for my book.

"They're kind of out there," he wrote. "But you might appreciate that."

"What are they doing, exactly?" I wrote.

"They call it 're-greening,'" he wrote. "Easier for them to explain. It's humble. But interesting. It might be something, might not. I don't know."

"Okay, I'm in," I wrote. "And thank you!"

That Saturday morning, under a low, chilly lid of clouds, I arrived at Phil's house, a sturdy Craftsman on a corner lot a few blocks from campus. I'd passed by it a thousand times in my life, never giving it much note, but on that day, suddenly, it became a place of significance—the home of my tutor. I had my backpack, with a water bottle and a brand-new notebook inside, and new hiking boots on my feet. I'd just climbed the steps, girding myself for a mountain adventure, when the door opened and Phil appeared, shirtless, waving me inside.

"Come in, come in!" he said. "Welcome! We're just getting things together here. Won't be long. Just hang out for a second. We're almost there."

I stepped into the fragrant warmth of Phil's domestic life. Two cats were asleep on the back of the sofa and clean laundry was piled on the dining room table. On the floor, there were bright Turkish rugs; on the built-in shelves, rustic outsider sculptures; on the coffee and end tables, antique lamps of oblong shape and citrusy glaze. There were books everywhere, mostly old, and above all else, house plants. Monsteras and ficas, a crazy jade, an origami-like purple shamrock, all flourishing. The house was a teeming jungle of art and life, the dwelling of clearly interesting people.

"Smells great in here," I said.

"Sarah made oatmeal cookies," Phil said, tucking a long john shirt into his Carhartt pants. "We're not going very far, but there isn't much food out there. We might get peckish. Hey, do you have gloves? You might want gloves. It'll be cold on the mountain."

"I've got gloves," I said.

"Great," he said. "And we can get ourselves more coffee on the way if you want it."

"I've had plenty of coffee already," I said.

"Well, I might need more," he said. "No greater pleasure than driving with coffee, in my opinion."

And it was then that Sarah entered the room. Nothing announced her arrival. There were no birds singing, no sunbeams streaming. She simply wandered from the kitchen into the dining room holding a Mason jar of lumpy cookies. By then, I'd heard a few things about her, in little asides and oblique references. She'd grown up in California, Phil had said. She enjoyed jogging. She didn't follow any prestige television shows. But my physical memory of her was bleary at best, more a suggestion than an actual image.

It turned out she was a tall, slender woman with wide shoulders and loose limbs coming to knobby joints and long, elegantly tapered fingertips. She had wild black hair and drowsy eyes and a very large nose. Her lips were full, the lower lip more so than the top, with a certain ironic smirk kinking the edges. Her skin was dusky olive, and she moved with a tentative, slightly pigeon-toed gait, but there was a certain gracefulness to her movements, too, like a heron's or a stork's. She seemed almost demure, but underneath that, I could already sense, she was more like coolly observant and wry.

"Hi, Arthur," she said. "Sorry the house is such a shithole right now."

Such were the first words I remember her speaking to me, as if we'd known each other for years.

"You should see my place. It's a lot worse."

"It honestly never looks much different," she said. "I might as well not pretend. Anyway, I hope it's okay if I come on the drive today. Phil's been talking about Merle and Candy for so long, I thought I should see what their deal is. Plus I really need to get out of the house."

"Of course," I said. "The more the merrier."

"Also, Phil's a pretty terrible driver," she said. "I have to watch him, especially in the snow."

"I'm a good driver," he said, lacing his boots. "My record is perfect. Insurance companies love me."

"That's what all the bad drivers say," she said. "They don't even know how bad they are."

"The truth is," Phil said, "Sarah is skeptical about Candy and Merle. She wants to meet them in order to prove a point."

"I'm not skeptical," Sarah said, mock affronted. "Phil talks about them so glowingly. I'm completely open to being amazed."

"You'll see," Phil said to both of us, donning a weather-softened leather fedora. "They're great. Anyone who finds a way to be hopeful in this world gets my vote."

"Mine, too," Sarah said, and disappeared back into the kitchen. Whether she meant what she said was impossible to tell.

We headed out. We took their Jetta, Sarah in the back seat and me in the front, and as we pulled off into the wintery air, heading south over the pass into California, we stuck to easy topics of conversation, the go-to complaints about Ashland, mostly. It was too cute, we agreed, too secretly uptight. The sense of moral superiority among its citizens was almost suffocating. There was no good pizza, either. By the same token, we agreed that the surrounding territory was even worse—a land of incels and secessionists driven insane by the Internet.

When the subject of our town had run its course, I started making inquiries into Sarah's life. Although on some deep level we already might have been entangled, on the shallower levels, I knew almost nothing about her at all.

"What do you do, Sarah?" I said, as the gray road rolled toward us.

"I'm a librarian," she said from behind my shoulder.

"You've been doing that for a long time?"

"About fifteen years."

"Sarah went to library school right out of college," Phil said. "It's the only job she's ever had."

"I've had other jobs," she said. "Ice cream scooper. Cheese counter girl. But this one is the longest, it's true."

"So you like it then, I guess," I said.

"It beats a lot of things," she said. "I might even love it. Yeah."

"And what library do you work at now?" I said.

"I'm at the high school," she said.

"Not for long," Phil said. "She'll be out of there soon. Sarah usually gets a job at whatever college we're at. They can usually arrange a spousal-hire type deal. But someone didn't retire this time. So it's taking longer."

"Doesn't matter," she said. "I like it at the high school. Teenagers are hilarious. I forgot. I get to hear everything about what's going on over there."

"And what are teenagers up to these days?" I said.

"Well," she said, pleased to report. "They don't wear enough clothes, that's for one thing. The girls seriously dress like prostitutes now. Tiny miniskirts and frilly halter tops and fake nails. And so much perfume! It's like they just walked out of a brothel, I swear. Toasted vanilla bean everywhere. And the crazy thing is they think it's empowering. 'My body, my choice.' 'Don't slut-shame me.' They have no idea what they're putting out there, though."

"And do you tell them that?" I said.

"God, no," she said.

"And what about the boys?" I said.

"Confused. Weird. I don't know. None of them can think because of their phones. I mean, it's actually incredible what they don't know. They don't know who Uncle Sam is. Never heard of him. I put up a poster the other day and they're like, 'Who's that guy in the stupid hat?'"

"But you like them," Phil said. "Some of the kids, anyway."

"Oh yeah," she said. "Some of them are great. There's this one girl, Elizabeth. Everyone talks about her. She crashed her scooter the other day and got a concussion. Then she did acid that very night! She's also having sex with her friend's boyfriend, Ronnie. And her other friend's boyfriend, Danny, too. She's a real mess. She's fantastic."

"What kind of books does she read?" I said.

"YA crap, mostly," she said. "Not a big reader."

"Don't you have to report that kind of thing to anyone?" Phil said, scowling ahead. "The drugs and sex and everything?"

"If I heard about her doing anything really bad, I'd probably tell a counselor about it," Sarah said. "But Elizabeth is just a kid testing boundaries. Nothing too scary. I'm keeping my eye on her."

"I think I'd want to know if my kid were doing some of that stuff," Phil said. "Wouldn't you?"

"Eh," Sarah said, and I could feel her shrug behind me. "I did a lot of things I didn't want my parents to know about at that age. It's all about becoming your own person. You have to make some of your own mistakes. That's my opinion."

"Sometimes kids want to be confronted, though," Phil said. "They want someone to take notice."

"Not really," Sarah said.

"Their brains aren't done developing," Phil said. "The prefrontal cortex—"

"I know, I know," Sarah said. "Planning, good decision-making. I know. But she's fine. It isn't anything too scary that she's doing."

"It's an important stage of development," he said.

"I don't regret any of the drugs I did as a teenager," I said, stepping in. "I don't think they hurt me at all. Granted, I might've been a genius if I'd been more careful. But I doubt it. I got a lot out of those experiences. Personally."

"Yep," Sarah said, and I could tell by the brevity of the syllable that she'd been one of the wayward kids, too, one of the kids who didn't believe what the grown-ups said, who'd had to find out everything for themselves. We didn't have to divulge any more.

"She's just bored is all," Sarah said in closing. "I can understand that. Anyway, these kids are living in a dying world. Let them have their fun. That's how I see it."

It was turning into a beautiful day, the cloud cover breaking apart into giant cauliflowers and hammerheads, throwing shadows onto the slopes of sugar and knobcone pine. Soon Mount Shasta appeared, and we peeled off into the foothills rising toward the timberline. The microecologies in the region were so drastic. In a matter of hours we'd passed from oak savanna, to mountain pass, to scrub canyons, to charred burn fields, and now into the volcanic draperies of conifer.

Around noon, we landed at our destination, an unremarkable clearing low on the mountain's hump, tucked on the side of a gravel service road. A green Harvester truck was parked at a faint trailhead leading into what one might call a meadow. We got out and mounted the low berm and stepped onto a field where thin, brown grasses spread between occasional shrubs and a few big-leaf maples and red firs. On the ground were wide patches of mud, along with thick streaks of ice and snow, the crusted remnants of winter.

In the middle of the meadow two people were staring at the earth. They were late-middle-aged, a little dumpy, a little grimy, well bundled in hats and scarves. The woman had plaited gray hair and a small, finely wrinkled face. The man was a shaggy giant, his loose clothes falling around his body like elephant skin. As we approached, they traded affectionate hellos with Phil, who introduced us all around.

"Merle, Candy, this is Sarah and Arthur," he said. "Sarah's been wanting to meet you guys for a long time. Arthur's the writer I told you about."

"Good to meet you," Merle said, shaking our hands. "You're writing a book about trees, we hear."

"Trying to," I said. "Thinking about it."

"Big topic, trees," Merle said.

"I'm still just finding my way in," I said. "Phil's been really helpful so far. He knows a lot about the subject."

"Phil's taught us a lot about trees, too," Candy said. "He's like an encyclopedia, isn't he?"

"Not as much as you've taught me," Phil said.

"He's also full of horseshit," Candy said. "But he's a nice guy. We like him."

"Before we get started," Merle said, "we wanted to ask you something. We have a little request, if that's all right."

"Of course," I said.

"We appreciate your interest in what we're doing out here," he said. "We're real happy if you want to get the word out. We just want to make sure you don't tell anyone exactly where this is. We'd like to keep this a secret location if possible."

"This is public land," Candy explained. "We're here at the pleasure of the Forest Service. A lot of herbalists, if they hear about a healthy, thriving patch of ground, they come pick it clean. Goldenseal, white sage, there's a big market for that stuff."

"They have decent intentions," Merle said. "They just don't know what they're doing in the big picture."

"That's totally fine," I said. "A secret location is great, actually. Even better."

"You're sure?" Merle said.

"Absolutely," I said. "Secrets are what make a book go."

A curious look passed over to Phil. The agreement seemed too easy. Merle only sort of believed me, and wanted Phil to guarantee my word. He did.

And so Candy began their full spiel. In this case, their story actually did go all the way back to the beginning of the world. Once upon a time, she recounted, this was an ocean planet, in whose Cambrian waters sponge spicules and worm tubes proliferated and evolved into things like mollusks and fish. Over time, landmasses emerged, and the fish climbed onto the dry land and became lizards and birds. Here in Northern California, the waters eventually receded enough that a band of mountains between the great basin and the fertile rain forest of the Pacific coastline appeared. Thus, the beautiful watershed of the Cascades and Sierra came to be.

For many millions of years, she said, all was well. The reptiles and mammals and fish and birds, even the human beings, got along fine. And then, only about two hundred years ago—two hundred years!—new humans arrived, white humans, who started destroying everything in sight. They rerouted rivers, leveled forests, strip-mined mountains. They killed anything they could put a price tag on. Then they invented the internal combustion engine and things really accelerated.

"In a hundred years," Candy said, "a single lifespan, the whole world got thrown out of whack. We've poisoned the air, spiked the rivers, turned the watershed into a desert. And now, here we are, standing on this ruined mountainside, staring into the abyss."

"They made the forest into a tree plantation," Merle said sadly. "Monoculture all the way down the line. All the trees in these sterile rows. Hardly any meadows left at all. Hundreds of millions of trees dead from drought and beetles, but no praying mantis to keep them in check."

"They never think about meadows when they're making their tree plantations," Candy said. "A meadow is the forest's negative space. It provides natural firebreaks. It sponges up the water to keep erosion from happening. Without a meadow, you don't have a viable system."

"This meadow we're standing in now," Merle said, "used to be a literal dump. People came up here and dropped off their washing machines, their old Christmas trees. But worst of all were the invasive species. Pampas grass. Cheatgrass. Scotch broom."

"Fucking Scotch broom," Candy said.

"So about ten years ago," Merle said, "we started cleaning it out. We started making trips up here on weekends and pulled out literally tons of debris. And then, a few years ago, we got permission to do a controlled burn. That was quite a bureaucratic feat."

"We burned out the saplings of the black oaks," Candy said. "We burned the invaders. And that nitrogen went straight back into the earth. The heat was exactly what the knobcone pine needed, too. We melted the resin from their seeds so they could pop out and germinate."

"We gave everything some space, gave it some air," Merle said. "Just gave it a chance to mellow out, basically. And as you can see, we managed to get it back to something more recognizable."

As they talked, they were touring us around, taking a meandering path from shrub to shrub. They pointed out the deer grass, home to wintering ladybugs; the milkweed, a habitat for monarch butterflies; the yarrow, good for medicinal clotting. They showed us the manzanita, the soaproot, the native flowering plants like curly dock. What had seemed an unremarkable plot was in fact a dense weave of interdependent life, no surprise.

"We've got tons of pollinators here now," Candy said. "Bird diversity is up eighty percent in the summer."

"We see bears, bobcat tracks," Merle said. "They like to come here and laze around. This has become a really prime hangout."

"And this is the coup de grâce," Candy said. We'd paused at a frozen patch of earth, a plane of ice mottled with encased stalks of grass. "The underground spring even came back."

We stared at the ground. It was just an icy patch of dirt. But to them it was a lot more, a miracle.

"It's pretty mind-blowing," Candy said. "We couldn't believe it when the water started seeping up again. It tells us the earth is healing down deep in her bones."

"The earth meets you halfway," Merle said. "More than halfway. When you do this kind of thing, the health multiplies. It spreads. What we're doing in this meadow is having effects all the way down the mountain chain. Down in Angels Camp, they're seeing birds reclaiming old habitats. They're seeing wind patterns changing, bringing back old cycles of pollen, old butterfly migrations. That's all from the meadow."

"This is a nerve ending of the world," Candy said. "We're doing earth acupuncture here, opening up larger channels. When you do that, big things happen."

For another hour or so, we hung around the meadow hearing more about their program. We heard about their lives, too. Candy had been the queen of the Chico punk scene back in the day. Merle had spent forty years as a lineman for PGE. They told us all about the rich lore of Mount Shasta, where many well-documented UFO sightings had occurred, and how the spacecraft often disguised themselves as lenticular clouds. They told us about the white-robed Lemurians who wandered the mountain's honeycomb of fur-carpeted caves, and about Chief Skell of the Klamath people, throwing hot lava from the crater, and Saint Germain and the other interdimensional ascended masters who occasionally appeared in the forest. They had a lot of interesting theories, those two, and they'd lived interesting tales. I could definitely see devoting at least a few paragraphs to them in the Tree Book.

It was midafternoon when we departed, and driving back home, the heater blowing, passing the cookies around, we did our debriefing.

"Well?" Phil said. "They're pretty cool, right?"

"For sure," I said. "They're fascinating. They're really doing something out there. I'm impressed."

"If more people were like them," Phil said, "we'd be living in a very different world right now. A much better world, I'd say."

"Too bad everyone isn't like them," Sarah said from the back seat.

"You liked meeting them, too, didn't you?" Phil said, glancing in the mirror. He could tell her words carried a trace of judgment.

"Yeah, they're great," she said.

"But you don't sound that impressed," he said.

"No, I like them, I do," she said. "I think they're awesome. I just thought their work would be more ... I don't know ... real. I thought there'd be more reality to it."

"What do you mean, 'real'?" Phil said.

"I mean, it all sounds kind of wishful, don't you think?" she said.

"Weeding this meadow is changing the whole bioregion's climate? I don't know..."

"It's all interconnected, though," Phil said into the mirror. "Their work could absolutely be having effects we don't understand yet."

"I know, I know," she said. "I mean, the butterfly flaps its wings and everything, I get that. But they're just weeding a meadow. I weed our yard."

"This is a long-standing argument between us," Phil said to me. "We have different ideas of cause and effect."

"Phil is very hopeful about a lot of things," Sarah said.

"And Sarah's not as negative as she thinks."

"I'm not negative at all," she said. "I'm just realistic. Phil believes in magic. It's sweet."

"I do," he said. "It's terrible. But I do."

"We knew some Wiccans in Mendocino once," Sarah said. "They told us a tree grew in their yard overnight. They claimed they walked outside in the morning and a whole, full-grown cedar was there. A hundred feet tall. Phil believed it."

"I appreciated their narrative," he said. "Arthur understands about that. A good story is a good story. It makes room for a lot of things. Look at, I don't know, Jules Verne. That was fiction that became reality. Storytelling is a kind conjuring, isn't it, Arthur? It's how we bring the future into being."

"Like *Mein Kampf*," Sarah said. "Or *The Fountainhead*."

"Oh please," Phil said. "That's not what we're talking about here."

"It is, though," she said, "Everyone has their own fantasy. You might like some of them better than others, but that's what they all are. A lot of people like to think controlled burns solve everything now. They think Indians used to groom the whole planet. There were so few people back then! They barely touched anything! Sleeping bears, romping bobcats. These are predators."

"Sarah thinks Nature is a constant state of war," Phil said.

"It is," she said.

"The way I see it," Phil said, "Merle and Candy definitely aren't hurting anything. And it's the spirit of the work they're doing. The citizenship—"

"Here we go . . . ," she said.

Phil rolled onward, ignoring her, and getting a little fiery as he entered the chamber of his deepest beliefs.

"We're at a point now where we have to try anything," he said. "This is what I've been saying for years, Arthur. I've spent my entire life trying to heal the planet. I've marched in the streets, I've educated in the schools. I've shouted from the rooftops since I was a kid. That's what's compelling to me about Merle and Candy: they're not waiting around for anyone to tell them what to do. They're just getting down to work and doing it. Tending their little garden. How can you not admire that?"

"It's totally admirable," Sarah said. "It just isn't true."

"Bah," Phil said agreeably.

"What do you think, Arthur?" Sarah said. "Did you buy their plan? Are you going to put them in your book?"

"I might," I said. "I'm not sure yet."

"And what'll you say if you do?" she said.

"Well," I said, and slowed myself down, wanting to navigate the schism between my two hosts as delicately as possible. "I guess I'd probably end up relating their work to writing. That's what I usually do. I'd frame the regreening program as a form of revision. I'd talk about how small changes can have big effects. How if you move a few words around, or rearrange a paragraph, a lot of energy can suddenly start flowing. A lot of writing is weeding and watering, in my view. I'd probably say something to that effect."

"There you go," said Phil, taking my words as a victory for his side.

"Whatever," Sarah said, disgusted by our mealy holism.

"Plus," I added, "there are a lot of good words attached. 'Yarrow,' 'acupuncture,' 'butterfly,' 'chaparral.' I don't have to literally believe what they say in order to use it in a book, you know."

"See, now that makes sense to me," Sarah said. "Practical."

After that, conversation returned to daily life. We talked about groceries, email etiquette, book bans. According to Sarah, the kids in her school only read banned books these days. Anything with a Pride flag on it, they loved, whereas anything over twenty years old, they found totally uninteresting. Phil and Sarah bickered for a while about the significance of this trend, in a way that was hard to tell if they were being affectionate or genuinely annoyed with each other, but such was the way with any couple, I thought; the subtexts were ultimately unreadable. By dusk, we'd retraced our path over the pass, and they'd dropped me off at the gate to my mother's property, where we said good night.

Inside, I poured myself a whiskey and sat in my little reading nook where I could ponder the day's raw information. I liked Candy and Merle. I could see how they might offer a whole chapter in the Tree Book if I chose to go that route. I could also see their figures from both Phil's and Sarah's points of view. Phil was a good person. He refused to let go of hope. Sarah was a good person, too. She refused to have false hope. I could see their argument as exactly the subject the section would explore. Theirs was exactly the unresolvable conversation I would restage in print.

I poured myself another whiskey and picked up a copy of *Earth's Shadow* from the shelf. I often enjoyed leafing through one of my books after meeting new people, scanning a few pages through their fresh eyes. This time I wasn't reading it through Merle's and Candy's eyes, however, but through Sarah's. I was wondering what she'd think if she ever took the trouble. As I read, my mind drifted from the page, revisiting our conversation in the car. I found myself trying out different phrasings on her, different arguments to keep her attention. I imagined comebacks I might have attempted, alternate quips to bring out the music of her laugh. When I finally returned to the words, I was happy to find the sentences seemed passable to me, even good. I didn't think I'd be embarrassed if someday Sarah decided to hold them in her lap.

3

I always enjoy the early phase of a book, the dreaming phase. You've made a decision about what you're doing, and then you get to walk around with a magnet in your head, looking for iron filings that might fit your design. Any stray scenes on the street that might be relevant? Any anecdotes at the party that might find some place? You're searching everywhere, open to anything.

This time the magnet was trees, and what more pleasant thing to think about than trees? My job became staring at branches and mulling the nature of a compound leaf, examining blade units and auxiliary buds. I learned about the gender of trees, how sugar maples avoided incestuous self-pollination by staggering the release of their pollen with the blossoming of their flowers, letting the wind and bees carry their powders away to finish the sex act out of sight. I learned about mother trees who feed the forest through their vast mycorrhizal networks. I learned that a living tree is 99 percent dead.

I scoured everywhere for relevant facts, landing interesting tidbits here and there on the web, but fewer than one might think. Ultimately, I believed, it took books to write a book. All kinds of books, new and old, relevant and seemingly not. For the new books, I headed to the bookstore, seeking to understand the current trends and titles and, sure enough, I discovered many tree books already in the Nature and Gardening and Spirituality sections. Collectively, the writers of the world were turning their attention to trees, awakening to the tree life all around them. But no one else, thankfully, seemed to be writing exactly the tree book I imagined.

I went to the library in search of the deeper ore. I wanted to find tree books going back generations, beyond Muir and Emerson and Thoreau. What did the Incas say about trees? What did the bushmen know? I started at the local city branch, checking out piles of books that I took home and devoured and brought back for more piles, knowing I had to aerate the new discourses with antiquated notions or else I was only drafting in our current moment's thought-stream. The new regime was all about interconnectivity, interdependence, rhizome thinking, but what about the other tree models that had come before? It was part of a writer's job, I believed, to resuscitate.

I visited the college's science library, too, where I wasn't allowed to check anything out, but where they gave me a carrel and let me read on-site. It was a certain impressionistic kind of reading I did there. These were tomes with graphs and charts I didn't really understand, filled with specialized language beyond my comprehension. But poring over them was still helpful as a form of contemplation. I was searching for exotic vocabulary words, interesting bibliographic entries, any scraps of data I might repurpose. If I decided a page merited more attention, I took a picture with my phone and then almost never looked at it again. I was collecting stray buttons and threads, weaving them into my growing structure. I was making room. I was becoming absorbed.

I could tell I was moving in the right direction when the universe started sending me signs. This was how it always went, little synchronicities and unexplained phenomena popping up on my radar. One day, walking home, I saw a postcard lying on the ground. The picture was a photograph of a silver birch, the very tree I'd been reading about in the library only minutes before. Another day, sitting on my back deck, a samara, the winged seed of a maple, came spinning into my hands, totally out of season. I spent hours staring at that tiny propeller, wondering who'd sent it, who'd made it, what the universe was trying to tell me with its elegant, aeronautical design.

The signs were all fundamentally insignificant things, but as anyone who has gotten deep into creative work knows, they're the kinds of communications you long for. They mean you're tuned to the right frequency, catching at least some of the world's subaudible whispers. They mean something is talking to you, telling you you're on the right path. In the words of Meister Eckhart, "God keeps on withdrawing, farther and farther away, to arouse the mind's zeal and lure it on to follow and finally grasp the true good that has no cause." Already, I sensed that hide-and-seek going on, the recent presence of some guiding, inhuman force.

When I ran into Sarah one day at the science library, I assumed she was a sign, too. I hadn't seen her since our trip to the meadow a month earlier, but I'd been getting news about her on and off from Phil. She'd visited her parents in California, and she'd bought a new Instant Pot. He hadn't mentioned anything about a new job at the college, but then, why would he? We barely knew each other. Seeing her there in the library, scanning books behind the main desk, I felt a mild shock. It seemed like a sign, for sure. Granted, in those days, as I drifted deeper into the Tree Book, pretty much any pleasant surprise counted as a sign.

"The famous author," she said, as I approached the counter.

"The famous librarian," I said. "I guess the college job came through."

"Careful what you wish for, right?" she said. "I already miss the kids. But the pay is better here. I couldn't really say no."

"Things happen for a reason," I said. "Just usually not at the right time, I find."

"Who knows why anything happens," she said. "Anyway. How's your Tree Book going? Making progress?"

"Still easing into it," I said. "Doing my homework."

"Are you looking for anything particular today?" she said. "Anything I can help you find?"

"Yeah, these," I said, and slid a scrap of paper with call numbers her way. They matched old issues of the *International Society of Arboriculture Journal*, and one *Journal of Arboriculture and Urban Forestry*. The bound volumes didn't go back far enough on the shelves, but they supposedly had them downstairs.

She looked at the call numbers, her fingers already flitting over the keys, double-checking the volumes' existence. Windows inside windows opened on her screen. The program looked ancient. She was wearing a green silk blouse with puffed sleeves that day. Her hair was up, making a loose, black bundle over her head, with flashes of blackness falling around her temples. On her wrist she wore a wide-gauge leather bracelet with a gold buckle.

"Okay," she said. "Just a second. I'll get them."

She got up and disappeared into a doorway and I stood at the counter waiting. The smell of the carpet was dry and woolly sweet. I could hear the sounds of pages turning, a pen tapping, a phlegmy cough somewhere in the stacks. I could hear a clock ticking, and in between the strokes, the gentle hum of the wheels inside. By the time Sarah got back, I'd come up with a reason to loiter a little longer.

"Anything else?" she said, sliding my volumes over.

"Maybe you could help me with a little search," I said. "I don't think I'm really maximizing the engines in here. I keep coming back to the same lists."

"Sure," she said, and sat at the monitor again. "What keywords are you using?" Already, her fingers were opening fresh windows, preparing to dig.

"Anything about trees," I said.

"That's pretty broad," she said. "Books? Articles? Anything to cross-reference that with?"

"Synapses? Ganglia?" I said. "Consciousness? That's the area I'm thinking about right now."

"Sounds like you've been talking to Phil, all right," she said.

Her words felt like a mild rebuke. "We have some similar interests," I said. "He's been really helpful."

"Uh-huh," she said. "So which one is it?"

"Which what?" I said.

"Which cross-reference?" she said.

"Uh, how about ganglia?"

"He likes talking to you, you know," she said, typing away. "He's happy to have someone interested in what he's thinking about. It doesn't happen very often."

"He's a very brilliant guy," I said. "I find out something new every time we talk."

"His students don't appreciate him," she said. "They're so fucking lazy. Any of these titles look interesting?" She leaned back, tilting the monitor to give me a view. Some of the titles were new to me, most of them not relevant. There were a few maybes. Leaning over the counter, I was close enough that I could see the fine hairs on Sarah's wrist, the wrinkles of her knuckles. I could almost feel the heat coming off the nape of her neck.

"Go down," I said.

She moved the list downward.

"Yeah. That one," I said. "'The Architecture of Quercus.'"

"What's quercus?" she said.

"Oak," I said. "The genus. I've learned that much already. Now a little more."

"Here?"

"Yeah. That one is something I'd love to see, too. 'Fungi Described and Recorded from Eucalyptus.'"

She wrote down the call numbers. "Keep going?"

"No," I said. "That's plenty. I can only deal with so much at a time."

She left again. By the time she got back, the clock had edged to noon. She said she was going to lunch. I happened to be going to lunch then, too.

We walked over to the grocery store together and ordered out of the deli case, with its bounty of ruby beets, iridescent tomatoes, shining bulgar, and glossy green beans, nested in beds of decorative kale. What amazing times for food, we agreed. How had people eaten before this millennium?

We took our boxes to a picnic table and ate in the fresh spring air.

It was only early April, but already warm. It'd been warm for weeks. The camellias had run their course by the end of February, and the rhododendrons had burst in mid-March. There were roses already budding. It was all wrong. And yet, smelling the fresh-cut grass, hearing the mellow buzzing of the bees, I had to admit, in the moment, everything was very pleasant. Maybe the calm glory of summer would come on and never end.

"So you don't talk about something when you're working on it?" she said. "Is that always how it is?"

"It just isn't really anything yet," I said. "Which makes it hard to talk about."

"When will you know if it is something?" she said.

"Not until the very end, usually," I said. "And even then I don't really know."

"I still haven't read any of your books," she said. "Sorry about that."

"That's okay," I said. "Books have long lives. They'll be there if you ever want them."

"I saw one at the bookstore the other day," she said. "It was called . . . what was it? *The Slow Game*. What's that one about?"

"That was my first one," I said, forking a tortellini. "Kind of an outlier. I hadn't figured out what I was doing yet. I used to have a whole sales rap down about it, but I don't really remember it anymore."

"I bet you can remember it," she said.

She was right. It was easy to fall back into my old grooves. I gave her the jacket copy overview of my first published work: a series of portraits of people who'd bloomed late in life, or who'd never bloomed at all, but whose influence had become apparent only long after the fact. It was a book about people who'd appeared slow but who'd in fact controlled the tempo of their times. That was how we'd framed it in the PR materials.

"Like who?" she said.

"Hakeem Olajuwon was a chapter," I said. "He was a center for the Houston Rockets. He was from Lagos, Nigeria, a beautiful guy. He was nicknamed the Dream. He looked like he was moving in slow motion out on the court, but when you checked the numbers, he was totally dominant. He led the league in rebounds twice, blocked shots three times. He hardly budged down in the post, but he just racked up the numbers. You could say that about a lot of big men. At least in a certain era of basketball. But Hakeem seemed especially slow."

"Interesting," she said. "Who else played the Slow Game?"

"Umm, Simon Rodia," I said. "He's the guy who built the Watts Towers. Every day, he'd go out into his backyard and add a new little piece to his structure. He'd bring out shards of broken glass, or seashells, or pieces of pottery. And gradually his sculpture grew like a coral reef. It took him thirty-four years, but he single-handedly created a ninety-nine-and-a-half-foot-tall monument that the whole world recognizes and loves. One guy, walking into his backyard every day and adding to his pile."

"I like that," she said. "He never made it to a hundred feet, though?"

"Nope," I said. "Stayed at ninety-nine and a half. He didn't fetishize the round numbers."

There were other examples, too, some famous, some just people I knew. I told her how I'd started collecting these stories in my teens, and eventually, in my late twenties, had realized I had some kind of book in my head. Through these portraits, I'd extrapolated the idea of the "slow universe," a pudding-like undertow to the bright, gaudy cosmos of streaking comets and flaming meteors. The slow universe was a place of belated consequences and time-delayed realizations. The book had ended up embodying the principle in a way, because I still got royalties off it, if increasingly meager ones.

"Funny, to write a first book about slowness," she said. "That book did pretty well, didn't it?"

"It did all right," I said. "People like to hear those kinds of stories, it turns out."

"Stories about slow people?" she said.

"Stories telling them they're doing better than they think they are," I said. "Or that they're getting something done by doing nothing at all. People like to hear that work is happening without really trying."

"Ha!" she said. "Was that your message?" Her eyes were suddenly alight. "It sounds so cynical."

"I didn't mean it to sound that way," I said.

"Because it sounds like you're a total charlatan," she said, pushing her advantage. "Feeding people stories to make them feel better. Telling them what they want to hear."

"Giving people comfort," I said. "I think that's part of what writing a book is about, giving solace. I'm not above offering solace."

"Call it what you want," she said. "Better an interesting charlatan than a hypocritical saint. In my opinion."

She sipped her sparkling water. We'd broken the skin of something.

We finished our lunches, but neither of us seemed eager to get back to work. I'd learn later that Sarah had already decided we were spending the afternoon together. At the time I only knew she didn't seem particularly worried about the library shift, and that my own workday was already shot. I rarely worked past 2:00 p.m.

We took a stroll through the farmer's market, admiring the spring vegetables. We had different methods for choosing artichokes, it turned out, and very different opinions about rhubarb. We paused for a while and watched a clown performing a juggling routine to a Beatles medley on a boom box. He had some incredible moves: two balls behind his back; three balls in front of his chest, hands swiping the air like a spasmodic bear; going wide, with high arcs; keeping the balls tight near his ribs; going under his knee. And then, as the crescendo of "Carry That Weight" surged, he sped through all of them, one after the other, a pyrotechnic sequence. We clapped and laughed and left a few dollars in his hat.

From there, we walked into the park, passing Hacky Sackers and Frisbee golfers, and circled the duck pond, where some geese were violently mating. We headed up the trail, spotting a hiker wandering down from Ashland's watershed, a dirty angel bounding through the tunnel of greenery. Now it became my turn to ask the questions.

"So you grew up in California," I said.

"That's right," she said. "Bay Area."

"And your parents are from Germany," I said. "Phil mentioned that."

"Yep," she said.

"What do they do?" I said.

"My dad is a coder," she said. "My mom is a schoolteacher."

"What grade does your mom teach?" I said.

"Every grade," she said. "Kindergarten to eighth. She's a sub now."

"And you always lived in California?" I said.

"I was actually born up here, in Oregon," she said.

"Oh," I said. "What part?"

"Out in the desert," she said. "In the east."

"What town?" I said.

"A town called Antelope," she said.

"That's where the Bhagwan Shree Rajneesh lived," I said. "Were you there when the Rajneeshees took it over? Turned it into the commune?"

"That was us," she said. "We did that. We call him Osho, though."

"You're a Rajneeshee?" I said. Here was real information, possibly even the key to a life. My full attention was locked.

"Yep," she said. "Born in the cult."

She told me the whole story. Her parents were both German hippies, she said, which was to say, very serious, real seekers. As young people, in their respective homes in the suburbs of Munich, they'd both discovered the writings of the Bhagwan and had each traveled halfway around the world to study with their chosen master. When they'd first met at his ashram in Pune, India, it'd felt like fate. They'd grown up about four miles apart, only to come face-to-face so far away from home. What were the chances?

Together, they'd gotten very deep into Osho's practice—the morning meditations, the calisthenics, the riddling out of his aphorisms. When he'd moved his congregation to the United States, they'd followed.

"This is when?" I said.

"This is the late seventies, early eighties," she said. "It was a little late for cults, but they'd missed the big flowering in the early seventies. So they ended up out in eastern Oregon when everyone moved there. This is kind of the Slow Game, isn't it? Belated cult activity! They really went for it, though. They had a lot of pretty out-there experiments going on in the ashram, even then. Osho's philosophy was based on free, open love between people, the destruction of the possessive ego. That's ironically why he had so many Rolls-Royces. They were symbols of how little he cared about material things. I was actually conceived in an orgy there."

"What a minute," I said. "What?"

"That's not how anyone puts it," she said.

"How do they put it?" I said.

"They never put it one way or the other," she said. "No one ever really talked about it at all."

"How did you find out then?" I said.

"I pieced it together," she said. "I grew up in a very normal way, actually. My parents left the ashram when I was still a baby. We moved down to California, started a life in the South Bay. My dad found work in the computer industry. It's funny to realize how close we were to those times, because to me, the ashram was always just a fairy tale. I have no memories of being there at all."

"So your parents were deprogrammed?" I said.

"No, no, nothing like that," she said. "We had pictures of Osho everywhere. They always had friends in the commune. They never stopped believing, in a way; they just moved on to other parts of their lives. People like to think there are these hard breaks in life, but nothing ever really ends or goes away. Don't you think?"

"And they didn't tell you anything about your conception?" I said.

"You're very interested in this," she said.

"How could I not be?"

"I don't think my parents really knew what to say about it," she said. "They didn't want to confuse me. It didn't really matter. But I remember the day it finally dawned on me. I was sixteen at the time."

"What happened?" I said.

"I was just looking in the mirror in the bathroom one day," she said. "Like a teenager does, you know? Wondering what I was going to look like as an adult, who I was going to be. And I just started to notice my features in a way I hadn't ever noticed them before. I don't look like my parents. At all. I have this black hair, these dark eyes. This nose. My parents aren't like Aryan blond Germans, but they're definitely not swarthy. They're kind of mousy-looking. Whatever was in me, it wasn't coming from them. Or from my grandparents. Or anyone else in the family. It was suddenly really obvious to me."

"But from one of the Rajneeshees . . ."

"We had pictures of Osho all over the house, like I said. He was always looking at us with those eyes. Those moonlike eyes, that little smirk. And he had this nose. He had this skin. I was putting on some makeup and it just kind of clicked. I finally saw it. My whole aspect changed."

"That must've been pretty bizarre," I said.

"It was," she said. "But it was also very subtle. It took a long time to process. It went under the skin, too, into the blood. I realized I'd kind of known for a long time, but somehow the idea had never formed into a full-blown thought. The whole shape of my life altered. I was still myself, but I was someone else, too. I had these two very different histories inside me."

"And then what happened?"

"Nothing, really," she said. "I didn't say anything about it. I kept going to school, hanging out with my friends. It changed everything, but it also didn't really change anything. It was strange. I saw my parents differently, obviously. I felt new things in myself. But I didn't feel Indian, either."

"What seemed different?"

"It's hard to say," she said. "New interests. New tastes. I got into Indian religions, Indian literature. I wanted to taste Indian food. I think this is true for everyone in a way, though. Everyone chooses on some level how to form their personalities. You have your Irish side and your Jewish side, or your Korean side and your Black side."

"Your mom side and your dad side."

"Right. Mine were just more pronounced sides. I felt like I had new choices. I wasn't just a German expat hippie child anymore. I had blood that went somewhere else, too. It was good, ultimately. It gave me access to more things."

"Did it pull you away from your parents?" I said.

"You're so full of questions!" she said. "But no. I wasn't suddenly some kind of identity warrior. Mostly, I didn't want to embarrass them. I almost thought they might not know! Germans of their generation have a certain relationship to the past and secrecy. My parents are very open, very transparent. They hate secrets. And yet, at the same time, they're very incapable of certain insights."

"But you talked to your parents about it eventually," I said.

"Not until I was in my twenties," she said. "By then, we'd been living in this cone of silence about it for so long that it didn't really matter anymore. I'd come home wearing kohl makeup, or a sari, and we'd all pretend it wasn't happening. Then one day, I was visiting home from college, and I just asked them who my real dad was, like it was no big deal, like we'd already established this fact. And in a way, it was true, we had. We'd already done all the processing inside ourselves. We were finally ready to have a calm conversation about it."

"And what did they say?"

"They said they didn't know. It could've been a handful of guys. My mom really enjoyed herself in those days. Or she'd been serially raped, depending on how you look at it. I prefer the former. That's how she sees it. She never seemed traumatized by her time in the ashram. All the men were quite nice, she said."

"But your parents weren't in touch with any of them?"

"No," she said.

"Did you want to go find him?" I said.

"Not particularly," she said. "I know the kind of guy he was."

"And your dad wasn't bothered by any of this?" I said.

"He's very German," she said. "He sees things in a very clinical light. He made a decision a long time ago that he was my father. He was going to play that role. No one was going to take that from him."

We'd made a full circuit by this time, up to the Japanese gardens and back down to the pond where the geese were no longer mating. A new batch of picnickers was on the lawn, a new circle of Hacky Sackers. We exited the park and reentered the traffic of town, heading back toward the library.

"You should really write about this someday," I said. "It would make a great book."

"Ha!" she said. "Why would I ever do that?"

"People would be interested," I said. "It's an interesting story. You tell it in an amazing way."

"No," she said. "I don't think so. I just told you all of it. Anyway, I'm not a writer kind of person."

"You could be," I said.

"Why do writers always think that sharing things in public is such a good idea?" she said. "You have this idea that sharing things in public is inherently positive. Some things are just private. Leave it be."

"We have to share our stories," I said. "That's how we understand anything about the world. That's how we know what's going on with each other."

"It doesn't change anything, though," she said.

"A librarian against books," I said. "Interesting."

"I'm not against books," she said. "I just think there are plenty of them already. Most of them don't have any reason for being. And anyway, there's life outside books, too, you know. I'm for life."

"I wouldn't know about that," I said.

"You should try it sometime," she said. "It's nice out here. Smells good."

We were getting back to the campus now, where students were dozing in the afternoon heat. A gardener was pruning the dogwoods lining the quad, clipping their pink limbs, which seemed criminal. At the library door, we paused before parting ways.

"Thanks for all the help today," I said. "I appreciate it very much."

"Of course," she said. "I mean, it's my job. And thanks for lunch. And the walk."

"My pleasure," I said. "Any time."

She opened the glass door. The reflections of the surrounding greenery slid and vibrated on the pane. "Phil is right," she said, stepping inside. "You are a good listener. I see why he likes your visits."

4

After that, I started seeing Sarah at the library fairly often. I'd stop and chat with her at the information desk when she was on duty or say hello when we ran into each other in the stacks. Sometimes she'd swing by my carrel and look at my pile, or bring me a reference book she thought I might find useful. Occasionally, we'd share a cookie or a brownie on her break.

I started seeing her around town, too, not in any organized way, but always by chance. It was one of those things that happens, where you go for years not noticing a person, and then, once you're clued in to their existence, they become ubiquitous. I'd hear her voice in the stationery store—that funny, almost-chortle she used in superficial conversations—or recognize her hair on the far side of the co-op vitamin aisle. I'd spot her hesitant gait and slightly hunched posture inside the bakery with the amazing spelt bread. Apparently, we'd been crossing each other's paths all this time without ever seeing each other, locked inside our parallel dimensions. Now, at last, our eyes had been opened.

Our big topic became the juggler at the farmer's market. We liked to keep each other up-to-date on our most recent sightings.

"I saw him without his makeup on," she said one day near the avocados at the grocery store. "At the DMV. I'm pretty sure it was him, anyway."

"I saw him with his clown wife," I said. "They were riding around on bikes together. They seemed very blissful."

"Yeah, I've seen his wife, too," she said. "She didn't smell that good when I saw her."

"No," I said, "not the cleanest clowns, those two."

We were always brief, always cheerful, always polite. I was always charmed by her quick laugh and subtle wickedness. She had a way of taking an idea and sending it back at a slanted angle, a little smarter, a little more colorful than before. I'd mention a kid with a bad Joker tattoo, and from her it became a Christopher Walken facial tattoo, a Johnny Depp pelvic tattoo, a Henry Kissinger ass tattoo, ad infinitum. At some point, I came to understand, she liked hearing funny complaints of any kind, anything involving a minor humiliation or gaffe, so I started preparing anecdotes of little disgraces I'd endured. I'd tell her about my argument with the cat lady in the neighborhood, or how I'd been caught by a neighbor throwing a broken table into his dumpster. She rewarded all my self-deprecation with avid delight.

"What did your neighbor say when he caught you?" she said, eyes gleaming.

"He said he had to pay for the dumpster by weight," I said. "He said I should've asked him first."

"And what did you do?" she said.

"I offered to take it back out if he wanted," I said.

"And what'd he say?"

"He said I didn't have to. This time."

"'This time,'" she said. "So you owe him now."

There was nothing going on. We were just two neighbors having a friendly back-and-forth. We liked each other, it was obvious, but she clearly liked a lot of people that way. She was the sort of person who touched people's forearms when she talked, and laughed at mediocre jokes, and relished almost every story she heard, even when it wasn't that great. I went away examining every conversation we had for special signals she might be sending, but I never found them. Not that I'd expect any. She was Phil's wife.

In that way, quietly, she entered my pantheon of unrequited crushes. There had been so many over the years. They came in the form of neighbors, cashiers, co-workers, actresses. Historical figures, students, friends' sisters. They were often people I barely knew, and yet who got recruited as the unwitting stars of my ongoing fantasy life. In my mind, they wandered into kitchens and living rooms wearing only towels; climbed stairs without underwear; entered bathrooms mid-shower. They played out roles rife with inexplicable submissions and offered their bodies willingly for incredible liberties. Now Sarah was one of them.

It was intriguing because she wasn't my usual fantasy object. Usually, I gravitated to women with compact bodies, small breasts, trim hips. I favored snub noses, chestnut hair. Who knows why? Sarah, by contrast, was long and languid. She had a substantial chin and a light dusting of hair on her cheeks. Her pores were noticeable. But it didn't seem to matter to my libido. I started imagining her in the library reading room after hours, wearing loose sundresses, or doing

Pilates in a private room at the gym, covered in a glaze of sweat. From there, the fantasies progressed as always.

Were my daydreams obscene? Abnormal? I didn't think so. If anything, they were probably more tame than most. I'd never find out. All I knew was, if everyone else wasn't walking around with these movies in their heads, these visions at once utterly depraved and utterly inconsequential, if they weren't imagining their fellow humans in every possible state of excitement and undress, I truly had no idea what was going on in the world at all.

In June, Phil and Sarah invited me to their annual solstice party. I was happy to have made the leap to mutual friend and party guest, and flattered by the invitation in general, even if I assumed it would probably be a party much like every other in Ashland—a mix of campus people, yoga people, transplants, and assorted architects and vintners, standing around talking about their vacations and where to buy the best fish. I'd been avoiding these gatherings as well as I could since getting back to town, protecting my personal privacy from the few friends and acquaintances I had left, but I RSVPed yes anyway, knowing I couldn't really say no. I figured I could always sneak out if I wasn't enjoying myself. Their house was only about two miles from my mom's.

And yet, as the days to the party narrowed, I found myself actually looking forward to it. If nothing else, the function would divulge some good sociological information. So these are the people a biology professor and a librarian consider friends. So this is what a biology professor and a librarian serve as snacks. One never knew when these little granules of data could be repurposed in the writing life.

And maybe, too, I thought, this party would offer other pleasant surprises. I wasn't thinking about Sarah, per se, but rather an entirely new person who might appear in my line of vision. Maybe Sarah would introduce me to her own replacement, the woman who'd finally unlock the deepest wellsprings of my passion, or at least offer a fun night or two. Maybe some graduate student would tell me she admired my work and take me home for a wild tryst. I'd been alone too much lately. And this was the ultimate reason for any social congregation in the end, wasn't it? The long-shot possibility of sex.

When I showed up at the door with my bottle of wine, Sarah and Phil seemed genuinely touched I'd come. They hugged me warmly and introduced me around enthusiastically, telling everyone I was their new writer friend. I did my best to meet the party halfway. I talked for a long time to a blond jewelry-maker about her love of the Girl Scouts, then to a man who said he produced independent documentaries, though his last efforts seemed like they were a few decades in the past. I sat for a long while with a group of San Francisco expats trading horror stories about the Tenderloin, bragging to each other about the profits they'd reaped when they'd finally cashed out of the Bay Area. All were fine, pleasant conversations, with thoughtful, interesting people, none of whom I'd be talking to again, I could already tell.

I'd been hoping to get in a little banter with Sarah during the night, but it turned out she was too busy for that. She was always in motion, filling wineglasses, guiding people to the hors d'oeuvres table, ripping apart heads of butter lettuce into a huge wooden bowl. I spotted her numerous times policing the front door and forcing people to take off their shoes. I could have cornered her and demanded a few minutes of time, but I didn't want to come across as a needy guest. Better to tip a glass in her direction as she lit the candles on the buffet table and receive a passing, apologetic smile in return.

It was a couple of hours into the party when I decided I needed a break from the small talk. It seemed too early to leave just yet—the paella hadn't been served—but I felt like some quiet would do me good. I broke away from the main group in the living room and went around looking for a space to hide. There was a line for the bathroom, and upstairs seemed off-limits, so I ended up drifting into what Sarah and Phil called their library, a bumped-out side room partly masked by a sliding, inset door. It was a nice room, with double bay windows, bushy houseplants, and a comfortable couch with a long-necked reading lamp. Best of all, it was empty.

The walls were completely covered in bookshelves. All of Phil's scientific tomes were there, bearing authoritative, no-nonsense titles like *Molecular Cell Biology*, and *Conceptual Biology*, and *Life on Earth*. There was a section of independent hippie publications of the 1970s, including a complete collection of the *Whole Earth Catalog*. There was a fiction area, and a history shelf, and a poetry zone. I spotted *Earth's Shadow* on the wall, which pleased me. I'd just pulled down an oversize book of satellite photographs showing demolished rain forests from a God's-eye view, and was leafing through its dismal, amazing pages, when Phil wandered in. Being a good host, he was keeping tabs.

"Everything all right?" he said, his usual good humor amped up a few degrees from the Negronis he'd been drinking. Not that he was drunk. It was only an extra flush in his cheeks, a warm flash in his eyes. He was never one to lose control.

"Oh yeah," I said. "Just admiring your collection here. So much great stuff."

"Feel free to borrow anything you want," he said, settling on the couch beside a shadowy zigzag fern. "We don't even have most of it out of boxes yet. After three years. Ridiculous."

"My books are mostly in boxes now, too," I said. "It's terrible. It feels like a lobotomy."

"We don't ever want to have to pack them up again. Moving books is such an ordeal."

"Are you planning on going somewhere?" I said, suddenly fearful. Already, I considered Phil and Sarah crucial people in my life. I didn't want either of them disappearing on me.

"No plans right now," he said. "But we'll see. The market dictates. If an opportunity came up I'd probably have to take it."

"I guess there are better colleges," I said.

"The college here is okay. It's more about the town. Ashland is great for retired people, or people with kids, but we're not either of those kinds of people. We've still got a lot of work to do. And we decided a long time ago we weren't going to bring any children into this world. Our little gift to the biome."

"Where might you want to go?"

"Oh, I don't know," he said. "Vancouver, BC? That's a nice town. With a nice rain forest attached. We talk about Rome. We talk about Vietnam. So many places you could live, theoretically. It's an ongoing fantasy. Do you think you'll ever leave again?"

"Depends on how the next book goes," I said, sliding his satellite book back on the shelf. I pulled out another. *Trees: An Illustrated Celebration*.

"That's a funny part of your life, isn't it?" he said. "You might always hit it big. Everything could change."

"But it won't. It never does. I've learned that by now."

"It might. You never know."

"Yeah, I doubt it," I said. "And anyway, it's not the motivation. It can't be."

"What is the motivation then?" he said, genuinely curious. Phil was a brilliant guy, but like a lot of readers at bookstore Q and As, he seemed to think I could offer him an answer to a question like that. He thought there was some personal dream I was pursuing with my writing, some agenda of self-discovery or self-glorification. He thought there was a therapeutic goal in there. In reality, the goal was even deeper and more ineffable. It was closer to the pursuit of divine communication. A way of feeling the presence of fate in my life. In other words, nothing I ever wanted to say out loud.

"To avoid real work," I offered.

He laughed and let the question pass. "I once had the idea I'd write real books, too," he said. "But it turned out I don't have the drive. I really admire what you do, Arthur. It's very difficult. I understand that, even from the work I do."

"Your books are real," I said.

"They're products of the academic industrial complex," he said. "They fill a certain need. Would they exist otherwise? I don't know. Your books, however..."

"... don't fill a need," I finished for him.

"No, not like that!" he said, laughing again. "They create their own need. They make their own context. It's different. It's more challenging, I think."

"It's all the same thing," I said. "It's all sitting in a room, sitting still. Tending the line. That's what you do, too. It's what we all do."

"Maybe," he said, and sipped his drink. His eyes drifted over the shelves, taking in all those books, with all their captured thoughts.

"But not really." He got up and ambled toward the wall. "Hold on," he said. "As long as we're in here, I want to give you something."

He went over to a corner and knelt and came back with a hand-stitched chapbook. It was bound in heavy, rough-hewn paper. The pages were deckle-edged and yellowing. It was a collection of poetry titled *Nature Loves the Number Five*. The author was Phil French.

"My Emerson phase," he said, handing it over. "That's where the title comes from. 'Why the star form she repeats.' A lot of pine trees in these poems. Five needles in their clusters. They're old poems, but you might enjoy some of them. Maybe even something you can use in there."

I held the book reverently. "Are you sure? I don't want to take your last copy."

"Oh, I have a lot of them, believe me," he said.

"I understand," I said, and gave a small bow. "I have those boxes, too."

We returned to the party, where Sarah was in the living room, talking to some botanists from Phil's department. After refilling my glass, I allowed myself to watch her for a little while. She was like a floating spark in the room, blowing around from place to place, shedding light everywhere she went. She laughed heartily at a remark by one of the botanists and listened incredulously to another one's intricate story, though on some level, I could tell, she was forcing herself. Overall, she seemed a little baffled by this invasion of people into her house, but was trying her best to be a good sport. I imagined she couldn't wait for everyone to go home.

Watching her legs, her long, bare arms, I imagined other things, too. I thought about bending her over the couch and running my tongue over her entire body. I thought about the damp heat between her legs. To see her standing there was to imagine the softness of her lips, the softness of her thighs, to picture sliding off her pants and placing my mouth on her belly, edging gradually downward.

It was so strange, I thought, how a person could picture these things unbeknownst to anyone else. Here I was, standing in the middle of a crowded living room, viewing the most lurid pictures in my head, and yet everyone continued walking around and talking to each other as if nothing was happening. What a bizarre thing, interior consciousness.

But then, something actually did happen. Or something might have happened, it was hard to say. It was so small, so subtle, I'm still not sure. If it did, it happened half an hour later, while Sarah was standing on a footstool in the kitchen, pulling a stack of dishes out of a cabinet, and I was standing nearby at the refrigerator, getting a fresh drink.

"Hey, Arthur," she said. "Can you help me out here for a second?"

"For sure," I said. "What do you need?"

"Would you take these plates out to the table for me?"

"No problem," I said, and went over and stood at her side as she pulled the plates off the shelf and rotated to hand them down.

"It's a big stack," she said. "Are you ready?"

"Yep."

I raised my hands. As the weight of the plates shifted from her palms onto mine, our fingers lightly touched underneath the bottom plate. It was almost nothing. The pad of my index finger merely grazed the back of her hand, and slid over a segment of her pinky. But as soon as the contact occurred, I felt a weird zing. It was like an actual electrical jolt flaring on the tip of my finger. Did she feel it, too? I couldn't tell, and I didn't want to ask. Her expression suggested she hadn't felt anything. But as I took hold of the plates and turned and walked away, I could still feel my finger throbbing from the contact.

The throb stuck with me the rest of the night. Maybe I'd imagined it, I told myself. Or, more likely, one of us had built up some static charge from walking around the house. We definitely didn't have some psycho-electrical connection that caused a spasm at the slightest touch. When people talked about sparks flying, they were speaking in metaphor. And yet, I couldn't stop caressing my finger and remembering the pulsation. It was nothing, I told myself. It hadn't happened.

Later still, when the party was really hitting its stride, and people were drunkenly staggering around and the music was loud and a few people were dancing, I caught sight of Sarah across the living room. This time she was staring straight at me. She had a look of misty affection on her face. Her eyes seemed almost swimming with warmth. It was too much. I had to turn away and pretend I hadn't noticed. I told myself again nothing was happening. Sarah wasn't staring at me in that way. She definitely wasn't plotting out her days to run into a minor writer of spirituality texts at the grocery store. I'd already given up on that idea. But isn't that the way it always goes? The moment you give up on something, that's when it springs to life.

5

All this time, I was making progress on the Tree Book. I was shifting out of the research phase and starting in on the writing phase, or at least the writing-things-down phase, which was still a prelude to actual grammar. The research wasn't finished yet, it never would be, but I had enough information to start piling words into files. I could start mushing them around, making fragments, fashioning the clay that would eventually be sculpted into actual meaning. I even had a loose structure in mind, or at least a few guiding concepts.

I'd decided the core chapter would be something about a mother tree, those hub trees connecting the network of life in a forest. That seemed requisite in this era of tree-related literature, though in my book it would be a different kind of mother. In my book, I'd talk about the mother tree as a controlling figure, persistently demanding, guilt-inducing, rationing her love, and making cruel choices. She'd be like a real mother, in other words, not the benign, giving force most people liked to imagine. I didn't think of it as a negative portrait, only more complex than usual. I loved my mother. But mothers were many-faceted, often manipulative. This was a technique I often liked to employ: take some given conceit and twist it the wrong way.

I'd also have a section rebutting John Muir and his latent monarchism. I'd go heavy explaining the eugenic implications of his grandiose worldview and compare him unfavorably to the lesser-known but more observant and humble John Burroughs, a confrere of Thoreau. And I'd definitely have a chapter about Candy and Merle, celebrating their simple, spiritual collaboration with the trees of their region, allowing for digressions into portraits of the bonsai master and a longtime tree dweller in Big Sur. I had a few other chapters in mind, too—a fairy chapter, a tree sentience chapter—all taking trees from different angles. It was a hodgepodge, which was always the case. Why write a book anyone else would write?

In June I decided I needed to pay another visit to Merle and Candy's meadow. It was becoming clear that their regreening project was going to be a load-bearing rafter for the book, and I felt like I needed to conduct a proper interview. Phil kindly put me in touch with Merle and we made a date. And then, a few days later, Sarah approached me in the library with her own ask.

"I hear you're going back to the meadow," she said.

"Yep," I said.

"You want any company?" she said.

"Sure," I said.

It seemed normal enough. We were new friends, going on a day trip together, nothing to be excited about. It would be interesting for both of us to see the meadow in a new season. Phil himself might have come along if he wasn't so busy. He certainly didn't object. I knew there were people who had the idea that women and men couldn't be normal friends, that men and women were for some reason unable to relate outside the project of procreation, but that was stupid in my opinion. Sarah and I were modern, sophisticated people, beyond any regressive rom-com clichés. We were capable of many kinds of mellow fellowship.

And how conceited to imagine Sarah would ever think of me like that anyway. She'd once looked at me kind of smolderingly at a party, big deal. I wasn't in her mind in that fashion. She obviously didn't consider me—a balding, potbellied, unrenowned writer—as some kind of paramour. We'd be taking a drive together, nothing more.

I arrived at Phil and Sarah's house late in the morning, and it was already hot. The shadows were shrunken little blots, bunched under the trees and bushes like creatures in hiding. I texted Sarah, and a minute later she emerged from the front door, and wended her way down the steps, and through the yard's riot of euphorbia, rosemary, heather, and lavender. She wore a cream-colored bucket hat that day, with a white oxford and a pale raspberry skirt, and moved with her normal slow, loping stride. She paused at the front gate and turned to make sure the clasp was latched before gracefully climbing into the car, pushing the clean cotton billows of her skirt down into her lap. Her beach bag went into the back seat, like she owned it.

"You're prompt," she said, buckling in.

"This is a business trip," I said. "There's business to do."

"I brought us snacks," she said. "Just in case."

"I made us some lunch," I said. "I hope you like soba noodles."

"Well, we won't starve on the mountain, at least. That's good."

We headed out, taking the same route we'd taken four months before, over the Siskiyou Pass, into the arid hinterlands of northernmost California. We followed the bends of I-5 through the Klamath Knot, as some called it, catching long views into the scrubby canyons opening and closing on either side. As before, we talked about Ashland's failings. The public art was gentrified hippie crap. The speed trap south of downtown was an insult to our intelligence. Overall, we said nothing we wouldn't say with Phil in the car, too.

"God, these fucking trucks," she said, as two eighteen-wheelers roared alongside us. "I hate these things so much."

"Seems like a lot of them out today," I said.

"There's always a lot of them," she said. "I guess most of the drivers are Sikhs now. Did you know that?"

"I did not," I said.

"I guess they came over and took all the long-haul trucking jobs in the West," she said. "Well, maybe not all of them, but a lot. I read an article about it. You get great curry at truck stops up and down I-5, they say. And in Utah and Arizona."

"That seems like an improvement," I said.

"Sort of," she said. "But the biggest rednecks in the world are Indians, you know. These drivers might be Sikh, but they're still rednecks. And they're just as shitty drivers as the white guys and the Mexican guys. Probably worse."

"I have a Chinese friend who claims the biggest rednecks are Chinese."

"I have Arab friends who say the same thing about Arabs," she said.

"Planet of rednecks," I said.

"Planet of shitty drivers," she said.

We broke free from the trucks, only to pass through another formation, and another after that. We arrived at the interstate agriculture checkpoint and didn't declare any fruits or vegetables even though I'd packed us bananas and Sarah had packed us grapes. Outside Yreka, Mount Shasta appeared, like a giant Chinese scroll painted across the sky, etched with inky filigrees, spotted with cloud shadows on the northwestern shoulder.

The gas gauge was getting low, but I kept passing up exits, holding out for better prices. Finally, after we'd split from the freeway and started into the foothills, we couldn't wait any longer. I had to pull over at a little no-brand roadside convenience store/gas station where the prices were the worst we'd seen, but I'd waited too long, and there was no going back.

"I told you Arco was the best," Sarah said.

"Yeah, yeah," I said.

The place had two pumps on a gravel apron, both of which were already taken. The front pump was serving a gray Honda; the rear pump was attached to an SUV. In line ahead of us was a giant white pickup truck, the kind that had become symbolic in our region of a certain phallocratic assholism. The bumper sticker informed us that the second amendment was not about hunting.

"He's literally driving inside a metal penis," Sarah said.

"You don't drive a truck like that if you don't have some kind of complex," I said. "Whereas if one drives a Subaru Forester such as this..."

"Pure understated confidence, yes."

Soon, the Honda drove away, leaving the front pump empty, but for some reason, the giant truck didn't budge. I gestured at the driver to go ahead and pull forward and back into the spot, but he shook his head, no. He made some gestures that I couldn't understand, maybe that he needed to use the rear pump, or something like that, so I went ahead and backed into the front spot and walked inside to pay in advance, per the signage.

When I came out, the rear pump was empty, but the giant white truck still idled in place. Maybe he was waiting for something other than gas, I imagined, not that I really cared. I started tanking up, but before I was finished, the pickup driver cut his engine and climbed out of his cab and stalked into the store, obviously in a huff. I followed a minute later to get my change and found him at the counter, complaining loudly to the cashier about me.

"Some people are such goddamn morons," he was saying, "they don't even know how to pump their own fucking gas. You end up waiting half an hour before you can get into a spot. I mean, Jesus Christ, people need to pull their heads out of their asses, I'm serious, who do they think they are?"

I pretended not to understand what he was talking about and eventually he stormed outside. The cashier shook his head.

"Sorry about that," the cashier said.

"Yeah, that was weird," I said.

"It's just that the pumps are too close together," he said. "My dad built this place fifty years ago, and he didn't leave enough space. You wouldn't know that if you haven't been here before. If you could move your car up a little bit, that'd be great."

"I'm done anyway," I said, and walked away, annoyed the cashier was giving the asshole truck driver any credence whatsoever.

I took my time getting back into the car. I made a display of climbing slowly into the seat, and slowly checking my mirrors, and slowly buckling my seat belt. The angry truck driver was now back inside his cab, glowering at us from behind his windshield.

"Did something just happen?" Sarah said, picking up on the negative energies.

"That guy in the truck is mad we took his spot," I said.

"This wasn't his spot," she said. "He said he didn't want it."

"I know," I said.

"You tried to let him go first," she said.

"I know," I said.

"So what's his problem?" she said. "Why doesn't he just pull into the spot behind you? Or back up into the spot when he had the chance? What a fucking asshole."

"I agree," I said.

"So then what's he so pissed about?" she said, craning her neck to see the guy's ongoing gesticulations.

"Ask him," I said rhetorically.

"I think I will," she said. And before I could start the car and get moving she climbed out and slammed the door, walking over to the idling white truck to instigate a confrontation.

"Sarah...," I said, but it was too late.

I watched in the rearview mirror as she tapped the guy's window and started talking to him in a way that looked hostile. Things quickly got heated. He was shaking his head, grimacing. She was talking a lot. Finally, I got out and went over to do what I wasn't sure.

"Is everything okay here?" I said.

"I'm asking this man what his problem is," Sarah said. "But he won't answer me."

"I told you," the guy said. "I don't have a problem."

"Is your truck too big?" she said. "You can't control your own truck?"

"Just waiting my turn, ma'am," he said.

"So why the attitude?" she said. "Do you have some issue with us? Do you have some kind of grievance?"

"Dude," he said to me. "What is this?"

"Why are you asking him the questions?" Sarah said. "Am I not here? I'm the one talking to you, not him."

"Dude," he said. "Come on. Get your wife off me."

"I'm not his wife," she said. "And even if I was, don't turn this into some man-on-man thing. I just want to understand what you're thinking."

"Sarah...," I said. "Maybe we should just—"

"I just want to understand what's going on," she said.

"Look," the guy said. "My tank is over on that side of my vehicle. You see that?"

"Yeah?" Sarah said. "So?"

"So the hole is over there, nozzle is over there," he said. "And the body of this truck is long. Do I have to draw you a map?"

"So you need both spaces to tank up," she said. "How are we supposed to know that?"

"Using your eyes, I guess," he said.

"Do you measure every car that comes into a gas station?" she said. "Do you note every gas cap?"

"I could've communicated better," he said. "I'm sorry. It's true."

"I don't see why you had to turn it into a thing," she said. "It was an innocent mistake we made. We're all just people here. We didn't understand."

"You're right, ma'am," he said. "We definitely are. We're all just people, trying to get along."

Ten minutes later, we finally managed to get free, but only after

Sarah had brought the guy completely to heel using her charms. She'd invited him to see a play in Ashland, and had been invited in return to visit a swimming hole outside Redding. The guy lived there, he told us, and although he harbored wishes to move somewhere else, he couldn't do that any time soon because he'd recently put his mother into an assisted-living complex so she'd quit giving her money away to scammers. Today, he was on his way to a fishing hole specifically to contemplate what the next three to ten years had in store. Pulling away, leaving the truck in the distance, I felt sorry for him, even as I could still feel the adrenaline numbing my fingers and toes.

"Glad he didn't have a gun," I said.

"Yeah, no kidding," Sarah said. "I didn't think about that. Shit."

Onward we pushed. We cruised along between towering walls of evergreens and wended our way up the northern shoulder of the mountain, and arrived a little after noon at Candy and Merle's meadow. They were busy making piles of brush, giving the plants and grass room to breathe, healing the world at their own turtle's pace. It was a lovely, peaceful clearing now, warm and fragrant and subtly colorful. Wild grasses spread between happy maples and conifers; the tattoo of a pileated woodpecker floated in the air. This was a patch of land that barely seemed like it needed healing.

Greetings were fond all around. I was now considered an old comrade in arms, and Sarah was practically a sister. I sat Candy and Merle down on a fallen pine trunk and got them to repeat their presentation for my phone camera, Sarah helping by holding the external lavalier mic I'd purchased. They explained their theories again and went on some new digressions about the Indian plantings that dotted the western landscape, how the Indigenous people had cultivated batches of yarrow, chamomile, and giant trillium, how all the American West was in a sense a man-made garden.

They also gave us a lesson on how trees drink, which was interesting.

"We don't even really know how trees pull water up their trunks to their crowns, if you can believe it," Merle said. "The old theories of capillary action and transpiration don't really account for the physics of it. Osmosis, either. Now they're saying the inner tubes of the trees have tiny carbon dioxide bubbles in them, and that's just more confusing."

"You can hear them drinking if you listen real closely," Candy said. "This time of year, especially, you can hear the water moving in the wood."

Sarah scowled, disbelieving.

"Come on," Candy said. "Come over here. Put your ears to the trunk."

Sarah and I followed Candy to a nearby Douglas fir whose trunk was mottled with lichens, slashed by a big, white bolt of crusted sap ten feet up. Almost shyly, we placed ourselves on either side of the trunk and pressed our ears to the wood.

"Just listen," Candy said. "Give it a minute."

We waited, feeling the fissured bark against our cheeks. It was a good feeling, rough and warm and almost pliant.

"Maybe I hear something," I said.

"Shhh," Sarah said.

We kept waiting, listening. I heard my own breath flowing in my nostrils, into my lungs. I heard a squirrel's toenails scrabbling on a branch. Between breaths, I might have heard the faintest murmur in the tree. Somewhere deep in the trunk, I imagined a trickle of moisture traveling upward through the grain, like a slow seepage. Whether I really heard it or not, or only willed myself into hearing it, I wasn't sure, but Sarah claimed she heard it, too. How could you not choose to hear it? How could you not love these kindly people?

"If you've got time," Merle said an hour later, as we backed into the dust cloud from our rolling tires, "there's a really nice waterfall a couple clicks down the road. It's on your way back, mile marker 9. It's worth a visit if you're out here already."

We had time. We still had our lunch to eat, and the days were long this time of year. We drove to the trailhead and collected our things and took another walk into the forest, through red earth this time, and more pine trees. The forest was drier this far south and east, without the dripping fronds and moist leaf litter of the rain forests on the other side of the Siskiyous. There were no other hikers on the trail. Apparently, we surmised, Thursday afternoon wasn't a big hiking day in these parts.

Soon, as advertised, we arrived at the falls, which were humbly impressive. Over a broken granite proscenium, a mountain stream tumbled in beautiful, rugged cataracts, pooling into a huge basin where giant, calm boulders were semi-visible in the mossy gloom, shafts of light bending in the green depths. The basin drained through a narrow granite throat that opened into an easy, free-flowing stream where trout were twitching, tadpoles squiggling. The air was filled by the raucous, peaceful sound of crashing water.

The air was a little chilly near the falls, so we made our way downstream to a spot where the current became almost slack. Water striders made tiny dimples in the river skin, and crawdads lazed on the floor in pools of Dalmatian sunlight. The rocks on the banks were nice and wide, offering ideal, sun-warmed tables for a picnic lunch. I sprinkled our soba noodles with sesame seeds and diced scallions, and spooned some chili sauce on top, nothing special, but after a day of hiking and rewilding, very tasty.

"This is nice," Sarah said. "I guess you've probably been here before, haven't you?"

"No," I said.

"Really?" she said. "I thought you would've been everywhere around here. Growing up here and everything."

"We almost never went into nature when I was a kid," I said. "My mom was against it. She thought it was better to leave Nature alone. It doesn't want us. The kind thing to do was stay home."

"My dad loved camping," she said. "He had all the gear. He really got something out of that. Being prepared for anything. I guess it was a kind of imperialism, it's true."

"I could see getting into camping," I said. "It's always nice, being out here. It's easy to forget."

"Even if it is a tree plantation," she said.

After that, we didn't talk much. Candy and Merle had tuned us to the mountain's silence, and now it was only more silence we craved. Sarah had an app for identifying birdsongs and we sat and allowed the phone to tell us about the life hidden in the boughs. She picked up seven different calls in a five-second window. Poorwill, nuthatch, chickadee, kingfisher. Hummingbird, killdeer. And then one faint, faraway water ouzel, that snob John Muir's favorite.

After lunch, we moved over to a grassy clearing and lay down in the dappled shade, still tuned to the mountain. Was anything happening now? No, I told myself. Nothing was happening. We were just two nature lovers, enjoying some quiet on a warm mountainside. It was summer, and this was what people did in the summer. It was what I'd do with anyone. If Phil were here, we'd all be doing this together.

We heard dragonflies whirring, bird wings flapping, the wind flowing through the soft needles of the trees. We heard a beetle scratching in the dirt. The water made a constant, calm background chatter, and the longer we listened, the more nuance we could hear in the stream's voice. We heard the water stroking the bed, wearing the rocks smoother and smoother, the occasional small rock rolling into a new placement. We heard the sun hitting the water, the sound of light tangling in the ropy current.

We remained still and listened to the blood in our own bodies, the hum of electricity in our nerves. The silence continued to ramify. We found rooms of silence inside the silence. We almost laughed a few times but we stayed quiet and kept listening until the forest seemed to forget we were there. A deer appeared in the tree break across the stream, browsing the leaves. We heard a dry rasping noise in the long grass that turned out to be a garter snake slithering through. It was an adorable little guy, with black and red patterning; tiny, shining dots for eyes; a flashing, elegant tongue. Off it went, happy to be free.

Still we were silent, breathing the scent of sun-warmed sap and cedar. Sarah rocked up onto her knees and leaned over to pluck a few blades of grass, allowing the neckline of her blouse to gape. I saw the curve of her breast cupped in her beige bra, not quite the edge of her aureole. She took a blade of grass and placed it gently between her teeth and dragged it out to dredge the droplet of milk from the stem. She tossed the blade and picked a few more. She handed me one and I bit gently on the milky tip. It tasted bitter and clean.

How do you know when something is actually happening? When you've waited long enough? How do you know when enough pressure has built up? You might feel something jangling in the airwaves, some invitation, but you're never sure if you're reading the air right. Maybe the other person doesn't understand the signals they're sending. The invitation is only ever half an invitation anyway. It can be rescinded at any moment. This was definitely a vague invitation. But it seemed like the moment had arrived. The moment when everything hidden came into view.

Sarah was looking directly into my face. She was close enough now that I could hear her breath and see the tiny pulse of her heart in her neck. I shifted my weight and leaned closer and she leaned closer and closed her eyes. Our lips touched. We pulled away, both in mild terror. And then, before saying a word, before a doubt, we went back again. Our lips touched and touched again, and the pulsation I'd felt at the party flared everywhere in my body, a warm, welcoming current spreading through my limbs.

My hands went to her arms, her shoulders. They slid under her blouse, and I felt the softness of her back, the heft of her breast. My thumb traced her nipple through her bra's fabric and then drifted up the neckline to trace her jaw and massage the warmth behind her ear. Was this happening? It seemed unbelievable, and yet also somehow not unbelievable at all. It occurred to me that Sarah and Phil might have some kind of agreement between them. This might even be a normal thing for her. She was the child of free love, after all. Maybe she lacked all the hang-ups and guilt reflexes around the body's natural wants that I had. In any case, I assumed she knew what she was doing. It wasn't the moment to distract her.

Her skirt came off and turned into a sheet on the grass. The earth became our bed. As we lay beside each other, kissing and caressing, I remained in complete awe that I'd been granted this permission. And it was more than permission. She had the same hunger I did.

Eagerly, we stripped off each other's clothes. My pale, hairy body came into view, harshly exposed, but she didn't seem to care. I definitely didn't judge the stray hairs or cellulite on her part. Not as she slid off her panties, and her black pubic bush appeared, with the fading trail leading to her belly button, and the shadowy cleft of her pussy. In those amazing moments, although she was breaking her wedding vows, and I was lying with my friend's wife, we were bizarrely unconflicted. We were two animals in a forest, feeding our bodies what they craved. Feeling her hands on my neck, her breath against my cheek, I told myself that we were doing nothing wrong. In fact, this was exactly what we were born to do.

The sex that afternoon was awkward at first. We were extra decorous with each other, seeking permissions, pausing to reposition or to move a fallen twig. I tongued circles around her nipples while she stroked me, and then she straddled my legs and explored my chest and neck. Our roles reversed again and I kissed a dotted line all the way down her rib cage to her curving hip. She clasped my fingers as I reached the silkiness of her inner thigh, and when I came to her labia I kissed them lightly along the seam, then parted them with my tongue, tasting the hot honey oil inside. Far away, I heard her gasp.

And then it wasn't so decorous at all. I kissed my way back to her mouth and she guided me inside her. I pushed my cock into her pussy gently a few times, almost questioningly, and then less so, until we found our rhythm. We proceeded to make love there in the sun on the mountainside in a state of stunned gratitude, giving ourselves over mindlessly to the moment and its sweet, wet, shared breath. It went by in a delicious blur, as it does, except for a single instant that stood out even at the time. The instant came in the throes of our fucking. I was staring into Sarah's half-lidded eyes, moving fluidly inside her, when I almost whispered out loud that I loved her. We weren't remotely at that point yet. It would have been utterly absurd and premature to say those words. And yet I could feel myself wanting to utter them. And I thought I felt her wanting to as well. And then, blissfully, the wanting was over, and we were done.

Afterward, we lay in the grass, legs entwined. My paunch married easily with the depression of her hip, and her head found a nice resting place on my shoulder. For a while, we didn't talk at all. We weren't second-guessing anything yet, or making any plans. We were simply lying there, touching each other's eyebrows and lips, occasionally kissing, letting the summer wind blow over us. But it wasn't long before the mental backchannels began opening, and practical questions started to circulate. I could sense Sarah's worries forming. What was she going to say to Phil when she got home? What lies was she going to have to tell? And what would I say when I saw him next? We were only seconds out from the act, and already the reality was starting to tighten around us like a noose.

Her skirt was a mess on the ground, and she propped herself up and started to brush off the dirt and push out the wrinkles, erasing the clues.

"Are you . . . okay?" I said at last.

"Yeah," she said. "I'm fine."

She kept brushing at her skirt, turning it around, looking for stray stains. She seemed to be making a point of not looking at me. I wanted to be there for her, if possible, and help her through whatever was going through her mind. I could see that on my side it wasn't as bad.

"What are you thinking?" I said.

"I'm just . . . I don't know," she said.

"Is there anything I can do?"

"No."

"That was kind of surprising, wasn't it?" I said after a pause. "Kind of unexpected."

"Are you that surprised?" she said. "Really?"

"Sort of. But maybe not totally surprised, I guess. Are you?"

"I guess I'm both of those things, too."

She found another spot on her skirt and wetted her finger to wipe it out.

"I'll admit," I said, "I've been thinking about it for a long time."

"Uh-huh?" she said. "When did you start thinking about it?"

"I'm not quite sure. A while."

"Oh, come on. You can tell me."

I started picking strands of grass off my legs. "The first day I talked to you, I suppose," I said. "Driving out to the meadow that first time. That's when it started for me. How about you?"

She thought for a moment, squinting at the sun-filled clouds. She sighed, not unhappily. "After our walk in the park, I thought about it," she said.

"And when did you decide it was going to happen?" I said.

"What makes you think I decided?" she said.

"It just seems like you were the one in charge," I said.

She laughed. "You're the one who took me to this creek," she said. "You made the noodles."

"I had no idea this was going to happen!" I said. "I mean, I've been thinking about it, but I didn't think it was ever actually going to happen."

"Thinking, wanting, plotting," she said. "What's the difference?"

"People think a lot of things that never happen," I said.

"But they only really want a few things," she said. "Don't tell me you didn't want this."

"Oh no," I said. "I wanted it."

"So did I," she said, and leaned over and kissed me softly. And then we sat and listened to the wind in the leaves.

"Maybe no one decided," I said wishfully. "Maybe it just happened by itself."

"If only that were true," she said, and started putting on her skirt.

We drove home listening to classic country music on the radio. The late-afternoon sky was tousled with clouds. The mood in the car was calm, with accents of melancholy creeping in. We didn't feel the need to burden ourselves with too many interpretations or expectations just yet. We'd acknowledged that we'd conjured this event into being, that we'd dreamed it, and done it, and now there was no taking it back, but about the future, we had nothing to say.

We climbed over the mountains back into Oregon, overtaking giant trucks paused on the shoulder, resting on the steep grade. I took Sarah's hand and passed a brushing kiss over her knuckles. She put her hand in her lap and turned back to her window. The moon was rising on the horizon. Already, it felt like Phil was in the car, witnessing our every gesture.

6

The Barn was a literary institution located in downtown Ashland, founded with the mission statement of "engaging readers, supporting writers and creating grassroots community around the written word." In practice, that meant putting on workshops, hosting readings, organizing weekend salons, throwing occasional free-form parties, and generally offering the readers and writers of the region a place to congregate. For some of us—the writers of the Rogue Valley with any publishing credentials whatsoever—it also provided occasional teaching and mentoring gigs, a much-needed stream of supplemental income.

The Barn had originally been housed in an actual barn, but that hadn't proven practical during winter months, so they'd moved the headquarters to C Street. The door was located midway down the block between Fifth and Sixth, and led to a narrow stairwell that rose to a shallow landing that opened into a warren of rooms that smelled like herbal tea and old paperbacks. There was a tiny kitchen in there, a little office for the bookkeeper, and two fairly spacious classrooms, the larger of which was organized around a grand, faux-walnut conference table, the smaller of which was strewn with mismatched reading chairs, a Persian carpet, and a corduroy couch that folded out into a bed.

It was in this smaller, frowsier classroom that Sarah and I began meeting twice a week, sometimes more. As a regular Barn instructor, I had a key to the office and a calendar that told me there was no programming on Sunday, Monday, or Thursday nights. Around dusk, we'd arrive separately, always careful to lock the door behind us and never turn on a light. In backpacks, we carried our supplies for the evening, usually peanut wafer cookies, or sweating bottles of rosé, or Sarah's favorites, whiskey and Pringles. We unfolded the hide-a-bed and, as the sky outside dimmed from periwinkle to inky blue, we lay and told each other our days' news. We went over our phone calls, our dental appointments, our naps, recounting whatever interesting or semi-interesting thoughts had crossed our minds, and asking each other the questions no one else asked. And, of course, we made love.

For that summer, the Barn became our private beach, turquoise water stretching in every direction. On the powdered sand, I learned Sarah's life from the beginning. I heard all about her childhood summer camp in Puget Sound, her teenage lovers, Dylan and Trent, her friend Melissa, who'd crashed her car on crystal meth. I heard about her parents' friends and her neighbors' dogs. I heard about the books that had formed her, running backward from Marguerite Duras to Dawn Powell to Sylvia Plath to Judy Blume to the Black Cauldron series by Lloyd Alexander, which was incredible, because at the bottom of my own reading life was Lloyd Alexander, too. What a moment that was, discovering we'd loved the same childhood books. In our faraway bedrooms, possibly at exactly the same moment, we'd turned the same pages and dreamed the same dreams. Gradually, the star of her inner life was becoming brighter.

She heard my stories, too, all the old myths, burnished and round. She heard about the enigma of my dad, who'd left when I was two, and our move to southern Oregon from Santa Cruz as part of the greater countercultural diaspora of the 1970s. She heard about the entry and exit of Mary, my mom's abusive wife, and about my early twenties, spent wandering Europe and North Africa, sampling hash and hitting all the beatnik stations. I even told her about my illumination on the banks of the Nile when I'd decided to become a writer, no matter if it meant a life of complete penury. I told her about the dishwashing and janitorial jobs that had followed, and my rave phase, and my former girlfriends, trying always to express to her just how solitary my life had become to make room for the writing.

"What was your first kiss?" she said.

"I don't remember," I said, kissing her shoulder, her elbow, her armpit.

"Are you kidding me?" she said. "How can a person not remember that?"

"I just don't," I said. "I don't remember having sex the first time, either."

"What?"

"It was so fast," I said. "It might not have happened at all the first few times."

"I find that ridiculous," she said. "You should choose a time and stick with it."

"I remember kissing a girl named Julie Strunk in eighth grade," I said, turning her over and kissing the small of her back, the curve of her ass. "We went to a dance together. I could've done a lot more with her. But I didn't like her that much."

"I didn't think that mattered to boys," she said.

"To some boys it does."

We learned each other's histories in that room, but most of all, we learned each other's bodies. I saw Sarah from every direction, above and below, in front and behind, from off to the side. I saw her belly button indented in its lovely pillow of flesh, her face swollen from sleep. There were images that became instantly iconic in my mind, like stained glass in my cathedral of memory. Her body moving on top of me as I fingered her asshole, her pushing her weight onto the tip my finger, my finger sliding deeper into her, and feeling the pressure of my cock pressing behind her inner walls. Her on her knees, twisting to catch my eyes as her hand reached back to cup me between her legs, pulling at me from the root. The wide-screen tangle of her pubic mound as I nosed the coarse hairs aside, trapping them between my lip and gum, seeking the wet blister of her clit. In that room, I came to know all of her—the taste of her lips, the taste of her sex. But best of all, I came to know how to make her laugh.

"Do you want me to put my pud in you now?" I said, her ankles latched on my neck.

"Oh, God," she said, "don't say that word, please."

"I'm going to put my pud in you now," I said.

"Stop it. Seriously."

"Oh my God, this feels so good on my pud."

We had to stop, we were laughing so hard. We couldn't go any further, we were crying. She said she hated it when I said that word, but in reality she didn't mind the idiotic boy stuff. She liked it.

We didn't think very far ahead. Inside that room, the future didn't exist, and the room itself didn't exist once we walked outside. To talk about any of it would only do it harm, reveal its utter impossibility. And so we stayed silent, even to ourselves. We were building a secret between each other, and as long as the secret remained unstated, we were safe. We were more than safe, we were happy. Our daily lives remained beautifully the same, unimpinged upon, but our secret shed new light onto everything, imbued every moment with fresh, bright suspense. How long until we got back to our room? How long until we could meet again and strip naked?

During those summer months, I was still seeing Phil every week, too, as terrible as that sounds. I wrote in the morning, spent the afternoon with Phil, and met Sarah at night, as if all the different pieces of my life had no relation. Such were my powers of compartmentalization. As far as Phil knew, Sarah was taking a memoir-writing workshop, something she'd been threatening to do for years. If she and I played tennis together, or attended a lecture, as we sometimes allowed ourselves to do, he helped us with the scheduling. He had no suspicions whatsoever, which was a further measure of his goodness. He saw only good in those around him.

He and I usually met on Thursdays and hiked into the canopy above town, wending our way through the white fir and weeping spruce, passing birders and hikers along the way. As we ambled the trails, he pointed out the many different species of plants and trees we encountered, and told me about all their special adaptations. He told me what was native and what was invasive, not that he particularly cared about that. He was pro-immigration in every way.

On our walks, he revealed things to me I never otherwise would have known, introduced me to words I never would have heard. He was an excellent teacher in that way, overflowing with information.

But it was more than that, too. He passed along more than facts. He was passing along a whole way of seeing. The reason he observed the natural world so deeply, I came to realize, was because he looked at it with such deep love. "You must have the bird in your heart before you see it in the bush," John Burroughs said. Phil had the bird in his heart. I walked away from our meetings filled with new insights, brimming with new understandings. And then I went home and transcribed his lessons almost verbatim.

"The madrone is such a remarkable tree, isn't it?" he said, pausing at a twisting trunk on a ridge overlooking the Rogue Valley, snowless mountains visible in the distance. "I mean, look at this guy. His branches are so gnarled, but his skin is so satiny. And the wood. Feel it. It's so cool. So smooth. Like the back of your arm. Really, the madrone is among the most individualistic of trees, don't you think?"

"There's a lot going on with this guy, all right," I said.

"In the spring, the flowers come in like little bells," he said, "and in the fall, they get these bright red berries. Tons of birds eat them. Cedar waxwings, thrushes, quail, juncos. Mammals, too. Deer, bear. When the berries dry up they have hooked barbs that stick to the fur of the bigger animals. So the deer and bear become the madrone's sharecroppers, in a way. They haul the seeds off and plant them everywhere they go."

"This one looks pretty happy," I said.

"It's sunny here, and they're sun seekers," he said, patting the trunk. "They'll grow any direction to get to that sun. They can't wait to bloom. This one's already impatient to do it again, I bet."

"You think a tree gets impatient?" I said.

"Why not?" he said, continuing along the trail. "They know what's coming. They want to show everyone what they've got. Imagine what it must feel like to be a blooming tree. Drinking all that light. The biggest madrone on record was in Big Sur. It was over 250 years old. It burned a few years ago."

"Fuck," I said. "That's awful."

"Yep," he said. "A campfire. Those people deserve life in jail."

He liked to talk about the inner mechanics of trees, that confounding transformation of light into energy, what he called the symphony of photosynthesis.

"Inside every plant are these little organelles," he said, crouching in a bed of wild strawberries and clover, touching their delicate stems and leaves, "which are what store the energy of sunlight. They're a subunit of a cell. And inside the organelles, there are these little disks called chloroplasts. And inside the chloroplasts are these things called thylakoids. It's actually the thylakoid membrane where the chlorophyll is stored. The light-absorbing pigment."

"The green stuff," I said.

"Yes and no," he said. "Sunlight is full-spectrum light, obviously. Way more light than we can perceive with our eyes. During photosynthesis, the chlorophyll absorbs the blue- and red-light waves, and it reflects green-light waves, which is why the plants appear green to us. They're green because the green light is no good for the plants. They're repelling green. Isn't that funny? You think of a plant as green all the way through. Green is exactly what they are not."

We talked a lot about the current popular obsession with tree intelligence, the whole, stupid metaphor of the "wood wide web." The wood wide web idea didn't go far enough, Phil thought. Trees were more than just circuit boards, trading practical information. They were more like the mind of the world, thinking and dreaming, above us and below.

"What kind of dreams do you think they have?" I said, passing under a shining drop ceiling of big-leaf maple.

"We don't know what our own dreams are doing," he said. "How would we be able to interpret a tree's?"

"You think they dream in pictures?" I said.

"They don't have optic nerves," he said. "But then again, blind people dream, don't they? And what is an image, anyway? How does an image appear inside the mind? When you remember something, you can see it. But what is it? Where is it? Think of an image right now. Something not in front of you."

I thought of his wife.

"So where is it, exactly?" he said.

"In my brain tissue," I said.

"So there's a picture inside your brain," he said. "Like a tiny negative?"

"In some synapse inside a neuron somewhere," I said. "Sure."

"So it has a substance," he said.

"Yes and no," I said. "I'm not sure."

"When you see something out in the world, is it actually out there, or is it on your retina?" he said. "This is an old Zen trick. Where do you think the image actually resides?"

"Both," I said. "Outside and on my retina. And then the brain interprets it."

"But in your memory, where does the image live?" he said. "You can see it, and yet I can't see it. Think of a blue elephant. I definitely can't measure the image you see. How will we ever gauge a tree's imagination?"

"Maybe someday we will," I said.

"Maybe," he said. "Or maybe it's in the nature of some things to be hidden."

"God attracts us to Himself," said the anonymous author of *The Cloud of Unknowing*. "He draws us to Himself." That summer, God was drawing me powerfully in two directions at once. I was drawn to Sarah and drawn to Phil both, stretched on an invisible rack. I was drawn to Sarah in the most complete and carnal way possible. I wanted to be with her at every moment. I wanted to be inside of her. And I was drawn to Phil too, in the way of an eager student to a mentor, or a humble disciple to a guru. Increasingly, I saw Phil as the very model of what a man could be: innocent, giving, voracious, submissive. I was always happy to place myself under his power.

There were moments, standing in the shower or lying in bed late at night, when I could see I was doing something wrong. I was deep in the woods, far off the path. I wondered if I should end the affair with Sarah, or the friendship with Phil, but I didn't want to end either one, not yet. All my life, I'd lived so purely, I told myself. I'd spent my hours practically like a monk in a cell, reading and writing and almost nothing else. So maybe, I rationalized, I could allow myself this one transgression. It was only a temporary situation, wasn't it? A passing, strange compromise. Soon, surely, Sarah would become bored with me. My conversations with Phil would run their course. We'd all drift back to the places we'd been and scan our horizons for the next objects of desire.

And if we continued living this lie? Maybe that was okay, too. There were so many crimes in the world that went unseen. So many infractions and misdemeanors that never got punished. For every betrayal discovered, every infidelity exposed, there were ten thousand that went unsuspected. Every day, I hoped ours would be one of those.

And then one night, my two realities converged. It wasn't my proudest moment. It was in mid-July, and Phil had invited me over for an evening drink again. I'd refused so many of his invitations by then that it was becoming a little ridiculous, and on this night, I felt like I had to say yes. Sarah and I consulted beforehand and agreed she'd make some excuse to leave the house when I got there, which meant the three of us would only overlap for a few minutes at most. We both assumed we could deal with that level of awkwardness. We could act our parts, play our roles, and then the discomfort would end. There was even a certain thrill to the prospect. What kind of acting chops would we end up having?

It was a lovely night. The sun was bathing the valley in gold, sending long shadows through the streets, and the last midsummer cottonwood fluff floated in the air. Children were playing hide-and-seek, sending their shrill calls back and forth from their ditches and cubbyholes. As I climbed the now-familiar stairs, preparing myself for the uneasy scene, I did a quick mental rehearsal, reminding myself to act confidently and look both of them in the eyes. Or maybe I should avoid Sarah's eyes, I wasn't sure. Was that more natural? In any case, it turned out it didn't matter. As soon as Sarah opened the door, I could tell something was off.

"Phil's sick," she said.

"Oh," I said, already playing my part. "Is it bad?"

"Summer flu," she said. "He's really out of it. He said he texted you. Maybe he forgot."

"I didn't get anything," I said. "I guess I can come back another night if that's better?"

"No, no," she said. "You're here now. Come on in. It's fine."

"You're sure?" I said.

"Now it'd be weird if you didn't."

She opened the door and loudly invited me inside. "Come on in, Arthur!" she said. "Phil's upstairs in bed! He's got the flu! He's sad to miss you!"

Her acting wasn't very convincing. She was projecting her words much too loudly, practically throwing them up the stairs. In a more normal voice, I told her that I could come back another time, but caught myself enunciating strangely. My volume was okay, but I was mumbling out the side of my mouth like James Cagney. And for the benefit of whom? Phil couldn't hear us all the way upstairs anyway. We had to relax.

I followed Sarah into the kitchen. It was different than I remembered from the party, not different in itself, but different in my perception. There was something almost poignant about it now, seen through the lens of our deception. The machinery of their daily life seemed almost frail, with its old, stained coffee grinder, its fragile dish rack. So this was the room where they stood around together in the mornings, half-dressed, sleep still pouring off their skin. This was where they swept up bits of egg and stray dried beans. It was a scene of lies, but, still, undeniably real.

I stood across the room as Sarah made us both margaritas. She was wearing a cotton smock, and when the light hit her from behind, the silhouette of her hips and thighs showed through the fabric. I watched her dividing the limes and inserting each juicy lobe into the press, as together we performed a generic conversation for the body lying upstairs. We finally started to hit our stride. Our voices and transcript became flawlessly banal.

"We've been having a lot of palomas lately," she said. "Summer is all about tequila around here. Today is a margarita day, though."

"I just read an article about tequila," I said. "Actually it was about jimadors, the guys who harvest the agave. They're very skilled workers, it turns out."

"Is that so?" she said.

She made a pile out of the squashed rinds and gradually filled the pitcher with juice. In two squat glasses, she mixed it with the simple syrup and the tequila and added a handful of ice, the tiny air bubbles releasing fizzy snaps and pops. Then we went to their library, the book-lined, plant-filled antechamber off the dining room.

I'd seen the room in the dark, but in the daylight it was even more inviting. The room was designed for comfortable contemplation. Two armchairs faced a sofa running under the bay windows overlooking the side yard. Outside were two plum trees, bleary in the marbled panes. A hanging glass prism splashed the room with rainbow fragments. We took seats well apart from each other, her on the sofa, me in an armchair, and continued our play.

"So what else is happening?" she said, pulling her legs under herself, smoothing her dress. "How's the book coming?"

We never talked about the book on our island. She knew I found it hard to talk about a book in progress, the action was so mental and slow-moving. There were never any good anecdotes to recount. But this play we were acting in was forcing us into new, more generic territory.

"I'm getting my daily word count," I said.

"How many words do you go for in a day?" she said.

"A few hundred," I said. "If I can. Five hundred is a good day. A thousand is great. That almost never happens."

"What's the title?"

"Right now it's just called *The Tree Book*."

"That's kind of a dull title."

"I have some other ideas. We'll see."

"Do you have a lot of files?" she said. "Or one big file?"

"A lot of files," I said. "But they'll all join together pretty soon."

"Interesting."

It wasn't that interesting. We talked about formatting for a while, and fonts. We kept it very superficial. Phil was our true audience, even though he couldn't hear a thing we said, and the words were only a shell game, anyway, a thin veil covering up the pulse of sex that had started beating between us. As we talked, Sarah was shifting her weight on the couch and stretching her arms so the straps of her sundress sometimes fell. She was taking satisfying sips of her drink that showed off the elegant curve of her neck. I leaned back in the chair, slouching, allowing my lap to spread. The signals passing between us were silent but constant. We hadn't been in a room without disrobing in weeks.

"Do you ever write longhand?" she said.

"I take notes longhand," I said. "And sometimes I'll write a whole first draft longhand. I print out a lot no matter what, and make a lot of notes with a pen."

"How often do you print out?" she said.

"Every couple weeks, I'd say," I said. "Inputting the written notes is a real pain. But I once made the mistake of not printing out often enough. It really hurt the book. I got lost. I need to see it on paper."

"Writing is such a graphic thing, isn't it?"

"The shape of a paragraph is a kind of sculpture."

We talked about handwriting for a while, and how illegible people's handwriting had become. Kids never learned how to write with a pen anymore. My own handwriting hadn't ever been any good. I had trouble reading it myself sometimes. Maybe I needed glasses, she said. I'd look good in glasses. And then she told me about where to find the best glasses. It was sometime during that lecture that she got up and went to the doorway between the library and the dining room and quietly edged the sliding door partly closed, though not all the way. To close the door all the way would have been suspicious, but to close the door partly seemed within reason, a courtesy.

On the way back to the couch she paused and crouched and kissed me on the mouth. The kiss was long, flavored with tequila. Her hand wandered to my lap. My groin rose to meet her.

Our kissing was only a dumb joke at first, a dare. We were both terrified of Phil only a matter of feet away, hidden behind a couple of thin walls. But when no one stirred, no sounds drifted down, she kissed me again.

"This is a very bad idea," I said.

"I know," she said.

But I guided her closer. She pivoted and lowered herself onto my lap and we kissed more deeply. The betrayal was building to a new magnitude. This was a true sin we were committing. To sneak off in the night, away from anyone's eyes, that was one thing. To do this here was a form of sadism. The cruelty of the act was unforgivable. But we kept going.

The next moments went by fast and hot. My hands slipped under her dress, running up her spine, cupping her naked breasts. Our breathing became ragged, our eyes blank. I stood up from the armchair and went down onto my knees, lifting her dress and going at her from the angle I knew she liked.

Sarah shuddered, her hands caught in my hair. I held her thighs as I licked her and kept going until she moaned quietly and pulled away. We weren't done yet. She grabbed a pillow from the couch and threw it onto the floor and lay down and pulled me along with her. A moment later, our hot breath was in each other's ears. She was fumbling with my belt and then my pants were at my knees. She opened her legs and I slid inside her. She whimpered. I groaned. Within a few strokes it was over, as quickly as it started, appalling but ecstatic.

Immediately, I peeled off my sock and swabbed our stomachs, looking at her with a mixture of gratitude and remorse. We both knew we'd crossed a terrible line. We'd thrown Phil into a boiling volcano, or maybe thrown ourselves in, we weren't sure yet. We'd definitely committed a human sacrifice, that much was clear, but of whom, and to what deity, we had no idea. In that moment, we didn't really care.

We didn't care, that was, until a few seconds later, when we heard sounds in the kitchen. Sarah was in the middle of handing me back the damp sock, and we both froze in place. We'd been so blinded by our desires we hadn't noticed Phil's footsteps descending the stairs. He must have come down right in the middle of our lunacy. What idiots! To take such a stupid risk!

We sat there on the floor for a moment, staring into each other's eyes. We didn't know what to do. We could hear Phil moving around, opening the cabinet doors, rattling dishware. Sarah was the first to collect herself and begin talking again.

"I bet handwriting has changed a lot in the last few years," she said, almost normally. She stood and tiptoed back to the couch where she'd been, replacing the cushion, softly lowering herself down. "I mean, with computers and all. Do girls still do the big, bubble letters anymore, I wonder?"

"Yeah, I don't know," I said, sliding my pants up to my hips. "I think maybe not? I don't have any idea."

"That seemed like such a forever thing," she said, locating her glass. "The big bubble letters, with the hearts and stuff. But I guess that was just a phase of history. I wonder when girls started writing that way?"

"Ballpoint pens," I said.

"Maybe," she said.

She fluffed her hair and I checked my shirttails and pants for any fluids. Her cheeks were flushed, but the margarita could probably be blamed for that. The whistle of a teakettle came from the kitchen. I projected the question into her mind: "Does Phil have any idea what we just did?" "I don't know!" she projected back. "I don't think so."

"I know an artist who works in ballpoint pens," she said. "She's really amazing. She can do anything with a Bic. Giant works on paper. Women and apes. And plants. Amazing stuff. Your mom's an artist, isn't she? What kind of art does she make? I don't think I know."

"She makes quilts," I said. "But the kind you hang on a wall."

"Do you like your mom's quilts?" she said.

"Yeah," I said.

"Tell me about your mom's art."

I didn't have any desire to talk about my mom's art, though there was plenty I could say. I was possibly the world's foremost expert. But before I could get started, Phil's footsteps exited the kitchen. We heard them crossing the dining room floor, growing louder. Would he peek in on us, we wondered, or would he go back upstairs? We waited to find out. The footsteps continued coming closer. We heard him shuffling to the doorjamb and pulling the door wider a few inches. His face appeared in the crack. His friendly, innocent face, haggard with flu, eyes red and baggy.

"Oh, Arthur," he said. "I thought I heard you."

"I hear you're feeling not so great," I said, with moist concern. "I hope you're doing okay. Are you?"

"Getting worse before I get better, I'm afraid," he said, wiping his nose. "Seems like a flu has to touch every part of my body before it goes away. This one started in the throat last night. Now it's down in my chest. It'll be up in my head tomorrow. Sorry, I'm too sick to come inside. I don't want to give you anything."

"Sounds like it's running its course, honey," Sarah said.

"I can hold on to a cough for months, personally," I said. "You should take it real easy, Phil."

"Arthur's right," Sarah said. "You should be back in bed."

Phil nodded, and his eyes roamed over the room, a bit longingly. He gazed over the books, the plants, and then my sock near the fireplace. I thought I'd stuffed the sock into my pocket, but apparently it'd fallen out in the scramble. Phil seemed to stare at the sock for a moment, puzzling over it. Probably he thought it was his sock. It was gray and wadded. My bare foot was tucked under my leg to avoid drawing any attention. For a moment, Phil seemed to hover in the doorway, pondering whether to come in and pluck the sock from the floor, but mercifully, a coughing jag hit him. He hacked uncontrollably for a few seconds, his face reddening, tears squeezing from his eyes. When the spasm ended he stood there in the jamb, swaying, shaking his head.

"I'll leave you two to it," he said.

"I'll bring you more tea soon," Sarah said. "You sound awful. I'm so sorry."

"I'll be asleep," he said. "I just took some Theraflu. That always knocks me out. Well. Good evening. Drink another one for me."

We bade him goodbye and listened as his feet heavily climbed the stairs. If he'd noticed anything, he'd disguised any signs completely. We didn't feel the need to celebrate, though, or even acknowledge our victory. Barring a moment of wide-eyed relief, we continued talking as we had been, about penmanship and the nature of art versus craft. Soon, Sarah fixed us another round of margaritas. It would've been suspicious to have just one.

7

The end of summer was always hot, but this year it went on and on, until the heat became almost sickening. By mid-August, the needles of the conifers were burnt, with patches of copper deadness mottling the limp green shag. By September, the creeks were dry. Always, a vague haze smeared the horizon, brownish smoke scum trickling up from California, or down from Canada, or from the Coast Mountains, or the Cascades. The fires never stopped. It was that summer when I noticed people talking about the earth in the past tense. They began referring to Nature as a thing long gone, and whatever world was in store as a sad compromise at best, a shadow of a shadow of the grandeur that our parents and grandparents had once taken for granted as reality.

I had farmer friends who were calling it quits. For twenty years, they'd been working their land outside Ashland using only trapped rainwater, taking almost nothing from the watershed, and still they couldn't get by. The sky wouldn't give anymore. Their tiny footprint would now shrink to nothing.

"Where will you go?" I asked one friend.

"I don't know," he said. "Where is anybody going to go?"

I read old books and watched old movies, and found the lack of despair around the planet anachronistic. To live in those olden times, when the dread of global doom wasn't woven into everyday existence, was almost unimaginable.

I had moments when I wondered why I was writing a book at all. It made no logical sense to write a book that would be born into a dead world. There was no way my book would change anything or usher in a new age of ecological renewal and rebirth. If the book had any effect at all, it would be in the most subtle, negligible way. A book was not like a hammer driving a nail. It was more like a wave in an ocean. Collectively, the waves might reshape a shoreline, but individually, they were practically nothing.

And yet, I never considered pausing. I focused instead on Merle and Candy, and their humble gardening, and pressed onward every day with my doomed enterprise. It wasn't any different than usual in that way. Every book is a doomed enterprise. It's an impossible prayer going out into a world that doesn't listen and doesn't care. In fact, it was exactly the doomed impossibleness of the enterprise that made it so compelling. A book had no use value. It barely even existed. It was just a batch of vaporous thoughts emanating into the public mind as a faint demurral, a vanishing, ephemeral ghost of all the time spent writing it. It might stir a little whirlpool in the atmosphere of meaning, maybe ruffle a leaf, nothing else.

As always around this time, I was hitting a tricky patch in the writing. After months of spinning out provisional words and clauses, telling myself I'd improve everything at some later date, I'd reached that date. This was the stage of the process where things slowed down. It was the time when I had to acknowledge that everything I'd written thus far sounded wrong and it would be necessary to peel everything back and basically start anew. I had to slash entire sections, bleed entire bodies of text. I had to break open every sentence and find the real sentence that lurked inside. It was always demoralizing how this part of the writing went, and it could go on for a very long time. In writing a book, you had to give up everything on a daily basis.

I wasn't sorry when Sarah left town for a few days because it meant I'd have more headspace for the book. She was going on a retreat to Mount Hood with a mindfulness group of hers, which meant meditating together, practicing breathing techniques, and spending as much time in the saunas and hot springs as possible. It was an annual gathering, a good group, and she'd been looking forward to the trip all year. She was excited, even though it meant we'd miss a couple of our precious nights.

"I'm gonna miss you," I texted.

"You'll miss my ass," she texted back.

"I'll miss the other stuff, too," I texted. "The stuff connected to your ass."

"Uh-huh, but mostly my ass."

The day she left, I woke early and brewed coffee and got to work. I sat down hoping for a major breakthrough but had trouble getting started. The coffee wasn't hitting very hard for some reason, and the day's headlines kept distracting me. "Hottest Year on Earth Recorded." "Heavy Rains Wreak Havoc." "Wildfires Rage." "Why Would Anyone Live in Phoenix?"

I moved onto the back deck and set up my computer and notebooks in the shade, but still couldn't force myself to concentrate. It was already so hot, and the oak leaves were rustling so loudly in the lethargic breeze. I skimmed through my pages again and checked the news a few more times. "Plastic Waste Spiraling out of Control Across Africa." "Many People Are Feeling Ecological Grief."

At last, I got a little traction. That's the thing with a daily practice: you're there when the attention focuses. You never know exactly when it'll happen, so you have to be there, just in case. This time, I was suddenly seeing redundancies that I could clip and finding entire new paragraphs between jammed sentences. A long-held tight spot was giving way to something smooth and soft and possibly poetic.

I was still working inside the pocket, forging some decent, fresh clauses about softwood versus hardwood trees, when Phil called and broke my spell. I didn't pick up the phone, not wanting to waste my time, but I listened to the message a minute later to make sure it wasn't an emergency. He said he wanted to talk to me. Did I have a few minutes? I thumbed him a text explaining my situation, how I was living underground this week, laboring on the book. Maybe we could talk in a day or two? He texted back and said he wanted to see me today, in person, if possible. He said he had something important to discuss. He'd been known to call with random factoids he assumed I'd find completely mind-blowing, so I texted him again saying I was too busy, maybe Wednesday? I was a little annoyed that I had to keep batting him away in the middle of my prime hours, not that I was in any position to scold him.

I watched the pulse of his typing on the other end. The bubble grew and shrank, grew and shrank. As I watched the ellipsis burble on the phone's screen, it occurred to me how odd it was that Phil would be so demanding. It was so unlike him, I thought. What did he want? And then, the next thought boxed me on the ears: he knew.

My fingers and toes suddenly went cold. What else could it be?

What other reason could possibly drive Phil to this uncharacteristic pushiness? He'd discovered some clue in the house. He'd found something in Sarah's pocket, maybe, or a stray text. We'd been so careful, but really, how long could this deception go on?

The bubble on my phone faded and didn't come back. My insides curdled with fear and shame. Apparently, Phil couldn't think of what else to say in text form, but I knew now what his message meant. My first impulse was to call Sarah, but she was already off the grid. I was alone to field Phil's anguish for another six days.

Now I really couldn't work. I sat and tried to pick at a sentence, but it was no use. The trail was cold. What was I supposed to do now? It was amazing how little I'd managed to think about this part of our story—the actual consequences, the horrible reveal. As long as Phil hadn't known about the affair, it had seemed almost imaginary. I'd been able to tell myself that it was practically normal. Millions of people had affairs, all over the world. It was the way of human beings. All of which was true enough, in its way, but far from the whole truth. What I hadn't been thinking about was Phil as a living, feeling person. I'd been ignoring the very specific pain that this betrayal would cause him. I'd assumed, on some level, that Sarah would deal with it.

But now, with only a text, Phil had thrown a nauseating light on the whole ugly scene, and without Sarah, I wasn't sure what the next move should be. If Phil kept calling me, I'd have to talk to him at some point. Which meant I'd have to lie to him and tell him he was wrong, his fears unfounded. I'd have to lie baldly, in other words, and I'd probably get called out on it at a later date. And if he pushed harder, and showed me actual evidence, what would I do then? I'd still deny everything. I'd try to convince him it was all a misunderstanding, that he was reading it wrong. And if he pushed even harder? Eventually, I knew, I'd probably give in. I'd end up telling him something true just to end the logjam. I'd tell him how we'd never meant to hurt him and how we both loved and respected him and how we were all caught up in an unexpected, star-crossed, uncontrollable romance. I'd end up informing him that his wife and I had fallen in love.

It turned out I didn't have to wait long to figure out what I'd say because a little before noon Phil showed up at my door. He knocked and clearly spotted me on the back porch through the windows and rapped on the door again. I couldn't very well pretend I didn't hear him. As I shuffled through the cottage, it occurred to me that he might want to hurt me in a physical way. I doubted it, but who could say what people did in this kind of situation? All kinds of crazy things happened, even among otherwise reasonable people. If he'd arrived to hurt me, I at least wanted to make sure he didn't get in a good punch to my face.

"Hi, Phil," I said, opening the front door a crack.

"Hi, Arthur," he said.

"You doing all right?" I said.

"I'm not sure, Arthur," he said. "I don't know."

"You want to come in?" I said.

"If it's all right, yes."

I let him in. The air was crackling, but already I could tell Phil wasn't going to attack. Now that I saw him up close, he looked the opposite of angry. He looked depleted, confused. His eyes were downcast. He hadn't shaved. He didn't seem to know where to stand.

"You want a drink?" I said. "I just made some lemonade."

"That would be great," he said.

"I'll bring it out to the back deck," I said.

I went and poured him some lemonade. From the kitchen, I could see him pacing around on the deck, literally clutching his hair. The canopy of walnut and oak filtered the golden, smoke-softened light. It was a beautiful scene, but not so beautiful for him. I wondered if this was an elaborate performance on his part. What if he was trying to catch me in a lie? What if he only suspected something but didn't actually have any proof? I told myself I wouldn't give him anything he didn't already have.

I went out and handed him a glass of lemonade. He took a long drink. The birds were panting in the trees. You could feel the earth baking, turning into a brittle crust.

"I'm sorry," he said at last, putting down his half-empty glass. "I know you're busy. But I had to come over. I have to talk to you about something."

"I'm glad you came," I said, girding myself. "What's going on?"

Phil stared out into the valley, as if seeking words on the faraway hills. He'd called me, and now he'd shown up unannounced, and yet he seemed unprepared to say whatever he had to say. I wanted to be there for him, assuming his problem had nothing whatsoever to do with me.

"I guess I should just say it," he said. "I think Sarah's having an affair."

"Oh," I said calmly. I was convulsing inside, but also immediately put at ease. If he thought I was involved in the affair, I doubted he'd be phrasing it like that. We were deeply embroiled now, but also looking at each other from different realities.

"What makes you think so?" I said, and found my acting surprisingly nuanced. My tone suggested at once surprise and *a priori* doubt about any theories he might have. I sounded ready to explain away any suspicions, as a real friend would.

"Little changes, little signals," he said. "I couldn't even tell you what they are. It's just the way she talks to me lately, the way she sits. I mean, things have been hard between us before. Don't get me wrong. Every couple goes through those periods. You wait them out. You give them time. But this one is different. It isn't hard. It's something worse. It's like she's already gone."

"How long have you been feeling this way?" I said.

"A while," he said. "It takes a while to understand that you know something is wrong, you know? There's no one thing that tells you. It's all so small. But at some point, you can't really deny it anymore. There's something."

I made a sound that didn't require a response, just a noise of general sympathy and regret. I wanted to keep the conversation as abstract as possible, separate from any actual activities or protagonists. We were only talking about a theory here, not a particular accusation of any singular person.

"I think I know who it is," he said, surprising me.

"Oh yeah?" I said. "Does it matter, really?"

"I think it's her meditation instructor," he said.

"Ah," I said. Again, the flying hatchet had passed.

"He's a very attractive guy," Phil said, "very friendly. I can see how they'd have a lot in common. She's been wanting new experiences in her life, I know that. She doesn't love living here. It's been hard to make friends. I can't say for sure, but I think that's why she went on this retreat, to be with him. It's very hard, Arthur, thinking about it all the time. I think about it, I try not to think about it, I think about it anyway. I imagine things I don't want to see."

"Have you asked her about it?" I said.

"She doesn't want to talk about it," he said. "I've asked her in a million ways if something is wrong. She says nothing is wrong. She says I'm imagining things. Maybe I am. I don't know." He sighed wetly.

"It sounds hard," I said.

"I mean, I want to believe what she says," he said. "I just worry she's trying to be kind. She wants to protect me from whatever it is. I don't know. It's not that I don't believe her. I'm sure she has her reasons."

"You want to know the truth, though," I said.

"It's the not knowing that's so difficult, exactly," he said. "I can handle whatever it is. Just let me know so we can move on. There's nothing I can't take. We're just people here, trying to get through our lives, doing the best we can. I only want her to feel like she can tell me whatever she needs to tell me and know I'll support her in whatever way she needs. I love her, Arthur. I don't want to stand in her way."

He gave a choked sob and pinched the bridge of his nose. Tears flowed over his fingers, and he wrestled himself under control. The buzz of a hummingbird's wings zipped in the air. The faraway traffic of I-5 whispered. The heat of the sun bore down everywhere.

Within an hour, I was in the car, driving to the Wy'East Resort, an august spiritual retreat on the southern slope of Mount Hood. It was a five-hour drive, north on I-5, east on 22, then up winding roads into the monument of Mount Hood National Forest. I didn't want to be making the trip—I hated losing my precious writing time or crashing Sarah's private vacation—but I felt like I had to go and tell her what was afoot. Phil's visit had transformed our affair in a moment. We were no longer living inside a closed system, safe in our secret room. Our actions had somehow seeped out into the atmosphere and infected Phil's consciousness. Now, because of us, he was suffering. It seemed like our duty to make it stop.

All the way up I-5, hot wind whipped me through the windows. I spent the first hour trying to convince myself that we hadn't actually done anything wrong. Again and again, I tried carving the facts into some self-exculpatory storyline. I'd met a woman. We'd had an affair. Where was the crime in that? The love between two people wasn't a betrayal of the third; it was something between the two lovers alone. Whatever Sarah and I had done, whatever we felt, didn't touch Phil or reduce him in any way. No one owned Sarah. She owned herself. But as much as I rationalized our actions, I could never quite get the arguments to click. There was no getting around the fact that we'd lied to someone we cared about, cheated on a person we both, in our ways, loved. For all our careful subterfuge, we'd let our pleasures blot out our basic decency, and caused Phil harm.

It was in the second hour that I moved on to thinking about the situation in more practical terms. As far as I could tell, there were a few paths forward, none of which were simple or attractive. Most obviously, we could simply continue lying. We could keep duping Phil, convincing him nothing was happening, and go on with our trysts at the Barn as we'd been doing. We could live in a state of secrecy as long as possible, enjoying ourselves as if no one else mattered. But it was hard to see that as a real possibility anymore. After Phil's conversation, the innocence—or ignorance, whatever you'd call it—was gone.

Another option was breaking things off. Sarah and I could go back to our lives and pretend nothing had ever happened. We could reestablish normal boundaries, maybe find some new, less compromising rapport. But that life looked paltry and sad now. From what Sarah had been telling me, she'd been looking for a way out of her marriage before I'd ever come along. She loved Phil, and they had an affectionate partnership, but she'd realized their time together had an end point. For years, she'd been plotting an exit, seeking the right opportunity, and then I'd appeared like the key to her escape, the tool of her transformation. But I'd turned out to be more than she'd bargained for. I'd arrived at the right time, but I'd exceeded her needs. Now the old order of things was no longer possible.

At this point, the path forward became trickier and harder to comprehend, and it quickly subdivided into multiple tracks. In one version, all of us went our separate ways. No one ended up with anyone. Sarah left us both, maybe with Phil never the wiser. Our tryst became the fuse that destroyed her marriage and exploded all the bonds. That seemed like a waste.

Another path involved going on as three. I had polyamorous friends who recommended this kind of arrangement. They claimed all love was good love. They argued that no love ever subtracted from another love, that all love could peacefully coexist in the same giant love blob. They believed the only answer to a problem of love was more love. But their way of thinking had always struck me as wishful, at best. In real life, love destroyed love. Love ate love. The fact was, we'd sent an exterminating love into Phil's life and he was awakening to the terror of his loss.

What did that leave? Sarah and I could go forward together alone, leaving Phil behind, mangled in the dust. We could rent a place in Ashland or somewhere else, and then what? I had no idea. This was an option almost too scary to contemplate. We didn't even know each other very well. It seemed too fast, too deep. I wasn't sure Sarah and I truly trusted each other yet. Sarah was obviously a person capable of deceiving her most intimate partner. And what was I? A writer, a professional sneak. Somehow we'd entered into a conspiracy without vetting each other. Now we were stuck together, mid-heist.

In the end, I realized I couldn't plot any of these courses by myself. So much depended on what Sarah wanted, what Sarah felt. To know what I wanted, I needed to know what she wanted, and only then could we create any kind of plan. So I drove onward, the wind pouring through the car like the breath of some devil on the other side of the mountains, shaking the crowns of the trees on the shoulder. All the way down the highway, I bobbed in and out of my fiery pit, hating myself, forgiving myself, explaining myself, apologizing, rationalizing, and trying my best to ignore that other, buried part of me that felt so powerfully alive, like some raging monkey beating his chest.

I skirted the Santiam River, speeding past the towns of Sublimity and Mill City, and headed up the throat of the valley to Detroit Lake, which was practically empty. I turned at the marina, now a dry dock, and followed the roads as they narrowed and darkened with evergreens. Soon, I was pulling into a dirt parking lot filled with Subarus and Priuses coated in dust, and opening the door into the quiet of the forest. The carpet of needles was fragrant and soft, the shadows cool even in the day's broiling heat. I pulled my backpack from the trunk, along with my computer, which I knew I wouldn't be touching anytime soon.

I walked through the familiar neighborhood of clapboard guest cabins, where I'd spent many serene evenings over the years, and entered the grand alley of cedars and Douglas firs leading to the main lodge. The trees parted, and there it was, a beautiful, many-windowed mansion dating from the 1920s, circled by a grand, wraparound deck, studded with dormers, topped by a lightning bolt weathervane. On the lawn in front of the mansion's stately wings were children playing, sunbathers reading, couples talking. Half-naked guests ambled the trails with their towels, shuffling to the hot springs that dotted the landscape, or to the saunas, or to the hidden gazebos and yurts where the healing workshops were held.

On the edge of the lawn, near a bed of ruffled foxglove and snapdragons, sat a wide circle of people engaged in some kind of sharing. They were passing a beach ball around, which seemed to confer speaking powers. In the circle was Sarah.

I stood in the shade of the cedars, watching her group. It looked like she was having a fun time, laughing, listening, nodding along. I couldn't hear what anyone was saying, but I could tell by the way the attention moved around the perimeter that the leader was talented. He kept the flow going. He was as charming and attractive as Phil had reported, a young-looking guy with a swimmer's build, long chestnut hair, a regal nose. I felt threatened by him not at all.

When the beach ball came to Sarah, she batted it away and fell backward, laughing. And when the ball came back again she held it in her lap and talked easily for a while, getting some laughs. I hated to spoil her special week, but I didn't see any way around it. As soon as I caught her alone, I'd make my approach.

At last, Sarah felt my eyes on her and glanced my way. A look of surprise crossed her face. Was something wrong? her eyes seemed to ask. Had I come with some kind of terrible news? I gave her a shrug and a shake of the head that said, Don't worry, nothing too dire, no one is dead. She seemed to understand, more or less, and went back to the group, turning toward me again a few seconds later with another curious expression. This time I gave her a look that said, It isn't nothing, either, we have to talk.

Sarah was too enmeshed in her group to break away just yet, and thus it was almost dusk, after I'd checked into my cabin, when I saw her again, in hot spring number 7, the silent pool. She was soaking with a few women from her group, winding down after a long day of sharing. Wisps of steam coiled around their shoulders, the refractions of light underwater turning their naked bodies into scrambles. I disrobed and rinsed off in the outdoor shower and climbed into the pool, taking a place on the edge of the rocky basin overlooking a field of dry grass. The river wasn't visible, but you could hear the current shushing the landscape, mixed with the rasp of the wind in the tan pasture. Beyond a curtain of riverside poplars, the mountain's dirt peak rose in the twilight, burnished with orange.

We weren't allowed to speak in the silent pool and thus Sarah and I were left to communicate by significant looks. I tried to express the gravity of the news again, and she manufactured an expression of appropriate worry mixed with a warning that she couldn't just up and exit the pool with a strange man. The other women in her group were Ashland people, after all, and Ashland people talked.

I turned away and looked at the sky, breathing with the passing clouds. I could feel Sarah watching me for any additional clues, but we both knew I couldn't explain anything without words. All we could do was soak in each other's emotional proximity. At last, her group got up and left. I watched as she climbed the stairs and showered along with the other women, and wrapped her body in a clean, white towel. Then she walked away with a final, lingering, querulous glance that I answered with a frustrated grimace. A few minutes later,

I rose from the pool as well, and left the silent waters to the next bathers.

An hour later, at dinner, I finally caught her alone at the buffet. The first wave of diners had passed through the line and people were returning for seconds of collard greens and quinoa pilaf. Sarah was grazing the trays, loitering, and I took a place next to her, allowing the low murmur of conversation to mask our talk.

"What are you doing here?" she said, scooping some pilaf onto her plate.

"I have to talk to you," I said, accepting the spoon and taking my own scoop. "It's important."

"What's it about?" she said.

"I don't think this is a good place to talk about it," I said. "Too many people."

"I have a session after dinner," she said. "I'm not free 'til eleven."

"Can you skip it?" I said.

"Laura Baldwin recognized you," she said. "She asked me if we were friends. In a way I didn't like. I don't think I can miss the session now."

"How about after the session?" I said.

"Where?" she said.

"The Sunrise Yurt," I said.

"Okay," she said, and drifted to rejoin her group at the center of the room.

I got to the yurt first. It was on the outer edge of the resort's grounds, bowered in a grove of cedars, buffered by beds of maidenhair fern. During the day, it hosted meditation sessions and group encounters, but at night it was empty, a clean, sheltered womb ideal for a secret rendezvous. Tonight, the air in the yurt was stifling hot, perfumed by the cottony scent of the padded flooring, mixed with notes of cedar armature and canvas wall, plus a strong hint of sandalwood incense. I closed the portal door behind me and waited in the pitch darkness, already sweating profusely. At last, I heard her footsteps on the earthen path and she entered the dome.

"Are you in here?" she whispered.

"I'm here," I said.

"Where?"

"In the middle."

She crawled toward me until she touched my arm and found my hand. Our fingers clasped and we held each other for a moment, and kissed, returning ourselves to each other's possession.

"It's so hot in here," she said.

"Yeah," I said.

"Maybe there's somewhere else we can go," she said.

"No, this is a good place," I said. "We don't want anyone seeing us."

"So what's going on?" she said, catching my graveness. "Tell me."

I didn't know how to break the news to her except bluntly. "Phil knows something is going on," I said.

"Fuck," she said, with more resignation than anything else. The word didn't come as any great surprise. How could it? For months, we'd been sneaking around, having sex in Phil's own house, right under his nose. It had only been a matter of time before he started putting things together.

"He doesn't know it's between you and me, though," I said. "He thinks it's between you and somebody else."

"Who does he think it is?" she said, mildly offended.

"He thinks you're seeing your group leader up here," I said.

"Yeah, right," she scoffed.

"In any case, he's really upset about it," I said. "He's suffering a lot. He cried about it. I saw him this morning."

Sarah moaned, hating this news. The reality we'd entered was already bleak and unforgiving. We'd fallen into the oldest story in the book, three well-intentioned people trapped in a triangle. At least she and I were in the pit together now, suffering alongside each other. We sat in the hot dome letting it all penetrate.

"So what are we going to do?" she said.

"I don't know," I said.

"I don't think I can deal with lying to him much longer," she said. "It isn't fair. It's awful."

"Yeah," I said. "I agree with that."

"So what are we supposed to do?"

We sat in silence, wondering. Hot wind blew through the trees, shaking the boughs, sending needles and cones falling onto the yurt's roof. The trunks were groaning up and down their lengths, creaking in their grain. In the darkness, I could hear Sarah breathing. I could sense her turning inward, away from me, having her own private thoughts about all that was happening.

"What are you thinking?" I said.

"I don't know," she said distantly.

"Tell me," I said.

"I'm just thinking..." She sighed. "I guess I'm wondering what's going on here, that's all."

"It's a good question," I said.

"I mean, what is this, Arthur?" she said. "We've been doing this for a while now. But we've never really talked about it. Not in a real way."

"No, I guess we haven't," I said.

"Maybe it's time we did," she said.

"Okay," I said.

I waited, hoping she'd go first. I wanted her to tell me what I was supposed to feel. But I could tell she was waiting, too, hoping I'd inform her of the same thing. There was no outwaiting her, I could sense. I was the one who had to begin.

"Well," I said, trying to proceed delicately. I knew we were in a fragile spot, and I didn't want to break anything by going too fast or being imprecise. "I think we have something very special between us. Something that I never expected. Something I value a lot."

"Okay," she said, not impressed.

"And it's also something that hurts Phil," I said, "which is really unfortunate."

"Yep," she said.

"But even though I know it's wrong," I said, "I don't want it to end. I can't really imagine that happening."

"Me, neither," she said. "I'm glad you said that."

"So where does that leave us?" I said. "I don't know."

"I don't know, either," she said. And again, we waited in silence. The branches of the trees were going crazy outside, roaring in wild gusts. A big pine cone dropped on the roof and rolled off the edge, plopping on the wooden deck.

Quietly, as if the words could barely make it out of her lips, she said, "I could leave him."

We let that thought expand in the darkness. In our hot bubble, it felt like we could hear the world's heart beating. She was taking the final path, the deepest path, the one that led into pitch blackness.

"It would be a big step," I said.

"It would," she said.

"It would mean some really big changes," I said.

"That's for sure," she said. "But what do you think? As an idea?"

I didn't know what to say. At the same time, I knew I wasn't allowed to wait long to answer. The more time that elapsed, the weaker my answer would become. My answer would become deformed by misgivings, even if the misgivings were well hidden or later denied. If my answer was going to give her any dignity, it had to come fast.

"I think," I said, "that that sounds good." And it was true, even as I heard the words exiting my mouth. Already, I could feel the rightness of the idea as it came into being. I could feel the rightness of our worlds melding and becoming one. It was almost like the idea had been there all along, waiting for us to voice it. My misgivings vanished for the moment. I could almost see the whole shape of the future resolving and making room for us. I could see that we'd been building it that way from the start.

"That's nice," she said.

And then we rested. It seemed like we'd already climbed a mountain. We'd clambered over a high, rocky escarpment, and the view of the country now spread before us in all its dazzling, sun-spotted hugeness. The idea of a life together was capacious and warm. There were landscapes of mystery and sweetness ahead. I saw a house in California with peeling paint on the windowsills and dripping nasturtiums in the front yard. I could see Sarah and me cooking a stir-fry in our humble kitchen. I could tell the images had been growing between us for months now, but we hadn't allowed ourselves to look at them. We hadn't realized how far up the mountain we'd already come.

It turned out, however, we weren't done climbing. There was still a major length to go.

"There's something else," she said.

"What?" I said gently. I was still enjoying the view into our future. I could feel Sarah's ribs breathing against me. In a gleam of wayward moonlight, I saw the finest grain of her hair, the curve of her cheek.

"I don't know if I want to say it," she said.

"We're here now," I said. "We should say it all."

She took a deep breath and exhaled slowly. "If we're really talking about this..."

And before she could say any more, she started to cry.

I didn't say anything, but only held her tightly, waiting for the squall to pass. I was starting to comprehend where this was going. I could already see that to live together, to leave a marriage, was something she didn't take lightly. It implied certain expectations, certain bargains. I could tell that the mountain we'd just climbed was not the real mountain after all, but only the base of the mountain. The view I'd glimpsed was suddenly overgrown with vegetation. We were entering a much denser territory than I'd imagined.

"I'm thirty-seven years old," she said, gasping. "I don't have a lot of time to mess around. Do you hear what I'm saying?"

"I think I do," I said.

"You think so?" she said.

"Maybe," I said.

"Are you going to make me say it out loud?" she said.

"Uh, yeah, maybe so," I said. "Just to be sure."

She whimpered a few times, trying to collect herself, but she couldn't seem to get her breathing under control. Finally, she went ahead, breaking into ragged sobs as she spoke.

"When I was little," she said, "I never wanted any kind of family. You know? I looked around at all the people in the neighborhood and I thought, no, no, that's not me. I saw all those stupid dads in their backyards. Those stupid moms in their pantries full of Doritos and Pepsi. All those huge, stupid cars. I hated it, Arthur. The waste of it all. It was all so fucking obvious. It was a fable that people were living in, and I hated it.

"And then I left home and met Phil," she said, "and it was great, because he saw it all the same way. Not in an angry way. Just in a smart, deep way. He didn't even wear shoes back then. He lived in his fucking van and slept in a hammock on campus. I don't know what we were thinking. I was so young when we got together. He was my TA, you know that, right?"

"I think I did," I said.

"But now, I'm having different feelings," she said. "My body is wanting things that I didn't want before. Do you know what I'm saying, Arthur? Do I have to spell it out to you? A bomb is going off in me."

"I think I understand," I said.

"I want a baby," she said, and gasped like she'd been punched. "I can't believe I'm saying this out loud. But I think about it all the time, Arthur. I do. I was thinking about it before I met you. I don't know if I knew I was thinking about it, but I was. I want a fucking baby. I want to see a baby grow up and learn to talk. I want to see it learn to walk. I want to see it grow up and leave me. I want to be abandoned by a baby, Arthur, is that so wrong? I feel like my life might be wasted if I don't do it. Oh, God..."

She wept harder, burying her face in my shoulder.

"It isn't wrong," I said quietly, kissing her hair, even as the earth seemed to dissolve underneath me. We were floating into a completely new dimension now, without features in any direction. I didn't know what kind of place it was. But in the moment, more than anything else, I only wanted to console Sarah. I wanted to make her feel safe.

"And you're saying I'm the one you want to do this with, right?" I said, buying a little time.

"I wouldn't be telling you this if you weren't, you dumbshit," she said.

"This really isn't what I thought we were going to be talking about tonight," I said. "Wow."

"Yeah, me, neither," she said, recovering a bit and wiping her eyes. "But now it's out there. You don't have to say anything right now. I just need to know if it's a definite no or not. Is it? You can tell me."

"No," I said, "it's not a no."

We sat in the darkness holding each other, sweating. At last, the real secret was out, and it was far beyond the meager secret of infidelity. The fable Sarah had rejected her entire life was suddenly the one she wanted to live. And for whatever reason, she'd deemed me good enough to live it with her. Why was Phil not good enough? Who could say? I was the one.

I kissed her wet forehead, her eyes. Her tears were salty and viscous. We were both covered in sweat but we didn't care; the sweat was clean and fresh. We began kissing each other with more ardor, feeling a new solemnity gathering between us. No matter what happened now, there was no going back. Her marriage was shattered.

I peeled off Sarah's shirt and she peeled off mine. We took off our own shorts and found each other again, our bodies gliding against each other, slipping and sliding almost like they were turned inside out. I ran my hands over her hips, over her nipples, over her beautiful, rounded ass. The sweat in the crevice was maddeningly arousing. She took me in her mouth until I made her stop and we lay down on the soft floor, the backward wind blowing in the trees overhead. She'd never been so open to me before. I'd never been so strong. As I thrust inside her, she held on to my back like I might float away, both of us wondering if we were conceiving new life that very night, in the very first, raw moments of our brand-new life.

8

I left the lodge in the morning before the heat got too intense. We hadn't talked any more about what the future held, the details were too much to contemplate, but we'd agreed on an immediate time frame. For the next few days, Sarah would stay at the retreat. She'd already paid for the session, and nothing was going to change before she got back anyway, so she might as well enjoy herself, inasmuch as that was possible. Meanwhile, I'd head home and keep working on the book. When she returned, she'd talk to Phil, and depending on how that went, we'd go from there. We wanted to make this the best possible betrayal for him, the best possible destruction of his life. We had time to do it properly. We were together in eternity now.

Wending my way back down the mountain, I tried to keep my mind on simple matters. I had a five-hour drive ahead. I'd get gas outside Eugene at the biofuel station, where I could pick up some lunch. They had quiche, bagels, and burritos at their food kiosk. They had kombucha on tap, too, but I wouldn't get any of that. I'd push onward and make it home by early afternoon, and maybe manage to get a little work done before dinner. Tomorrow, I'd have steel-cut oatmeal for breakfast, and a solid workday.

Mostly, though, I found myself thinking about the future and all it held. It was impossible not to think about it. Even as I drove, tectonic plates were shifting. Massive reorganizations were underway. Was I really ready for this? In the moment, in the yurt, I'd expressed my readiness, if not in words than in deed. But in the light of day, as the tree shadows flickered on the windshield, my readiness seemed much less certain. Already, I could sense doubts creeping in, second thoughts blooming. I'd extinguished the doubting part of myself in the yurt in order to avoid hurting Sarah, but now that I was alone, those parts were growing back like ivy.

Questions of money, housing, friendship, and time swirled all around me. Sarah probably didn't understand how limited were the wages of a writer of syncretic, quasi-academic spirituality texts. She might think that my life was built on a solid foundation, when in fact, without the subsidized rent at my mother's house, I wouldn't be able to survive at all. I wasn't sure what I'd be able to swing as far as family life went. And the thought of betraying Phil continued stabbing at me. I hated to think of myself as a betrayer of friends. Phil was a good person, thoroughly brilliant, utterly undeserving of our treatment. What were we doing?

Most of all, though, it was my writing that worried me. I'd worked hard to build a life empty enough to contain my daily practice. My solitude was a precious substance that I'd sacrificed to create. It was that solitude that had always led me away from relationships in the past. I'd always feared losing my quiet mornings, losing my thread. I loved my writing life. Was I ready for that to change?

An hour into the drive, I pulled off into Amethyst Creek, a

pocket of old-growth forest just east of Salem, feeling like I needed a little ritual of some kind—a moment of reflection, or cleansing, or celebration, or I wasn't sure what. Amethyst Creek was one of the last stands of old growth in the western United States, a few thousand acres of Douglas fir, red alder, and Pacific yew, where two creeks joined to become the Little North Santiam. I was stopping there because it seemed like a good time for some ancient tree wisdom.

Stepping into the forest, I felt my mind immediately calm, become green. The trunks were tranquil and enormous, rising in giant, five-hundred-year-old pillars. They were coated in moss, with little ferns sprouting from the crooks of their limbs, lichens dripping. The ground was a plush blanket of microbial life, dank with hornwort and diverse mosses. As I walked, thinking about our new life, the new life we might create, I allowed my feelings about this absolutely world-changing step we were on the cusp of taking to unfurl completely. What did it all mean?

I'd never thought much about being a father before. I wasn't against the idea, necessarily, I just hadn't actively considered it. My own father had been a nonentity in my life, gone before I'd even been aware of him, although I'd met plenty of happy, dutiful fathers over the years. No one I knew seemed to regret having children. On the contrary, they loved it. I supposed I'd assumed I'd have one someday, when the right situation came along. I'd thought of fatherhood as something that would happen to me somehow, not something I'd actively pursue. I didn't doubt I'd be a decent father. How hard was it? Look at all the baffled people out there who managed it. Yes, I could become one of them.

Walking in the ancient forest, I enumerated all my thoughts again, all the arguments, pro and con, and found, passing under the boughs, that the cons didn't hold much energy. I searched my body for grave misgivings, checking my gut, checking behind my sternum, but I didn't find anything negative. We'd make our way, I reassured myself. Did a tree choose when to send out its shoots? Did a raccoon debate whether or not to mate? Like everything in Nature, they simply obeyed the drives that entered them, without conflict, without qualm. Only human beings could turn the basic act of reproduction into a problem, mired in stupid, human complications. Sarah's body was calling out to mine; my body was answering. It was that simple.

Would Phil forgive us? I could only hope so, but I couldn't worry about that, either. "The cut worm forgives the plow," as the great William Blake said. Though easy for the plow to say. Better were the words of the sage Meister Eckhart: "And so anyone is quite wrong who worries about the means through which God is working His works in you, whether it be nature or grace. Just let Him work, and just be at peace."

Walking the leafy trail, listening to the warblers and swallows, spotting centipedes and banana slugs, I felt at peace. I thought about all the ways that life in the universe divided and multiplied. I thought about chickens pecking out of eggs; kittens mewling in litters; giraffes dropping six feet to the ground from their mothers' haunches. I thought about halibut spewing their millions of eggs; sand tiger sharks cannibalizing their sibling embryos; weird toads squirming out of holes in their mother's backs. I thought about the oak's pollen blowing from the catkin to the female flower and the bee's hairy, pollen-covered legs touching the sunflower's stigma. The spectrum was mind-boggling. Why not us, too?

I came to a creek where soft mossy banks curved over the melodious current and stripped to my boxers and took a plunge. It was exhilarating. Every cell of my skin vibrated with the shock of the cold. I pulled myself onto a boulder and let the sun dry me. It was hot, and the wind was blowing again, harder than ever. The crowns of the trees were bending and swaying. I jumped into the water again, and this time the cold was less jarring. I came back to the boulder, still thinking about life in all its myriad forms. Birds, bees, snapdragons, jellyfish. Algae, salamanders, ostriches, tulips. I'd lived alone long enough. Phil would forgive us. The planet wouldn't die, at least not for many generations.

I was thinking about jumping into the water a third time when I noticed the fuzz of gray coming over the sky, and the sun going blood-orange. I squinted up and saw what looked like fine particulate floating in the air. The sun was rapidly dimming, turning into a dull gray circle, and by the time I'd put my shoes on, chunks of ash were floating down. An eerie quiet was taking hold, and the temperature had noticeably dropped. On the way back to the car, knocking water out of my ear, I started to smell the char.

I found my phone and did a quick scan of the news. In the mountains, not far away, a forest fire was raging. It was only hours old. All summer long, we'd been getting small- and medium-size burns up and down the coast, but this fire was big. Yesterday, it seemed, the wind had blown down an electric line near Suttle Lake, due east, and sparks had sprayed onto a dry pasture. The wind had then carried the sparks into the trees, and now, overnight, forty thousand acres were burning. I'd been driving only a few miles ahead of the smoke this whole time.

I called Sarah but it went straight to voice mail. She didn't have service on the mountain, I remembered, but I called her again just in case. I kept scrolling the news. The Santiam Valley was like a wind tunnel, they said, shooting the flames down the flanks of Mount Hood toward the lower ground. I looked at the fire map again. The orange blobs seemed to be coursing directly toward the Wy'East Lodge.

I called Sarah a third time and got no answer. And not knowing what to do next, I called Phil.

"Are you seeing this fire?" I said.

"Yeah," he said. "I'm driving to Wy'East right now. I'm almost to Grants Pass. But still four hours out, goddammit. What kind of world are we living in?"

"Have you talked to Sarah yet?" I said.

"No," he said. "I've been trying to get through to her all morning, but she isn't picking up. It's so fucking annoying. It's so typical."

"So you don't know if she got out yet?" I said.

"I have no fucking idea," he said. "They're evacuating the lodge right now, I've heard that much. Apparently, they're dropping people at the gas station at Detroit Lake. But I'm not sure if she's with them or not."

"I wonder why she isn't calling or picking up," I said.

"Her phone is always dead," he said. "Or maybe she's still up there, out of range."

"She could use someone else's phone if she wanted to," I said.

"You'd think so," he said. "I'm sure it's pretty chaotic wherever she is right now. I guess that's an excuse."

"Is there anyone else to call?" I said.

"I tried a few people in her group," he said. "But she's not with them. Some of them are already driving home. They got away from the lodge an hour ago."

"I drove up to Salem yesterday afternoon," I said, half-truthfully.

"I had some errands to do. So I'm actually not that far from Detroit Lake right now. I could go and see if she's waiting at that gas station."

"You don't have to do that, Arthur," Phil said. "I'm sure she's fine. She almost never picks up. It doesn't mean anything."

We spent a little longer going back and forth, Phil trying to dissuade me from driving into the fire zone, me offering to go again and again, and in the end, he gave up. The road would be closed down soon, we agreed, and it seemed imperative that someone get to the gas station as quickly as possible. So, minutes later, still damp from the stream, I was back in the car, driving the road I'd just driven, hoping to find Sarah sitting on her luggage in the parking lot of a gas station waiting for someone to fetch her.

Within five miles, the smoke hit. It was like a soft wall approaching, and then, silently, it was all around me. The whole world went yellow, and the surrounding landscape disappeared in a hot, brackish haze. I had my windows up, but the campfire smell was already in the car, stoking a deep, animal fear. My primate nerve endings started screaming to get away, to turn around and get to clean air, but I ignored them and kept going.

As I headed deeper into the cloud, I spotted cars streaming in the opposite direction, in full evacuation mode. They appeared dimly and disappeared quickly, filled with boxes and clothes pressed to the windows, or loads of garden equipment, or loose bedding. Some seemed well-organized, as if the drivers had practiced for this event, go-bags ready, while others were a mess. I saw a masked woman riding in the open trunk of a Toyota. I saw a RAV4 full of goats. Even the most disorganized drivers were smarter than me, though, traveling in the wrong direction.

I tried calling Sarah every few minutes but got nothing. Please,

I thought, let her be at the gas station. Please, let her phone just be dead. And please, for that matter, let me be able to make it there at all. Driving through the yellow soup, I kept assuming I'd be stopped by some authority, but mile after mile there were no barricades, no flashing signs. I pressed onward, skirting Detroit Dam, or so I imagined, as I could only see the silhouettes of the trees along the shoreline, and, at last, rounded the lake's edge to the gas station. But when I got there, no one was waiting. The parking lot was empty. The gas station was closed. I called Phil and told him what I was seeing.

"What?" he said. "That's where the sheriff said people were supposed to be."

"Well, no one's here," I said.

"Goddammit," he said. "Why isn't she calling back? This is what happens all the time. Her phone is useless."

"Maybe she didn't get down from the lodge yet," I said.

"Goddammit," he said again, "I'm still three hours away."

"I don't know what to do now," I said. The smoke was so thick I couldn't see the road twenty yards in the distance. The smell was filling my clothes, coating my hair. My eyes were burning.

"You've done everything you can, Arthur," Phil said. "There's nothing else you can do right now. You should come home. I'll be there soon. This is my job. I'll find her."

We hung up. The smoke was thick and inert. I got out of the car and peered into the yellowness. No cars were on the road anymore. Beyond this point, I knew, the cell signal crumbled. I took a shirt from my backpack and dampened it with water from the gas station spigot and wrapped it around my neck and lower face the best I could. I ignored the evacuation alerts on my phone and called Sarah's number one last time, going straight to voice mail. I called Phil.

"Yeah," he said.

"I'm going up," I said. "I wanted someone to know."

The last handful of miles were very slow going. The road I'd floated down only hours before was clogged with smoke, peppered with smoldering firebrands blown in from the main fire. When the road turned to dirt I had to inch along at blind-slug speed. I was feeling my way, catching glimpses of raw fire in the duff beyond the shoulder, hoping there was enough oxygen out there to keep the engine running.

Somehow, I burrowed my way back to the parking lot, which was now almost empty. The few remaining cars were so coated in ash they looked like they'd been abandoned years before. I cracked my door and climbed into the sludge, and it was then I first heard the fire. The sound was enormous, voracious, like a rumbling train in the not-so-far distance. The volume of trees being consumed on the mountain was insane.

On the edge of the lot, a van was idling, the headlights making pale yellow globes in the smoke. A few people were packing the cargo hold, while others were frantically dragging what they could from the cabins. One woman was standing perfectly still, consoling a younger woman who seemed to be hyperventilating. When a guy in a damp bandanna came lurching by, dragging a cart with a single piece of luggage in it, I stopped him. We had to yell over the ongoing detonation of the fire to hear each other.

"Hey!" I said. "I'm looking for Sarah Weber! Do you know her?"

"No!" he said.

"So she isn't with your group?!"

"No!"

"Are there still people at the lodge?!"

"I don't know!" he said. "I don't think so! But good luck!"

And he pushed past me to the van, where he flung his luggage into the open cargo hold and climbed into the flapping doors. He was smart. He wasn't waiting.

I made my way into the neighborhood of guest cabins, all of which appeared abandoned. I found Sarah's cabin and opened the door to discover all her things still there. Her toiletry bag was on the narrow wall shelf and her clothes were strewn on the unmade bed. Her sandals were in the middle of the floor. She might have left it all in the rush to get out or she might have left everything for some other reason. There was no telling.

I walked out and spotted a group of people near the bathroom. One of them was her team leader, whatever his name was, and my heart leapt. He seemed to be shepherding the remainder of his flock to the waiting van, and although none of them were Sarah, my whole body flashed with hope. Her group, at least some remnant, was still here, terrified but intact.

"Hey!" I said. "I'm looking for Sarah Weber! Is she still with you guys?"

"Are you her husband?!" the team leader said.

"No!" I said. "But I need to find her! Do you know where she is?!"

"I don't know!" he said. "We've been looking for her, too! She took a hike this morning! And we haven't seen her since then! The fire came on so fast! We've been trying to get word to her husband! But we don't have any coverage!"

"Where have you looked?!" I said.

"Someone saw her going up a trail!" he said. "She had her backpack on! And a sleeping bag! We went as far up as we could! But we can't wait any longer! I'm sorry! We have to go!"

"What trail?" I said, as he started to the parking lot with his people.

"Mountain View!" he said, and pointed in the direction of a trailhead near the cabins. "That's all we know! We'll call her husband as soon as we have a signal!"

And he rushed off, eaten by smoke.

I stumbled over to the trailhead and tried to peer into the haze. The world disappeared five feet beyond the sign, swallowed in yellow ooze. I took a few steps, but I couldn't convince myself it was a good idea, the sound of the fire was so thunderous, the smoke so thick. I was hovering there on the threshold, debating my next move, when a shadow emerged from the parking lot area. Quickly, it gained shape and mass, and resolved into a striding man in a plastic gas mask, his forehead black with grime.

"Hey!" the man said, spotting me. "Don't go up there! That's where the fire is!"

"I think someone's up there!" I said.

"They're gonna have to wait!" he said.

"For how long, do you think?!" I said.

"Until the wind shifts!" he said.

"When will that be?!" I said.

"Fuck if I know!" he said. "If you're going to wait, and you want to make yourself useful, you can follow me! We need hands!"

The guy barreled down the trail, heading toward the main lodge. I wasn't sure what else to do, so I followed him. He was moving fast, fluxing in and out of visibility, but I kept his shadow in sight, adrenaline making my limbs light. My mind had already detached from my body, and was floating a few feet above me, polarized by fear. Only two hours ago I'd been swimming in a beautiful mountain stream. It turned out heaven and hell are only one tiny step apart.

When we reached the main lodge, I could barely see the building, it was so erased by smoke. I could make out only a faint outline, with pale windows, and the general roof shape. On the lawn, a handful of guys were doing what they could to prepare for the tidal wave of fire about to crash on their heads. It didn't look like much.

Two of them were wetting down the lodge with garden hoses, but the streams barely made it to the second level. Another two were digging a trench in the lawn using hand trowels. I didn't understand how this could possibly help against the monstrous sound approaching, and for a moment, I considered heading back down the mountain and taking up a vigil at the gas station. I could wait there while Sarah was rescued by professionals, I thought. I imagined a helicopter churning the smoke into vortices, landing on the empty highway tarmac. Brawny men carrying her, smiling, from the metal bubble. A tearful embrace. Phil, somewhere off-site, waiting. But then, before the fantasy could complete, the man in the mask reappeared and dashed my plan. He handed over a paper mask and leaned in to yell, "The road's blocked now! I just heard on the radio! Looks like you're stuck here for a while!"

He turned and started to lope away. "We need to get water!" he said over his shoulder. "You coming?"

I followed. He was taking me ever farther from Sarah, but I didn't feel like I had any choice. I didn't know what else to do. I couldn't get down the mountain anymore, nor up the mountain. If I wanted to survive, I had to follow him. It was amazing how quickly a person adapted to hell.

I followed my guy along a dirt pathway, passing the sauna building, zigzagging by the eternity pools. We crossed a pebble mandala on the river's floodplain and came to the bank where the water was flowing in a gorgeous, liquid ribbon, pure antidote to the incoming flames. I didn't see how we were supposed to transport the water up to the lodge, however, as we didn't have any vessels, and we needed to move it in great volume. I didn't have time to ask because already the guy was walking again. He seemed to have an idea that involved striding across the footbridge to the other side of the river. I followed and, midway across the span, looked up and tried catching a glimpse of the mountain's peak. It was usually visible from this point, but not today.

I followed the guy along a dirt track into the staff housing area, a collection of humble cabins decorated with prayer flags and potted plants. He went to a large metal shed and opened the door, revealing a gleaming, miniature fire truck inside. It had Japanese writing on the side, and little ladders, and a heavy-duty spool of canvas hose. It was a cute, tiny fire truck, imported from Japan. But when he went to start the engine, it wouldn't catch.

"Fuck!" he said. He turned the key in the ignition again but got no action. The battery was dead.

"Unfuckingbelievable," he said. "Who lets this happen?" He looked around, seeking any kind of solution. I could hear my breath scraping in my mask. I had nothing to offer by way of advice. I could tell he was calculating the amount of space and time he had to work with, what might still be done given what we had.

"There's another truck down the road!" he said. "Not as good, but we'll have to get that one!"

We headed back onto the road, going deeper into the staff housing complex. Already, the fire was infiltrating the neighborhood. Firebrands were floating down from the sky, landing on the rooftops, setting cozy homes smoldering. I could see the new calculation my guy was making. These were cute homes, but rebuildable. The main lodge was not. That was the priority.

We came to another tin barn at the end of the road and rolled open the door and found a beat-up flatbed truck inside, with a big plastic tank on the back. It seemed more like a farming rig, used for watering fields, but the keys were in the ignition and the engine started. We pulled some canvas hoses from the wall and piled them alongside the tank, which, of course, was empty.

"We need to get water!" the guy said.

"How?!" I said.

"The river!" he said.

We got into the truck and backed out of the barn and bounced down the dirt road, ignoring the fires growing on either side of us. For a moment, the shadow of a double-propeller helicopter appeared in the haze, but it disappeared as quickly as it came. On a walkie-talkie, the voices of the other guys were filtering in, crackling and barking. *"Wind might be picking up from the east again!" "Lost power in the office!" "Roger that!"* My guy didn't respond to any of it. He was too busy pressing onward, in search of good river access.

We couldn't take the footbridge back because it was too small, so our goal became the trestle bridge a mile downriver. By the time we got there, it was already on fire. My guy didn't hesitate at all. He barreled directly across, and then, once we were over, he immediately reversed and backed us down to the river's edge and nestled the truck into a spot.

There, we plunged our one thick rubber hose into the water and let the suction engine do its work. As the tank filled, we finally had a second to introduce ourselves. The guy's name was Gary, he said. He was from Montana. He'd been working at the lodge as a groundskeeper for three years and loved the whole landscape and philosophy of the place. It was a beautiful, spiritually important site, he believed, where the veil between worlds was thin. He'd been asleep when the fire bell rang, and he hadn't had a chance to put on his underwear, so his crotch was chafed from all the running and sweating, which was a little more than I needed to know.

"Have you ever fought a fire before?!" Gary said.

"No!" I said.

"First rule: always have an escape! Okay?!"

"Okay!" I said. "Any other rules?!"

"That's the only one I know!" he said. "We're kind of making this up as we go! The fire department bailed on us! It's just a few staffers now! And you!"

When the tank was full we drove up to the lodge. Gary knew the roads well and avoided the worst gulleys and potholes, and soon we emerged onto the main lawn where, only hours before, children and parents had been peaceably playing, and where the previous afternoon, Sarah had batted a beach ball with her fellow retreaters. The memory of her turning toward me, shading her eyes, pierced my mind. I let the image pass through me and disappear, knowing it would serve no purpose now. I'd have to look at those pictures later.

Gary parked the truck sloppily on the lawn and we jumped out and pulled the hose from the flatbed and uncoiled it. Gary attached one end to the tank, and I yanked the nozzle end all the way to the wall of the lodge. I gave the twirling-hand-in-the-air sign that meant "send water into the hose," and moments later felt the bulge of water coming. Out it splashed, the hose becoming a giant, vomiting snake, spewing fluid.

We got a decent stream going, shooting all the way to the roof of the lodge, and a cheer went up among the volunteers. I managed to douse the top of the roofline, guiding the water back and forth until a large segment of shingles was wet, but as soon as the good news came on, bad news came on stronger. A floating firebrand had landed on the hose and the hose was on fire. Gary ran over and stomped it out, but it didn't bode well. The wind was blasting us, sending heavy sprays of sparks ahead of the fire line. We were still far from the main flames, but we were already in trouble.

When the tank ran dry Gary went back for a refill and my job became firefighter. I was handed a shovel and a rake and told to put out anything I saw. There were small fires everywhere, in the bushes, under the boughs. I went from shrub to tree to grass, stomping embers, shoveling dirt, raking duff. At some point, the propane tanks in the staff housing across the river started exploding, causing loud blasts every few minutes for an hour. At another point, a guy got trapped in a ring of fire and we had to stop everything and cut a channel and drag him out. He was practically unconscious from smoke inhalation, but he was back on the line within forty-five minutes.

Into the night, we labored. The sun set and we fought the fire in the dark. Our express purpose was to preserve this magical compound anchoring the land where humans had gathered for millennia to collect huckleberries and soak in the mountain's sacred waters, but all the while, digging trenches, chainsawing fallen trunks, I was thinking only about Sarah. I kept a lookout for her at all times, hoping she'd appear from the woods. I went to the trailhead every half an hour and tried to push my way up, but I was blocked by the fire every time. As the night went on, the outbuildings burned. The massage building burned. The guest cabins burned. The yurts burned. We heard loud reports of shattering glass at random intervals and breathed caustic smoke from melting plastic and metal that made the woodsmoke seem almost pleasant. Around midnight, I moved my car down the mountain to safer ground. And through all of it, Sarah never appeared.

I'd never been a big praying person before. I'd grown up outside any praying tradition, and as a general concept I found it a crude idea. The asking for favors, the wishing away of guilt, it had always seemed childish to me. I'd worked instead on dwelling in gratitude and acceptance, living inside the mystery of existence as it actually was. I'd become a ponderer of koans, an acceptor of unexpected fate. Maybe occasionally I'd put my thoughts toward manifesting some goal, but never anything irrational or desperate. If anything, I'd worked to expunge as much desire from my body as possible. I'd tried to reduce my sense of selfhood into the smallest particles and let them blow away in the wind. But now, thinking about Sarah trapped on the mountain, I prayed with a selfish, desirous vengeance. I wanted Sarah to be all right. I had no idea who I was praying to.

Be alive, I prayed. Be safe. That night, I sent hundreds of prayers up the mountain, in hopes any of them would find Sarah and give her some comfort. I sent my prayers streaming into the inferno like little missiles, seeking contact with her terrified mind. I sent prayers of protection, prayers of safety, prayers of love and survival. I talked to the mountain itself, imploring it to help her and to give her shelter.

Over and over, I silently called out her name, thinking as long as I kept talking to her, she was still alive. I'd feel it if anything was wrong. I didn't feel anything yet.

I was still praying when Gary sent out a call to come back to the main lodge. He and the other guys had been laboring under the notion that if we could only guard the lodge until morning, the structure could be saved. The new day would bring rain, they believed. Even a shift of the wind would be helpful. If we could make it until sunrise, all agreed, we'd be okay.

We doubled down on protecting the area just around the mansion. We doused the whole building again and widened all the firebreaks. We stockpiled water so we'd be ready in case any fires erupted inside our cordon. We arranged our barrels and hoses and shovels in neat rows. We really thought we were getting somewhere, but when the sun finally began to rise, we could see we'd been fooling ourselves. The sun was brightening and the flames were only getting bigger, the flying sparks becoming more crazed. And it was even worse than we'd realized: it turned out the sun wasn't even rising. The morning hadn't come. The light we were seeing was only the main body of fire.

Through the bands of trees, we were finally seeing the raw plasma itself, a wall of coursing orange, rising from duff to crown. The fire had arrived, pitiless and hungry for more fuel. We all staggered from our spots and gathered on the front deck and simply stared. We were too exhausted to move anymore. Yellowjackets riled by the heat were buzzing and attacking, but all we could do was lean on our shovels and watch the flames come.

The fire was like an orange waterfall flowing into the sky. A terrible, shaking beard. A thousand golden snakes writhing out of the earth. The sound was like a gang of 747s pummeling us at takeoff.

The heat was brutalizing, wave on wave of crackling fury. We had a decent path of escape behind us, and enough buffer that we weren't in imminent danger, but within an hour, the lodge would surely be vaporized. The whole mountain would be ash soon enough.

I stared into the fire, hypnotized. The flames blurred between orange and yellow and blue, bending into delicate new forms with every riffle of wind. Here it comes, I thought, the thing that arrives for everything, the thing that remakes the world. It's all fire in the end. The violent transmutation of one substance into another, the liberation of energy from one form into the next. I stood before the ravenous, annihilating essence and watched it feast.

I barely noticed when the guys all around me started cheering. At first I thought they were seeing something I didn't see, like a battalion of helicopters, or some thundercloud massing, but it turned out they didn't see anything. They were watching exactly what I was, but to their credit, they'd already given up. As it turns out, this is what you do when a tsunami of fire is cresting in front of you. You give up hope. You welcome whatever is on the other side of that curtain. I joined in, screaming at the top of my lungs.

And then, incredibly, the fire paused. The sparks slowed their zigzags in the air. The falling ash ceased. The smoke suddenly thinned. We all stared in disbelief as the flames began pacing back and forth, like a lion at the limit of its hunt. We looked at each other down the line, confirming what we were sensing. Was it possible? It didn't seem possible. But it was true, the wind had shifted. The fire had turned.

9

We stood in front of the lodge, swaying in the giant heel of black ground, unsure what to think. The earth around us tinkled with the sounds of embers dying. The remaining trees were haggard and shocked. Word came in on the radio that the wind had indeed turned, and the fire line was indeed tacking strongly south and east, which meant we were now inside an eye, or in the clear, we didn't know yet. As dawn drew closer, the wind started blowing even more forcefully south, bringing more hope.

We kept pumping river water onto the roof of the lodge and stomping out all the orphan fires scattered around the grounds. A few guys tried to sleep, figuring if another wave was coming, this was their window. It was also the window I'd been waiting for, the window in which I could possibly climb the Mountain View trail and find Sarah. I had no idea how far I'd be able to go, but I could at least abandon the other guys in good conscience for a while and take a walk in the fire's charred fingers.

"It's not a good idea," Gary said, when I told him my plan. We were sitting on the deck of the lodge eating half-thawed microwave curry bowls from the dead freezer, possibly the most delicious thing I'd ever tasted.

"I have to try," I said. "If I can't make it, I'll come back."

Gary gave me a long look. We'd been through lifetimes together in the past few hours. He leaned over and gave me a hug with his hand on the back of my head and wished me good luck.

I strapped on a headlamp and filled a bottle of water. I found a fresh mask in the supply case and put another one in my pocket for Sarah. Then I walked from the lodge, through the torched remains of the guest cabins, alongside the edge of the parking area, where the carriages of two melted cars wheezed liquid magma. I kept going until I came to the trailhead, where my lamp still barely sent a beam of illumination onto the ground. Somewhere, up above, the wind was blowing, but down here, the smoke was still thick and opaque.

I edged onto the trail and took a few more steps into the darkness, testing the ground. The first handful of steps seemed all right. There might be stretches of fire ahead, but for the moment, as far as I could see, the way seemed passable. I told myself I'd climb as high as I could and make sure at every point I didn't get stranded. Always, I'd have a way out.

I started moving, unsure exactly what I was traveling through. At my feet, orange galaxies of embers seethed on the mossy ground, but otherwise, the world was all smoke. My strained breathing and crunching footfalls were the only sounds I heard, which I took as a good sign. It meant the fire was far away, busy devouring some new territory.

Through the haze, shadows of trees emerged, sometimes smoldering, sometimes untouched. The fire was fickle in that way, destroying one thing, leaving its neighbor unscathed. I took that as a good sign, too. It meant Sarah might have avoided the worst. Maybe she'd found some furrow of ground between the flames.

The poor trees. Only now did the scale of the destruction hit me. It was unimaginable how many millions of these creatures had been incinerated. It'd taken hundreds of years for them to grow, and in a matter of hours, they'd been eradicated. Over their lives, they'd experienced sun and snow and rain and drought. They'd been hit by lightning and clawed by bears. They'd sprouted children and watched their friends and family wither and die around them. And now they'd been smote. I could almost hear the survivors keening in pain.

But I put the trees out of my mind and kept going, concentrated on Sarah. I was exhausted, and having a hard time moving, let alone marshaling any thoughts, but I tried to get the prayers going again. I prayed in a practical manner now, asking for simple favors. Let me find her easily, I prayed. Let the trail be unblocked. I prayed to avoid any problems or delays. Don't let there be fire in the way, I prayed. Don't let the smoke obscure my visibility. I've come this far, I prayed, just let me go a little bit farther. What thought directed toward the future isn't a prayer? What thought, period, isn't? Please let me keep going, I thought. Let me keep going and I'll do the rest. Let me find her at the end of this trail.

After a few bends and switchbacks, I started gaining more confidence. I was passing trees still on fire, the crowns burning high in the air, but nothing that looked imminently threatening. I had the feeling I understood the fire now, and that we'd come to some kind of agreement. I passed a patch of largely unburned foliage and climbed a steep slope to an exposed ridge. For a moment, the air cleared, and the sky appeared, dead gray, only the faintest daylight visible, not yet lavender. For a moment, I felt like an astronaut floating into space, the thin oxygen line unraveling behind me.

The sky closed again. The smoke returned. I kept climbing and it wasn't long before I'd reached a fork in the trail. I'd been on the trail before and I knew that the right fork went to a spring-fed mountain stream with a little Zendo overlooking the bank. It was a beautiful spot, and a beautiful building, constructed by a Japanese master craftsman. In my memory, it was a simple tongue-and-groove box, with flaring eaves and a veranda that floated a few feet off the ground. The whole structure was held aloft on hefty river rocks. People often went there for their private meditation sessions, enjoying the elegance of the sliding wooden doors and smooth tatami mats. I suspected it was where Sarah had been headed.

I took a brief rest and sipped some water, but I didn't wait long. I had a bead on my goal now and kept moving, pushing through a stand of juniper and a grove of smoldering oaks. Soon I could hear the stream up ahead. The landscape was still only partially visible in the smokey dawn, but I could tell it was a disaster. Shriveled branches lay on the ground exhaling smoke. The ground itself was a blackened waste. I knew I was getting close to the Zendo now, but for a long time I couldn't seem to find it. I paced around, back and forth, until eventually I realized it was gone. The building was only a blackened sketch of its former self.

"Sarah!" I called out. But there was no answer.

I called her name a few more times, my voice already hoarse from the smoke, but nothing came back. I went over to the remains of the house and looked at the crumbled pile of charcoal. Sarah wasn't there in any form. There was no body, no semblance of a body, no body-shaped pile of ashes. She had to be somewhere nearby, I thought, but where?

I walked out in a spiral from the former Zendo, making larger revolutions with each pass. Every revolution, I called her name. I looped the burned structure three times but I found nothing, heard nothing. There were no sounds out there at all—no bird sounds, no animals. Only my footsteps on the blackened earth and the sound of rushing water, muffled by the heavy blanket of smoke.

When I came to the creek's bank I paused and watched the messed-up water gurgling downstream. It was marbled with ash and gunk, swirling in snotty whorls. It occurred to me that Sarah would have gone to the water when the fire landed. It would've been a primal response, to go to the water. It was a terrible thought, imagining her panic in that moment, surrounded by flames, but I put that out of my mind. I wouldn't think about that yet. I would only think about her now, her living, breathing body completely intact. Of course, the water was her refuge.

I started walking downstream, calling her name every few steps. I walked a quarter mile but didn't find anything, so I turned around and walked back, yo-yoing another quarter mile beyond where I'd started. Still, I didn't see a single trace.

I crossed the stream and walked the opposite bank, pushing through scrabbly bushes and climbing over fallen snags, keeping as close to the water's edge as possible. The forest on that side was still crackling and sighing from the fire's assault, burning in the undergrowth, and although the smoke continued to brighten with the rising sun, the visibility didn't get much better. I kept calling Sarah's name, partly to make myself feel less alone.

I came to a beachhead backed by a low cliff. It was just a shallow strip of pebbles, scattered with a few bigger rocks, the cliff face rising about twenty feet. The soft dirt had been carved by years of spring flooding so that it almost overhung the narrow spit of beach. The ledge was topped with what looked like poplars or cottonwoods, judging by the trunks. It was hard to be sure as the upper parts of the trees were lost in the jaundiced fog.

Midway down the beachhead, I came to what looked like an avalanche. At the base of the cliff lay a slump of debris, a chaos of smashed tree limbs and fallen rocks among a mess of dirt. The main piece in the jumble was a toppled birch, its trunk crazed with branches extending out into the rushing stream. The tree's root ball was tilted sideways, wires of root flailing everywhere. The whole tree had evidently come loose from the overhanging ledge, bringing down a tonnage of dirt and rock along with it.

I walked to the pile and that was where I found Sarah's hand.

It was the back of her hand, limp and dirty. Her hand was connected to her wrist and her forearm, which led into the pile. I could see part of her shoulder and the top of her head, but the rest of her was obscured by branches and debris. Her face was turned away. The trunk of the birch had fallen almost directly on top of her, which had also shielded her from some of the rock and earth, but only partly. She hadn't been entirely crushed, but her body had been cruelly battered.

I said out loud, "No." I couldn't believe what I was seeing. I stared at her hand, her beautiful, graceful hand, lying on the ground, lifeless. I knelt down and brushed dirt from her forearm and from her hair and shoulders. I could see that Sarah had been huddled at the base of the cliff, sheltered from the flames, and how the wind and fire had wracked the trees above her until one had loosened and fallen. The cave-in had taken her from behind, pinning her to the beach. How idiotic, I thought, in the middle of a fire, to be swallowed by a landslide.

I held her hand even though I could tell there was no life in it. The utter limpness was appalling. I felt for a pulse and felt nothing. I said her name and shook her wrist and got no response. I saw no breath filling her ribs.

I tried pulling her out of the pile but her body was trapped under the tree. I couldn't move her. I watched again for any breath but I still didn't see her chest moving. Her face was in shadow, caked with mud. Again, I said, "No, no, no." I stared at her grimy fingernails.

I wasn't sure what to do so I got up and stumbled a few feet away and numbly sat down on a rock. The water swirled past me, carrying ash and tree garbage. The smoke was still so thick I could only see a few feet in any direction, which meant I couldn't see Sarah anymore, which was both good and bad. I didn't want to abandon her, but nor did I want to look at her body. The beach at my feet was covered in gray pebbles. I stared into the listless smoke, knowing I had to dig her out soon and figure a way to carry her home, but I was unable to start just yet. I still had the irrational feeling that some change might occur, that the needle of time might loop backward and make a different stitch.

My feet were so heavy I couldn't move. I closed my eyes and started muttering things to the universe. The praying hadn't worked thus far, not exactly, but what could I do but pray more? Pray harder? Now, on the blackened mountainside, I found myself praying in the most florid way imaginable. I was praying for a miracle. Praying for a different outcome of time. When the moment arrives, a person finds the frequency and starts pleading.

Bring her back, I implored. Please, bring her back to life. Let her live.

I kept repeating the phrasing in different ways, and almost without thinking about it, I began to offer up deals. People had always struck bargains with the universe. They'd feasted and danced, giving their energy and love to whatever god they believed in. They'd left burnt offerings on the temple altar. They'd killed goats. They'd even made human sacrifices. They'd bloodied their own sons and daughters to demonstrate their fear of the implacable power that dictated their fortunes. So what would my offering be? What could I give that would demonstrate my adequate devotion? This was what the creator wanted, wasn't it? To exact some kind of pain from the supplicant.

It had to be something valuable, I realized, something I'd acutely miss. What did I care about enough? In that moment, it was Sarah. Immediately, I could see the symmetry of my prayer locking into place. Let her live, I thought, and you can have her. Let her live, and I'll give her up. I'll give you the most important thing I can imagine if you only allow her to continue to exist.

I thought these new words over and over, in different formulations, honing the bargain. Each phrase was like a balloon floating up into the smoke, seeking contact with the divine mind. Each utterance was a jewel pressed into the wall of the universe. Or maybe a wire shoved into the door of the cosmos, blindly seeking the heavy latches of the lock. There were a million metaphors I could use. I was seeking whatever purchase I could find.

What happened next, I don't know how to describe. Whatever it was, it happened quietly, almost unnoticeably, though going back, I might have had some kind of inkling. Something in the world seemed to reorient a degree, some channel opened. Some scaled, lidded eye cracked awake.

I heard a sound and I turned and stared into the torpid smoke. At first, I couldn't see anything but the slow-coursing tendrils and the splashes and sunbursts of my own corneas. And then, out of the gloom, a shadow appeared. The shadow moved a step closer, gaining detail, and with one more step, I could see it was Sarah. She was standing there on the pebbly bank, alive, covered in ash and singe. Her face was caked in blood. Her black hair was lank. But she was swaying on her feet, definitely alive.

I've been poisoned by smoke, I thought, or deranged by sleep deprivation. There was no way she'd climbed out of that pile. And yet, somehow, she was there.

I got up and went to her, still not convinced she was real. She shook my arms off, not ready to be touched yet. She was real.

"What happened?" she said.

"You had an accident," I said. "You got hurt. But you're okay now. Thank God."

"What kind of accident?" she said.

"A tree fell on you," I said. "It knocked you out."

"And where are we?" she said.

"On the mountain," I said. "You don't remember?"

"Not exactly," she said.

"You hiked up here yesterday," I said. "And then there was a fire. You were trapped in it. But you're okay now. Everything's going to be okay."

She winced, thinking all this through. She tried shaking her head to clear her thoughts, but the movement seemed to hurt her skull so she stopped. She raised her finger to her temple. "And when did you get here?"

"Just now," I said. "I'm going to take you home, okay?"

"Okay," she said.

"We should go before the wind changes," I said.

"Okay."

Before we went anywhere, I strapped the mask onto her face. I also took off my shirt and soaked it in the stream. I wrung it out and wrapped it around her neck, hoping this would feel refreshing. Then, as delicately as possible, I braced her body against my body and guided her across the stream. We hobbled past the ruined Zendo and back to the trail. All the while, I was holding her close.

We walked slowly, careful not to jar her in any way, back along the path we'd both come before. It didn't seem important to tell her about the miracle yet, or the whole deal I'd made with the universe, if that was what you'd call it. We were both in shock. I didn't want to add any more disturbance to her mind than necessary. And I wasn't thinking about anything very clearly myself. The only goal now was to get her to safety.

We navigated every rock and root, and by the time we got back to the lodge, the smoke had cleared. Raw sunlight was falling onto the roof, shining off the wet shingles. The guys were still digging fire lines and spraying water onto anything they could find, but the danger was past. When they saw us emerge from the trees they all paused and stared. Gary strode over and helped us to the deck and gave us some water, while the other guys gathered around in reverent silence and began murmuring their praise and astonishment.

Sarah needed medical attention, Gary and I agreed, so the rest period didn't last long. Gary helped me carry Sarah the remaining distance to my car, and helped me get her into the passenger seat, and helped me find the way out of the lower lot. I drove the road back to the lake in a daze. Another miracle: someone had already chainsawed the fallen trees on the road.

As soon as we got to the highway, my phone flooded with messages. They came from everywhere, from my mom, from Barn people, from neighbors, from students. Somehow everyone I knew had heard I was on the mountain. I skimmed through the messages until I came to Phil's name and touched it with my thumb. His voice said he was waiting for us at the rest stop at exit 34. He'd been stopped by state troopers. He was awaiting word. He wouldn't leave until he saw us.

I drove the remaining miles gingerly, rarely speeding, while Sarah slept. I wasn't sure if sleep was a great idea, considering her head injuries, but I didn't want to wake her, either. She looked so vulnerable in the seat, coated in mud and blood, her hair matted, her clothes ripped. I could give her this moment of rest. I glanced at her often to make sure she was still breathing and noticed her eyes twitching with dreams. I put my hand on her bare leg and fixed my eyes to the road.

At the rest stop, I turned in and found Phil immediately. He was standing at attention beside his truck, looking desperate but unyielding. Sarah was still asleep, and together, we lifted her from my car and placed her in his cab and buckled her in.

Phil hugged me for a long time. "Thank you," he said through tears, and gripped my shoulder. He looked into my eyes for a long time. And then, purposefully, he got in his truck and drove away, heading for the hospital in Medford. I stood in the rest area, too exhausted to move. The air was clear. The sun was already hot.

10

I tried to sleep in the car for a while but I couldn't settle down, so I drove home, wondering what the hell had just happened. Outside, the off-ramps to Corvallis, Eugene, and Cottage Grove swam by, and soon the road was lifting me out of the valley into the black woods between Roseburg and Wolf Creek. All the while, a dim kaleidoscope was revolving in the back of my brain. Every twist of the cylinder sent new shards of color into the pattern, new shadings of fear, awe, gratitude, and disbelief. Every arrangement a new consequence, a new ramification.

It was a miracle I'd witnessed, there was no other way to describe it. I'd been present at a miracle, the resurrection of a dead body. I'd seen it with my own eyes, more or less, and possibly even manifested it with my own mind. On the charred mountaintop, in the brightening smoke, I'd bowed my head and focused my thoughts and somehow, through me, the strings of the universe had been strummed. Invisible circuitries had been reversed. It turned out performing a miracle was nothing like the religious movies would have you believe. There hadn't been any shafts of light beaming through clouds, no arias resounding in outer space, only a sense of extreme smallness and humility. I didn't feel power or glory whatsoever. I felt like a tiny bug.

Did I even believe in a miracle like that? I asked myself, driving alongside the shining Umpqua River. In some ways, I supposed I did, generally speaking. I believed in the miracle of existence itself, which was to say, the universe as an unbeginning, unending explosion bringing forth everything that ever was and ever would be. That was a miracle, wasn't it? And then, in that tumult, somehow, fragile life had occurred, which was also a miracle. Everything was a miracle from this point of view. A plum was a miracle. An oak tree growing from an acorn was a gigantic miracle. Overall, I felt like I experienced an appropriate sense of wonder at the miracle of creation on a fairly daily basis.

But what about an actual miracle abrogating the laws of nature? That was a little tougher, though in some ways, I guessed I believed in those, too, or at least didn't entirely not believe in them. Within the swirling cosmos, I could acknowledge that many strange things occurred. Inexplicable healings, odd transfigurations, bizarre coincidences. I had a friend who'd had a stroke at the very moment his mother had died across the country. How could you explain that, except as his mom's soul somehow transporting across time and space and touching him? I had another friend whose father's voice had appeared on his answering machine days after his father died. How could that happen, barring a small miracle? I didn't see the universe as some rational computer, running on glassy algorithms. It was more like a cloud of chaos, filled with wormholes and wind shears, built on strange resonances and entanglements. Science had already proven that.

But the thing I'd experienced: that was something else again. A miracle in the old style, a Lazarus-type event, a Jesus kind of thing. It was a miracle implying communion with an omnipotent consciousness, possibly a personal covenant with a divine force. Did I believe in that kind of miracle? That kind of God? It was easy enough to believe in the little miracles of normal life, the minor serendipities that came from a positive attitude. That was just the basic law of karma. You got what you gave. You reaped what you sowed. Sometimes things came back in unexpected, mystical-seeming ways. But magical favors from a hidden, all-powerful creator? A distant being capable of remaking reality at will? Was that really how the universe conducted its business?

I drove onward, passing dark valleys and open vistas, thanking God, doubting God, too exhausted to come to any conclusions. I was still too deep inside the experience to see anything clearly, still too tangled up in the mountain's energies. I caught sight of my pinched eyes in the mirror, my face coated with ash. The long days of smoke and fire had utterly wiped me out. It was too soon to put words on anything.

Somehow I kept the car inside the lines and wended my way home. I left my bags in the back seat and went directly to bed. I woke up hours later in darkness, the room hot, the moon a white hole in the black sky. I had smoke in my hair and in my clothes. I got up and showered and went back to sleep. I woke up again and it was morning.

I stayed in bed for a long time, letting the world reknit around me. My muscles were sore from the hours of digging and raking but my bedroom was the same as it had been a couple of days earlier. Two dresser drawers were still open, and a pair of jeans was spilling onto the floor. My nightstand still held the same stack of partly read books. I could hear the familiar squeak of a hummingbird outside, interrupted by the familiar croak of a crow.

I got up and dressed and went to the kitchen and made my oatmeal. I put on water for coffee and used my favorite cup. As I ate, I checked the news. I discovered the fires were still raging in the Cascades, metastasizing out of control. The Suttle Lake Fire had bled into the Barrel Fire and was oozing toward the Orient Creek Fire. They'd called up crews from as far as Kansas. The volume of trees being incinerated in the Cascades was equal to a nuclear bomb going off. And yet, here at home, the air was clean. The wind was favoring us.

I thought about driving back to the mountain to help the guys on the line, but sitting in my kitchen, surrounded by my familiar pots and pans, I had a hard time convincing myself it was a good idea. They needed manpower, but I knew I wouldn't be much use. I had no training. I probably wouldn't even be able to get up the road. Already, it seemed, my normal life, with its normal parameters of risk, was reasserting itself.

I scrolled through my messages and wrote to all the people who'd checked in, reassuring them that I was okay. Only then did I allow myself to think about the miracle again. I sat at the table and tried to reconstruct the last few days step by step, searching for the moment when reality had warped and delivered me into the ear of God. I remembered driving to the lodge; I remembered fighting the fire; I remembered finding Sarah under the collapsed earth at dawn. Up until that point, the laws of nature had held fairly steady, but somewhere in that area they'd gone astray. I thought about touching her. I thought about those few steps I'd taken away from her body and imploring the universe to bring her back, and the minute later when she was standing there, alive.

Already, my memory was getting tricky. There were big blank spaces in my recollection, abrupt jump cuts, lots of smoke. Certain angles and sense impressions were heavily favored. Was it possible that I'd misjudged? That I'd failed to notice some major clue? Sitting in my kitchen, I had to allow for the possibility that Sarah hadn't been dead when I'd found her, even if in the moment I'd been absolutely certain. I remembered taking her limp wrist and searching for a pulse. I remembered watching for her breath. I remembered staring at her and believing that the weight of the landslide was terminal. But maybe I'd been too hasty. If only I could go back in time and get another look, I thought, I could erase the doubt. But time didn't open its back door like that.

I kept approaching the moments from different angles, at different speeds, rotating the information in my mind. I thought again about driving back to the mountain, this time with a measuring tape and some chalk and string. But what would a pile of rocks and trees tell me? The site was already compromised, blasted by fire and wind. The suspects had all vanished. There was no video to watch and rewatch at superslow speed.

I was left with my own meager powers of memory and reason. At the moment, I couldn't decide whether it seemed more ridiculous to believe in the miracle or to doubt it. Eventually, I knew, I'd have to fall on one side or the other. I couldn't just pretend this was one of the false choices that life presented. Whatever truth I drew from this experience, whatever interpretation, excluded the other completely. I'd always assumed miracles were meant to confirm faith, but apparently not this one. I knew one thing, at least: now that Sarah was alive, I didn't want to lose her.

Washing my oatmeal bowl, tidying the house, I found myself

thinking about Abraham. That was another miracle on a mountain; that was another deal with the Almighty. Kill your son to prove your faith, God had said, and Abraham had obeyed without question. He'd walked Isaac to Mount Moriah, bound him, raised his dagger, and then, at the last moment, the ram had appeared and Isaac had been spared. Would the universe let me off the hook like that, too? Would I be shown that kind of mercy if I kept my promise?

Granted, Abraham had never asked God for his miracle. He'd simply received his order and performed his task, which, one could argue, also made him a kind of a psychopath. He was a person willing to murder his only son because a disembodied voice had entered his brain—madness, by definition. It was also the source of the story's great power. If you doubted the existence of God, Abraham was a schizophrenic child-murderer. If you believed, Abraham was the father of faith.

Granted, too, Abraham's was a much more extreme case than mine. To kill your child was a bloody, irrevocable act, whereas mine was more soft-edged. To "give someone up," I thought. What did that mean, exactly? Was Sarah even mine to give? And giving her up, did that mean to give her up entirely, as in, never see her again, or did it only mean to give her up physically and emotionally, to simply withdraw? I assumed in this case the deal definitely meant giving up having sex with Sarah, and with it, our whole dream of procreation. Definitely that. But did it mean we could never speak again? Was a platonic friendship permissible? What was the core intimacy here? What was the real her of her?

My thoughts kept turning this way, making analogs, seeking loopholes, as the morning shadows slanted and dissolved. When I was done cleaning, I put on my shoes and went out for a walk, thinking some movement might bring more clarity. I was already starting to wonder if I'd made a bad deal. I was curious whether my prayer would have been answered if I'd made a lesser promise. Abraham had talked God down from destroying Sodom unless a hundred pure souls could be found. He'd worked Him down to one soul, which of course couldn't be found, and God had destroyed Sodom anyway. I could have promised to give up drinking or using plastic. I wondered if a person could renegotiate a thing like that, if a prayer could be returned. Apparently, anything could be returned. Death could be returned. But how could I get back in touch with the store manager?

I walked into the trails near the house, fondling my phone, wanting to call someone but not knowing exactly who. The main person I wanted to call was Sarah, of course, but she was the one person I was apparently prohibited from talking to. Not that I could call her anyway. I'd been getting texts from Phil all morning, telling me Sarah was in the hospital in Medford, just down the highway, recuperating nicely but not yet ready for contact. She'd been diagnosed with a concussion and a broken wrist and collarbone, he said. She'd be fine, but needed some time to heal. So the resurrection hadn't been a complete success after all. She hadn't been returned from death totally intact. Maybe that gave me some leverage.

Other than Sarah, I couldn't think of anyone else to call. I had a lot of friends I could talk to about normal problems, the mundane issues of family and work and such, but this situation was too complicated to explain. Also, I'd have to confess the adultery part, which was embarrassing and a betrayal of Sarah's trust. It was too much to put on anybody. And I could already predict what they'd tell me: see a therapist; get some sleep.

I arrived at a giant cedar at the edge of the neighborhood, a tree that I loved. It had a massive, fluted trunk with branches starting about fifty feet up that radiated in near symmetry to the crown. It was like a huge, circular stepladder into the sky, I always thought. I stared up the tower, through the arms, at the bright sky beyond, smelling the tree's spicy scent, listening to its soft needles whisper. Craning my neck, I half expected to see horsemen or seven-headed beasts come galloping through, but there was only the slow movement of the clouds. Already, the events on the mountain were becoming a dream.

I made it through the afternoon and cooked myself a stir-fry for dinner. The smell of sautéing garlic brought me another step back into my body. I had some beets and I roasted them as well. The swirl of color inside the pink beets was beautiful to behold, these splashy watercolors on every cut face. These were the kinds of miracles I understood. If Sarah had been with me in the kitchen, I'd have forced her to stop and appreciate the beets' beauty, too.

I ate out on the deck and watched the traffic on the distant freeway. The more time that passed, the more comfortable I was feeling in everyday reality. Back in the normal world, where people drove up and down I-5 and drank beer with dinner, it was getting easier to explain the miracle away as an elaborate hallucination, images lighting in the synapses of an exhausted, smoke-poisoned brain. I could see that a genie God who granted desperate wishes was fundamentally ridiculous. If He existed at all, He wasn't some Old Testament vaudeville act, extorting promises from His children with His rickety thunder-and-lightning machine.

By the time the sun went down, I'd begun folding the events

into a story that I'd tell Sarah as soon as she was able to hear it. I was beginning to appreciate the events in all their secular danger and suspense. What a wild tale. I could see how we'd look back on it one day as our fiery passage from one chapter of our lives to another, the ultimate stepping stone on the path of our romance. We'd tell our children about it someday around the dinner table.

As our lives went on, and our love grew, we'd bring it up every once in a while to remind ourselves of our dramatic beginning in this miraculous universe without miracles.

After dark, I made tea and lay down on the couch, planning to watch a movie. I'd barely opened my computer, however, when my mom called. She'd already called a few times during the day and although I'd reassured her of my safety a few times via text, I didn't see how I could refuse her any longer, so I picked up.

"Arthur!" she said. "Jesus Christ! What happened? I can't believe you were in that forest fire. I've been watching the news! Are you okay?"

"I'm fine," I said, already feeling assaulted.

"Are you sure?" she said.

"Yes," I said. "How did you even hear about it? I haven't talked to anyone yet."

"Jane told me," she said. "She says everyone at the bookstore is talking about it. It's big news. They say you're a hero. What were you doing, running into a fire? Are you crazy?"

I didn't want to tell my mom the whole story. I loved her, but I didn't always want to give her the details of my life. Still, I felt obliged to tell her something, so I gave her the abridged version, spinning my relationship with Sarah as chastely as possible and downplaying the firefighting scenes, knowing she didn't want to hear about her only son almost getting annihilated by flames. I only slowed down once I got to the miracle itself. I hadn't intended to tell her so much, but I found it interesting to hear myself narrating the episode.

"My goodness," she said when the story was done. "That is quite an adventure, Arthur. You're sure you're okay?"

"It's been pretty intense," I said. "But yeah. I'm all right."

"That smoke can really do some damage, you know," she said. "It can poison your whole system. You should probably see a doctor."

"I don't have smoke poisoning," I said. "Don't worry, Mom."

"And your friend is doing all right?" she said.

"She's in the hospital now," I said. "But yes, doing okay."

"And you're sure you're fine?" she said. "You sound a little . . . I don't know . . . confused."

"I'm fine," I said. "It was just a very strange thing that happened."

I could feel her letting the story settle on the other end. She was smoking a cigarette, her lifelong vice. I could almost see the gray sails curling out of her mouth, dispersing into the darkness above her frizzy head. Some of my earliest memories involved smoke carving its elegant whorls. Even three thousand miles away, I could almost smell that wonderful, acrid scent.

"It's funny," she said, exhaling. "I didn't even know you believed in God."

"I don't know if I do," I said.

"You write about religious things so beautifully," she said. "But always in such an abstract way."

"Thanks, I think," I said.

"You know I love your books, honey," she said. "I just never thought of you as a praying person, that's all."

"I'm usually not," I said.

"Seems like God really did you a favor this time, though," she said. "He helped you out, big time."

"I'm sure there are other explanations," I said.

"Like what?"

"I don't know," I said. "But I'm sure they exist."

"It seems like you were talking to somebody up there," she said. "Seems like someone answered. Why would you doubt it?"

I could tell she was fascinated by the whole situation. She wasn't someone who adhered to any particular system of belief, but she loved nothing more than processing a complicated, morally opaque dilemma. I could see how this event held all the mysteries and metaphysical conundrums she most craved. Not to mention she still sensed details regarding my relationship with Sarah to extract.

"Strange things happen all the time," she said. "Blessings. Portents. I've had a lot of things happen to me that I can't explain."

"Oh yeah?" I said. "Like what?"

"Well," she said. "Once, when you were a baby, we didn't have any money. We were really poor back then, if you recall. We were about to get evicted, and then a check came in the mail from your dad. Only one he ever sent. Just in time to keep us from getting thrown out on the street. That seemed like a miracle at the time. Boy, I'll tell you, it sure did."

"I guess you could call that a miracle," I said, though it didn't really compete with a resurrection.

"Another time," she said, "I had a bad feeling about a plane, and I waited so long to pack that I missed the flight. And then the plane actually crashed. I've told you that one before. These kinds of things happen, Arthur. Not like yours, I guess. Not a *miracle* miracle. But signs and messages."

"So you believe in God," I said. "I guess I didn't know that, either. I thought you were more of a Goddess person."

"Goddess," she scoffed. "Who cares? It's beyond gender, whatever it is."

"But you believe in something," I said.

"Of course I do," she said. "Not a man-in-the-clouds kind of thing. But something."

"So how would you describe it?" I said. I was curious to hear. After all these years, we'd never directly discussed our ideas of the divine. We'd talked about many issues grazing on the topic—questions of religion and mysticism and magical thinking—but never that very personal conception of what may or may not exist at the bottom of it all. I hadn't discussed it with almost anyone, for that matter. It was one of the topics that no one wanted to broach out loud, which was partly why I wrote my books.

"Oh, I don't know," she said. "It's hard to explain. The thing I believe in, I don't know what it is. I don't call it God. It's like God, but it's not God, exactly. It's not *not* God. But it's not God."

"So what do you call it?" I said.

She seemed almost embarrassed. "I call it Goddy."

"Goddy?" I said.

She laughed. "Like, 'Hey, old buddy, old pal.' Goddy. I say, 'Okay, Goddy, let's roll up our sleeves and figure this out.' Or, 'What do you think, Goddy?' Goddy is someone with good common sense. Or then sometimes it's like, 'Here, Goddy, Goddy, Goddy.'"

"Like a cat," I said.

"Yes," she said. "Sometimes. Goddy can be like a cat. Not that he's a 'he,' like I said. But I'll say 'he' right now. You never know what Goddy is thinking. You can only treat him nicely and hope for the best. Give him what he wants. Hope he doesn't bite you. That's Goddy."

"Sounds like God to me," I said.

"But in my mind," she said, "it's something different."

We talked more about God, and all the different forms He or She could take in people's imaginations. We concurred that the idea of a Goddess was mere semantics. As if women weren't as cruel and unforgiving as any patriarch. We talked about the prohibition of writing God's name, or representing Him in images, which we both felt made sense. We entertained the idea of the Godhead as something like a cosmic fountain or a mysterious cube. And all the while, my mom kept asking about Sarah, too, trying to gather more intelligence. It would all come out eventually, I knew. It would be a scandal. But for now I didn't want to talk to my mother about my sex life.

Thankfully, she was mostly interested in the miracle, and we kept returning to the theological plane.

"I'm sure I told you about the time my sister had a religious experience, didn't I?" she said, lighting her fourth cigarette. I heard the lighter spark, the pop of her lips, the exhalation. By then I'd moved into the kitchen and was pouring myself a third whiskey.

"If you did, I don't remember," I said.

"This is back when we were in our forties," she said. "You were in your late teens, I guess, off in Asia or something, on one of your trips. She got way out there. I suppose calling it a religious experience is debatable, but to me, that's what it looked like. She was under a lot of stress at the time. She was getting divorced from Terry. And Sam was only six and having those asthma attacks. She went deep into a state and kind of snapped."

"I don't think you ever told me this," I said.

"She didn't sleep, literally, for months," my mom said. "There were tons of endorphins coursing through her body, tons of fear. For a while, she was just super alert, getting everything done. But then she started telling weird jokes that no one else got, and then the revelations started. Her eyes got all glassy and intense, like a saint's eyes. And she started doing weird things. In her house, she built this circuit of gongs. She had meditation bells, sleigh bells, handbells. And they corresponded to exercise stations. She had to go around the house and gong every bell and do some push-ups or jumping jacks or ride her stationary bike. Then it got worse. She started tying bottles and cans to her clothes, walking around with smeared makeup all over her face, offering guys on the street hand jobs. It was terrifying. We ended up having to take her to the hospital."

"Poor Aunt Ellen," I said. "Sounds like she had some kind of breakdown."

"You could call it that," she said. "But it was something else, too. She was comprehending things during that time. She was communing with something on a different level. It was hard not to see it. She still claims she learned a lot from that experience. It was like something came into her. Like a possession. After that, I understood why people believe in demons and witches. She was taken over by something."

"But she came back," I said.

"Yeah, she got medicated," my mom said. "But it was in the ER that I met a doctor who told me something I'll never forget. I was so scared during that time, honey. It was her experience, but it was intense for me, too, you know? Extremely intense. I was looking for any kind of reassurance I could get. And this doctor, she was terrific. She took me aside and told me she saw this kind of thing all the time. All the time. And she said it was always the same, too. For women, she said, it was always about the body. They got obsessed with their holes. They'd start having really inappropriate sexual relationships, talking really dirty. It was all about mortifying the flesh. And it was true, Ellen did some of that.

"And for men," my mom said, "it was always about God. Men would hear voices. They'd receive commands from outer space, uncover secrets that only they could understand. They'd comprehend conspiracies that no one else knew about. God and sex, she said. Those were the ways people communed with the divine. Or the way the mind broke. I'll never forget that conversation."

"So you're saying I'm delusional," I said. I was back on the couch, staring at the ceiling. It was two o'clock in the morning where she was.

"No," she said, from across the continent. "Not at all. I don't think you're crazy at all, sweetheart. I would never say that. It's just interesting is all. What's real and what isn't. It's very hard to say, even on the best days. Tonight, I'm just glad you're safe."

11

I wanted to talk to Sarah about what had happened on the mountain. I wanted to hear what she remembered from those hours under the rubble. Had she felt any cosmic messages? Had she seen any mystical light? I felt like I couldn't truly understand what had happened until I heard her story, but unfortunately I had to wait.

For days, she was stuck inside the hospital, with Phil and the doctors guarding her every movement. She was prohibited from having any visitors, or even access to her phone, because the doctors didn't want her taxing her brain while it healed from the concussion. Phil kept me updated on her progress and assured me she was getting better all the time, but for the moment, she remained unreachable.

"She wants to talk to you," he said. "She can't wait to thank you for all you did, Arthur. Both of us feel that way. We owe you everything. She'll tell you herself soon enough. But not quite yet."

"I'm glad she's healing," I said. "Does she remember anything? Has she said anything about what happened?"

"Not very much," he said. "And we're not pushing it. She just needs to rest right now. All I can say is, she's getting stronger. It's incredible, isn't it, what the body can do. God, we were so lucky. We'll never be able to repay you, Arthur."

During those days, she became a kind of Schrödinger's cat, alive and dead, depending on my mood and train of thought. She was a miracle; she was an invalid; she was my lover; she was Phil's wife. She'd been resurrected; she'd been lucky; she was now; she was then. She was my destiny; she was my tragedy. I still didn't think I'd performed a miracle, but at the same time, I was curious to know what she'd experienced. Had she floated into a tube of light? Or encountered any dead family members on a hazy beach? Just how closely had she grazed death?

And then there was a part of me that didn't want to talk to her at all because I didn't want to break the compact. It was silly, I knew, but the old stories were pretty clear on the failure to obey a divine command. In all the fables, the disobedient one was left broken and alone. I didn't want either of us turning into pillars of salt or getting cooked in a witch's oven. I didn't want my wings melting or to fail to recognize Buddha on the road. Over and over again, the ancient wisdom agreed: obey the order, even if you don't understand it. Humble yourself before the mystery, no matter what.

On the third day, we finally spoke. I was sitting at my desk, working on the book, or pretending to work, when the gentle bell tone of my phone struck and her name appeared on the screen. An immediate flare of dread went through me. Here it was, my first test. Was I going to breach the contract and accept the call? I had to think that talking to her on the phone wasn't such a big deal. Giving her up would be something that happened in stages, even in the most severe case. You didn't sell your house and evacuate the same day. You got a few weeks to implement the task. And how bizarre that I was thinking this way at all.

"Hi," I said, and no lightning hit me.

"Hi," she said. "Where are you now?"

"I'm at home," I said. "How about you?"

"In the hospital," she said, "but I'm alone. Finally. Phil went to the gym. I told him to stay a while."

Her voice was an immediate balm. She sounded so normal, so unambiguously alive. Whatever worries I'd been nursing receded to the edges of my mind. There was nothing more natural than talking to Sarah, the woman I loved, listening to that lovely little timbre of amusement in her voice.

"Are you doing okay?" I said.

"I'm okay," she said. "I mean, this bed rest kind of sucks. But they're taking really good care of me here. Phil's been incredibly sweet. He says you saved my life. Is that true?"

"You don't remember?" I said.

"It's pretty vague," she said. "I mean, I was pretty out of it up there."

"Maybe that's for the best," I said. "It means your brain is healing."

"It's not like I forgot everything," she said. "I wish."

"What do you remember?" I wanted to hear the story, but at the same time I didn't want to press too hard. I definitely didn't want to plant any thoughts.

"God," she said. "I mean, where do you want me to start?"

"From when I left you."

She told me her version from that point. She began with the moment of waking up in her cabin on the day I left. She said she'd gotten up feeling the need for some space to think about everything that had been happening. She was happy about our conversation in the yurt, and the plan we had, but also sad about Phil, and it seemed like some kind of ceremony was in order. Her idea had been to hike to the Zendo near the creek and spend the night as a ritual of gratitude, or maybe just a period of silent contemplation. Something to mark the moment, which was significant.

"I was feeling a lot of guilt about Phil," she said. "I mean, I still am, obviously. He deserves a lot better than what I'm giving him. I know people get divorced all the time. It isn't a big deal in a way. But it doesn't really matter when it comes to your own marriage, it turns out. You know? It's like it's never happened before. We've spent a lot of time together. And to hurt a person who really loves you, and who you still love, too, is really hard. It's really fucking complicated. Anyway. I just needed to take a walk."

"So you went up to do some kind of penance," I said.

"Maybe a little," she said. "More like a purification, or at least some kind of acknowledgment."

"Were you having second thoughts?" I said.

"No, no!" she said. "I wasn't doubting anything at all. I was only feeling it. It's a big deal, what we're doing."

She told me she'd hiked to the creek and found the Zendo and had sat down on the creek bank and listened to the branches thrashing in the wind. The wind had been crazy that day, she said, the way it kept attacking the trees, bashing them from every direction. It'd seemed appropriate somehow, the violent, all-over-the-place wind. It was how she'd felt. She'd sat there thinking about me, and Phil, and all the things they'd been through, and all that we had ahead, but in the end she hadn't gotten very far in her thinking because, suddenly, the fire was all around her. It came on so fast, she said, she barely understood what was happening. She'd tried running down the trail but already a wall of flames was blocking the way. The wind was so strong, whipping sparks all over the place. The fire was jumping from branch to branch, bursting the trees into candles. She was trapped.

"I can't stand to think about it," I said.

"I was thinking about you the whole time," she said, "and about everything we're about to do. It was so horrible, Arthur. I've been telling myself for so long that I don't want a family. And now, after I finally met you, and made the decision, to die in this fucking fire. It seemed so idiotic."

"Did you pray?" I said. For some reason, I wanted to know if another channel had been opened ahead of mine, not that I knew what that would have meant, exactly.

"No," she said. "I didn't have to, because I knew I wasn't going to die up there. I wasn't going to let it happen."

She'd gone and submerged herself under the water, just as I'd guessed. It'd taken a while to find a spot where she could get all the way under, and she'd waited there, in this pool, going under and coming back up, as everything around her burned. This had gone on for what felt like hours. The air became so hot the whole world seemed to warp and ripple behind its waves. The flames roared and reached out, trying to grab her, but they couldn't quite get there. She'd gone under, come up, breathed the scalding air, gone under again. The water had filled with ash and twisted branches still on fire. She had no idea how long it went on. It'd seemed like a year. And then, eventually, the fire had started burning itself out. She'd been able to get out of the water and sit on the bank. The sound of the fire was still like thunder, all the wood and needles evaporating, but she'd felt safe for a moment, like she was going to make it. And then she remembered this other sound, this sudden roar. It was like a sound inside of a sound. She'd been looking at the fire whipping in the wind and then... she didn't know...

"You don't know what?" I said. We'd come to the very moment I most wanted to understand, but I could hear her voice faltering, leaving the next passage blank.

"I don't know what happened," she said. "It goes black."

"You don't remember anything at all?" I said.

"No," she said. "I guess that's when the rocks and tree hit me?"

"And then, when do you start remembering again?" I said.

"I remember you," she said tentatively. "You were sitting on the rock. In the smoke. I could barely see anything through the smoke. But that's what I remember next. The sound, and then you. It's fuzzy."

"But you don't remember anything while you were out?" I said. "You don't remember the rocks and everything actually hitting you?"

"No," she said. "I don't remember it happening at all. Thank God. It's all so mixed up now. I was on the bank, and then you were there, and it was morning. And I was all banged up."

"No dreams?"

"No."

"You don't remember getting out of the pile?"

"I don't remember being in the pile at all," she said. "Why are you so curious? I wouldn't even know it'd happened if Phil hadn't told me about it. And if my wrist wasn't broken. And if I didn't have a concussion. Tell me what you saw. Phil told me what you did, but I haven't heard it from you. I want to know what you did."

I told her my version. I told her about fighting the fire and climbing the trail at dawn to find her under the pile of debris. I told her about touching her wrist and feeling no pulse and trying to dig her out from under the rocks and tree, but not being able. I told her how I'd taken a few steps away and prayed. And how I must have somehow unlocked the tumblers of the universe because I'd turned around and there she was, living again.

"So you levitated me out of the pile or something?" she said. "Is that what you're telling me?"

"I don't know," I said. "Not exactly. But it did kind of seem like it at the time."

"You roped my soul back into my body?" she said. "Wow. That's pretty crazy. Thank you for that."

"I'm just telling you what it seemed like," I said. "I'm not saying it actually happened."

"Maybe you really did," she said. "Maybe you're, like, an angel of light. Did you smell any celestial perfume up there? Did any birds talk to you?" She couldn't help the sardonic twist. It was her way.

"There were no birds," I said. "I should also tell you, I kind of made a deal with the universe up there."

"What kind of deal was that?" she said.

"I said I'd give you up if you lived through it," I said. It seemed like she should know, even if she found it unconvincing. "That was my deal with God. You for you."

"What does that mean, exactly?" she said.

"I don't know," I said. "I didn't read the fine print. But I think I'm not supposed to be with you anymore." As I said them, the words seemed more absurd than ever.

"I thought when you saved someone you became their servant for life," she said. "That's what I always heard."

"You'd like that, wouldn't you?" I said. "A live-in butler."

She thought about it for a second. "You really think God cares that much about us?" she said.

"I think He cares about everything," I said. "That's what they say."

"He has a lot of other things on His mind," she said. "That's what I think." And then she laughed. "That would be pretty stupid, wouldn't it? If we had to leave each other now, after everything? I really hope that isn't what's happening."

"Me, too," I said.

We shared another moment of silence, pondering what it all meant, and then she laughed again, washing away our doubts.

"I'm not too worried about it, Arthur," she said. "I think I'd probably know it if I'd been dead or not. The point is, you came and found me. That's what I find amazing."

A good thing about a book is the way it fills up your time. It's always there, ready to distract you from enormous tracts of your life. You can always burrow down into the clauses of your language world and put the other, real world out of sight. It can be sad, really, how selfish it makes a person. I'd once liked to believe I'd become a writer because it connected me to other people, but sometimes, I had to admit, the opposite was true. Writing allowed me to isolate. And with Sarah stuck in bed, and Phil standing guard, I went in deep.

It helped that I was entering a fertile period in the process. The binding energy was starting to gather, and connections between far-flung chapters were starting to make themselves known. I could see the text reaching out to itself and knitting into a big, beaded web of associations. The Tree Book was itself becoming a kind of tree, branching toward the light. Around the invisible trunk of research, a skeleton of language was building, leafing out into a shaggy bloom, sprays of color budding at the very tips. It was such a mysterious process, writing a book. Every new pass brought you a step deeper inside, and also laid a new layer on top. Deeper and higher, around and around, the coursing energy of revision.

Whenever Sarah had a few minutes alone over the next week, she called from her bed. I always picked up, not wanting to seem like the kind of person who succumbed to superstition. As long as I wasn't physically touching her, I told myself, I was still inside the letter of the law. Not that I believed in the law, per se. But if I did, I wasn't breaking it. It became a joke between us. The miracle had both happened and not happened. I wasn't exactly giving her up, but I wasn't wallowing in her presence, either. We were drifting in a kind of bardo together, some in-between zone. We were two bodiless voices communicating in the ether. On her side, she wasn't concerned about the situation at all.

"Are you worried about it?" she said. "Really?"

"No," I said. "Are you?"

"No," she said. "I don't believe in God. Not like that, anyway."

"Not at all?"

"Not really," she said. "Do you really think He exists?"

"Not exactly."

"Do you think I really exist?" she said. "Or is everything in the universe just a projection of your mind?"

"I think you exist," I said.

"Are you sure?" she said. "This might all be a dream you're having."

"It's not my dream," I said.

"How do you know that?"

"Because in my dream I'd be fucking you right now."

Sarah loved hearing about the miracle. She wanted me to tell her the story over and over again, like a fairy tale. She'd text me teasing notes.

"Is God watching you right now? Is he putting your name in his little book? Oh, that's Santa Claus, sorry. I always get my omnipotent guys with white beards who defy the logic of space and time mixed up. My bad."

Or: *"Can you do me another miracle? My back itches. I can't reach it. If you could deal with that, that'd be great...."*

For her, the story of the miracle was evidence of my all-too-human mind in the grip of oxygen deprivation. She also saw it as proof of my obvious, exultant love for her, and that made her happy. I'd climbed a mountain to rescue her. What more could anyone ask? It was the story that would seal our love. A story to tell our grandchildren. The test was over. We'd won.

"I'm really glad you're not like Abraham," she said one night, late, as we lay in our respective beds, drinking our respective cups of tea. I was still working on my pages. She was finally back at home, but still quarantined, staring at her walls. "I doubt he told his woman anything."

"I think the deal between Abraham and God was extremely private," I said. "That was part of the bargain. Maybe I shouldn't have told you about this, either."

"It's such a strange bargain, isn't it?" she said. "Kill your child to prove your faith. It's totally abusive, really."

"God was giving Abraham a test," I said.

"Yeah, I get that," she said. "But it's sadistic."

"An act of faith only works if it's kind of insane," I said. "If it were reasonable, it would just be a normal, transactional agreement. I do this, you do that. If it isn't crazy, it isn't really a pure relationship to the divine. That's one theory, anyway."

"Thanks, Kierkegaard," she said. "But why is God so needy? You'd think He'd be more above it all. I would think that, anyway."

"You'd have to ask God that," I said.

"I doubt He'd give me a straight answer."

I escaped ever deeper into the book. I was spending hours in there, late into the night, to the exclusion of almost anything else. In the mornings I woke up and made coffee and went directly to work. I carried the manuscript around and made notes in the coffee shop, at the bar. I walked away from the desk only to have another thought and go straight back and get it down before the brightness faded. It had its claws in me.

I was becoming happy with the Merle and Candy chapter, which I felt captured their warmth and optimism. I liked the chapter on Muir, too. Writing against something was always a pleasure. Sometimes I felt like all writing was against something or other. The fairy chapter was turning into something surprisingly moving.

Between those pieces, I had a sturdy foundation in place. I was able to read them through without a single complaint, which was about all I could ask for. There was nothing in the sentences that bothered me anymore. To go beyond that, to raise the hairs on my own neck, or to weep over the poetry of it all, was more than I could expect. But to feel unbothered. I could get there. I could navigate by the negative path once again.

As the days went on, the meaning of the miracle continued

shifting in my mind. I still worried that I was failing a test of some kind, succumbing to temptation, or lack of faith, but the more I bantered with Sarah on the phone and over text, the more the worries dissipated. The whole meaning of the miracle seemed to be evolving. I started understanding those blazing, smoke-filled moments as only one passage in a larger arc of meaning. The interpretations surrounding the experience were fusing with the experience itself, changing it, blurring its lesson. All the doubts were part of the greater event. If it had even happened at all, which it probably hadn't.

What did it mean to give someone up? I kept asking myself, as I got dressed or checked the mail. That sense of ownership inside the agreement never totally made sense to me. I didn't own Sarah any more than she owned me. And if I didn't own her, then how could I give her up? Maybe this was the real intention of the pact, I thought—to allow me to relinquish the sense of ownership itself. This was the agreement at the root of any marriage, wasn't it? Of any true, equal relationship, for that matter. To give oneself wholly, to commit entirely, without expectation, without claim. In a sense, Sarah and I were being asked to cast off our previous selves and to meet nakedly on this new, conjugal plane. We were being asked to love with our hearts open.

Sitting at my desk, watching the clouds, I became more confident of this reading. It was the lesson of almost every faith, wasn't it? Lose yourself, submit yourself. In every tradition, the highest, most noble act was to discard the petty distractions of ego and serve another. By promising to give up Sarah, I was in effect promising to humble myself before her as my new God. I was no longer backing into our life together, checking over my shoulder. I was striding forward confidently, without qualm, emptied out.

Brushing my teeth, getting ready for bed, I went through the whole contract in my mind again, confirming my new understanding. Yes, I thought, the universe, or my own mind, whatever it was, was bringing us together in this generous way. It was preparing us for our ultimate, joyful, giving union.

Did the complete reversal of the miracle's stated meaning seem odd to me? A little bit, but not really. The universe was built on exactly this kind of reversal, by my thinking. It was always about the rich becoming poor, the celebrated becoming despised, the meek inheriting the earth. Every role bled into its opposite over time. Just as the seed became the tree became the seed again, every meaning turned around and become its mirror version. Lying in my bed, turning off the light, I came to the conclusion, as I had so many times before: the only immutable law of the universe was irony.

All of this was happening without my ever seeing Sarah in person. We remained locked in our different rooms, the proverbial bride and groom before the wedding. She was back at home but being kept under close watch by Phil and a hired nurse. The doctors had strictly limited her range of activity, allowing her to amble around the house and watch TV, but not much else. The librarians were giving her as many sick days as needed.

But eventually she couldn't stand it any longer, and we began plotting our reunion. She told Phil her memoir class was starting up again, and she wanted to get back into it. The workshop was a nice, sedate activity, she argued, without any physical perils. Not that she needed anyone's permission. We agreed to meet at the Barn on our usual night, at the usual hour, with all our favorite provisions, and although I felt some flickers of doubt around the plan, I didn't say anything. It turned out my faith in Sarah was much stronger than my faith in God.

The cold rains started up again that week, which meant the last of the summer was truly gone, devoured by the incoming season. I went to the Barn early and prepared our room. I unfolded the bed and sprinkled it with a few rose petals from Safeway. I opened a bottle of pinot noir and let it decant. I would've lit candles, but our love was still a secret from the world, at least for the time being, and we didn't want to give ourselves away with a telltale light. The people of our town were too curious and not to be trusted.

Sarah arrived after dark. I watched her car drift down the street and come to a stop in front of the puzzle shop, the rain making jagged slashes in the lamplight. I saw her get out of the car and open her umbrella, the black membrane snapping to. I saw the pulse of light as the car door locked. I saw her cross the street to my side and disappear from view.

I heard her footsteps as she climbed the stairs and paused on the landing. I heard the main door open and the footsteps continue down the hall. It was a delicious moment. For weeks we'd been apart, our only touch our voices on the phone. Now, at last, she was coming close. Her body was walking toward the door to our room. She was almost there. Had I ever loved her so purely before? I wondered. In that moment, on the edge of her presence, I thought I might have loved her more than I'd ever imagined possible.

At last, the door opened, and she was there, standing in the shadow, backlit by the low hall light. She had on a yellow raincoat and a cast on her wrist. Her cheeks were a little sallow, her eyes a little dark and bagged, but her skin seemed softly to glow. Her aliveness was so vivid and yet so delicate in that moment, it seemed like she could vanish again at the slightest sound. I couldn't believe I'd come so close to losing her.

She took off her coat and leaned her wet umbrella against the wall.

"Hi," she said.

"Hi," I said.

"It's cold in here," she said.

"Is it too cold?" I said. "I can turn up the heat if you want."

"No," she said. "It's fine. I'll warm up."

I didn't go to her at first. I wasn't sure if I was allowed to touch her or not. She didn't come to me, either. For whatever reason, we both seemed tentative. Not because of God, but only because we'd been apart long enough that the open invitation to each other's bodies had lapsed. We had to rediscover our rules again. It was kind of sweet. There was no rush.

She sat on the hide-a-bed and I poured us both glasses of wine.

"So how was your day?" I said, handing her the glass.

"It was fine," she said. "Yours?"

"It was fine," I said. "I got some work done."

"The book is going all right?" she said. She knew it was still a boring question. The status didn't change much day to day. It was like asking about the weather.

"I got my words in," I said.

"Good for you," she said.

I sat down next to her on the squeaking bed. The mattress was so thin the metal frame pressed against the backs of my legs. Someday, we'd have a beautiful mattress of our own, I thought, with memory foam, covered in clean sheets with a high thread count, but for now, this was our nuptial bed. The windows were streaked with rain, a patter of droplets blowing against the glass in light gusts.

"You're feeling okay?" I said.

"I'm fine," she said. "Just the collarbone and wrist are a little stiff. My head is okay."

"And driving over here was easy?" I said.

"I'm seriously fine," she said. "You and Phil, such worrywarts."

"You can't be too careful," I said.

"I think you can be, actually," she said.

I leaned toward her and we kissed. Softly, the seal was broken. I leaned back and sipped my wine.

"How do you like your nurse?" I said. I didn't want to rush anything, much as I wanted her. Now that she was back, her body was doing all its tricks on me, working its power.

"She's amazing," she said. "Nurses are the best people in the world."

"Have you been watching anything good on TV?" I said.

"Mostly just nature documentaries," she said. "I just saw one about grasshoppers today. They molt five times in their lives, did you know that? It's so incredible, to see them squeezing out of their old bodies. Five times. It's only on the last one that their wings are finally fully grown. What a life."

"Are these the grasshoppers who eat their husbands?" I said.

"That's a praying mantis," she said. "The male grasshoppers sing a mating song. They have eardrums in their abdomens."

We didn't want to hurry anything, but we both understood we had a finite amount of time in our room. She had to be home in a matter of hours, or else she'd be missed. We were there for a reason, which was to reconsecrate our love, and so there was a certain seriousness as we finally got started. There were no sideways glances this time, no double entendres, no jokes. We were here for an almost ceremonial union, and we didn't want any distractions.

Carefully, we took off each other's clothes, with special attention around Sarah's cast, making a great effort to avoid stretching her arms over her head or getting anything snagged. We managed to get our shirts off, and our own shoes and pants. We helped each other with our respective underwear. And then, naked, we knelt facing each other on the bed, taking our time on the verge of this sacred transgression.

"You're sure you're okay?" I said.

"Just a little headachy," she said. "But it's nothing. I'll be back at work next week. How about you? Are you feeling okay?"

"I'm fine," I said.

"You're sure you're not a little scared of God?" she said. "You seem a little nervous."

"Maybe a little," I said.

We kissed longingly, and our bodies pressed against each other. We were warming up. We kissed again, with more ardor, and she began stroking me. My fingers grazed the slickness between her legs.

"You're worried that God is watching us?" she whispered.

"Kind of," I said.

"I didn't think you were the type," she said. "Such a believer, it turns out."

She continued stroking, and nothing dire happened. No locusts descended, no floods came. We kissed again, and no thunderclouds appeared. We were still there, together, in the darkness of our room. Her body was pliant, full of heat.

"He likes to watch people, doesn't He?" she said.

"He must," I said.

"He kind of gets off on it," she said.

"I guess so," I said.

"Why don't we show Him something then?" she said. And like Adam and Eve, we lay down beside each other on the creaking hide-a-bed and fucked.

12

We agreed we had to tell Phil what was happening. It was evil to keep him waiting any longer, living this lie. With Sarah becoming healthy again, and winter coming on, we had to go forward with the awful scene.

We decided the conversation would happen between Sarah and Phil alone. At some point, maybe, I'd have my own talk with Phil. And maybe someday we could all talk together, but that day was a long way off. I could imagine a time when we were old and mellow and forgiving of our younger selves for all our trespasses, but for now, the married couple were the main protagonists here. This was their tragedy. It was Sarah's confession to make. I would wait in the shadows and hear about the conversation after the fact.

"Do you think he has any idea what's about to happen?" I said. We were on our respective phones again, sitting at our desks, eating our lunches. Outside, the last, ragged maple leaves were clinging to the branches. The sky was the shade of wet concrete.

"I don't think he has any idea what's about to happen," she said. "Poor guy."

"I feel really bad for him," I said.

"Yeah, me, too," she said. And we sat through a long, anguished silence memorializing our regard for Phil. What was there to say?

She made a plan to drive with Phil to Summer Lake, an empty playa in the desert beyond the Cascades. Their final destination would be some hot springs with supposedly healing waters, and the long drive would give them an opportunity to talk in private. The prehistoric geology of the desert would offer a backdrop of proper dignity for the conversation, she thought. Time was like a physical presence out there, striated into the faces of the canyons and mesas, dwarfing all human suffering.

The morning they left was cool and damp. I woke up and took my place at my desk as usual, but found it impossible to work. Thoughts of Sarah and Phil rattled in my mind. I thought about them in the car, surrounded by all that space. What were they saying?

I took a walk earlier than normal, heading into the hills, up through the aspens and into the sword fern under the Douglas fir. The trail was becoming a slurry of decomposing leaf litter. I could hear the calls of crows, song sparrows, juncos, and spotted towhees, all the usual suspects. By now, Sarah and Phil were probably climbing the pass. They were possibly even east of the mountains. Soon, they'd be coming out into the high plains sage of Christmas Valley, with its big sky and tabletop mesas. I wondered where their conversation had gotten to now. If only I could listen in.

I arrived at a bluff overlooking the valley and checked the time: 10:00 a.m. I knew Sarah would be as kind as humanly possible in their conversation. She'd couch all the ugly news in many layers of love and sympathy, and yet there was no way around the pain it would cause. In my mind, I could almost see the curdled look on

Phil's face as the truth landed. I could feel the waves of disbelief, anger, and sorrow rolling off him. I could imagine all the questions and clarifications that would follow. They'd have to renarrate their entire lives together. The silences would be hellacious. They'd have to confront the fact that the love between them was over.

It was all terrible, but in the end, I knew, Phil wouldn't fight. He'd take the news into himself and surrender to Sarah like the decent person he was. He wouldn't try to convince her of anything or lead her to doubt herself. He'd wish her only happiness in her new life, and blessings in her new love. And in that surrender he'd display the true strength of his character once again. He was a generous, profoundly mature person.

And then they'd come home, and we'd be free. We'd been talking about moving to California, maybe Sonoma or Glen Ellen, someplace with rolling, golden hills and wildflowers. We were hoping to find a house close to Sarah's parents, but not too close. Wherever we ended up, I already saw our new life in a series of snapshots misted with nostalgia. I saw a baby lying on a clean quilt in the morning sun. A baby's hand touching a silky California poppy. I saw Sarah standing on the limestone steps of a public library, holding a swaddled baby. Around the edges, I could smell dry grass and sun-warmed blackberries. I could feel the heaving shadows of a heritage oak on my eyes.

Who would our child be? A boy or a girl, it didn't matter. What would the child bring out in me? There would be new streams of experience, new forms of inspiration. A baby and writing, all worlds together, nothing sacrificed, only gain.

I headed back home to wait for the future to begin. I waited all afternoon for an update from Sarah, but Sarah didn't call that day, which only made sense. They were way out in the desert, probably beyond cell range. I made myself pasta for dinner and watched a documentary about black holes on TV. I was doing my best to get my mind off the distant scene, but I couldn't help picking at it, worrying it, wondering what was going on. I imagined their conversation progressing in all its many stages and detours. I wondered if Phil was fighting harder than I'd expected, or if Sarah was waffling. Maybe they'd gotten drunk and were having a final go-round of tragic breakup sex. None of it seemed impossible, and none of it bothered me. I forgave them everything in advance.

Before bed, in case Sarah found a hot spot, I left her a message telling her not to worry, to just be there with Phil, however long it took. In the morning, I got up and did a little work. Around noon, I ate a sandwich. And not long after that, as an afternoon nap started to loom, a call finally came in. I rushed around the house looking for my phone, which had slipped into the cushions of the couch, worried and excited to hear Sarah's summary of the last twenty-four hours, but when I pulled it out, the name on the face wasn't Sarah's. It was Candy's. I tapped the button and said hi, and she asked if I'd heard the news.

"What news is that?" I said.

"The news about Sarah and Phil," she said.

How incredible, I thought, that the word had already traveled. Phil had barely received the news himself, and already Candy had it. Phil must have called her in the night, I thought. He'd needed to process his grief and he'd found a signal. And now, already, Candy was turning around and calling me to process her secondhand grief. It seemed like Phil hadn't given Candy the full story, however, because she didn't seem to understand I was part of the news she was passing along, too.

"I haven't heard," I said. "What's up?"

"Oh. No," she said. "I hate to be the one to tell you this then, but... oh boy..."

"It's okay," I said. "Go ahead. I might have some idea."

"Well, there was an accident yesterday," she said.

"Wait, what?"

Candy kept talking but already I was having trouble following her meaning. The news she was telling me wasn't the news I'd been expecting, the news of Sarah and Phil's breakup, but rather the news of some kind of crash. Phil and Sarah had been driving in the woods yesterday afternoon, Candy said, when out of nowhere, a buck had jumped the guardrail and plowed into their car. The impact had caused the car to veer into the oncoming lane just as another car had been rounding a bend, and the rear bumpers had clipped, sending Sarah and Phil's car off the road. They'd spun over a ledge and tumbled into the Klamath River, rolling at least twice. While Phil had made it out with a broken leg and major contusions on his face and chest, and was now resting safely in the hospital in Medford, Sarah hadn't been so lucky. She'd probably been unconscious when the car hit the water, and she'd drowned.

"I don't think this is right," I said. "I just talked to Sarah yesterday."

"It happened yesterday afternoon," Candy said. "Late in the day."

"I texted her in the afternoon," I said. "I left her a message last night."

"Well, yeah," Candy said. "I don't think she got that."

We went around for another ten minutes, with Candy explaining the events to me, and me disbelieving, even as more proof piled up. She told me it was rutting season right now, and the bucks were jumping across the highway all the time, driven crazy by their mating instinct. The only thing in their minds was the scent of the females. I kept asking Candy questions, trying to find a way in which she'd gotten her facts wrong, or garbled them in the retelling somehow, but as many ways as I asked her to recount the story, it was always the same.

By the time we hung up, the world had disappeared. Everything had drained completely out to sea, leaving me alone on an empty beach. I didn't know what to do, so I went over to the window, half expecting to see bloody writing in the sky, but there was only an airplane traveling silently through the atmosphere, drifting south.

I still didn't believe Candy's story because, by believing it, I thought I might make it real. I would have sensed something, wouldn't I? Sarah's voice would have called out to me, or some animal would have appeared in my path. But nothing like that had occurred. I went through the previous day in my head, looking for any signs or portents, but I couldn't find any, not a single ripple in the fabric. How was it possible that Sarah had exited the physical plane without telling me?

I walked outside to get some air as flashes of guilt began detonating on my skin. They clustered on my arms, my toes, and my scalp, coming in hot waves. Already, it was occurring to me that the accident might be my fault. Was that possible? I had to admit, the universe had been pretty clear on the matter. The whole idea had been to let Sarah go in order that she might live, and yet I'd walked away from the agreement and done the exact opposite. For the past weeks, I'd been seeing her, touching her, ignoring the whole covenant, assuming I was living in a rational universe. But now, too late, I was seeing the consequences. I'd disobeyed a divine command and I was paying for it with Sarah's life.

I felt like I was being x-rayed by God. I was suddenly exposed in my deepest recesses. What a fool I'd been! Willfully blind to His authority, willfully ignorant of His absolute might. All this time, He'd been shining His light in my face and I'd pretended not to see it. I understood now, too late, that God was in fact everywhere. He was the author of everything, rationing every moment, coloring every image. His moods of mercy, anger, love, and boredom were the very texture of our days. How had I not been aware?

I bowed my head and tried to pray, imploring God to bring Sarah back like He had before. But this time, the prayer didn't catch. I couldn't seem to marshal the right concentration. I kept murmuring the words over and over again, in different configurations, but they were leaden and flat. They didn't pick up any energy, they didn't float. I tried orienting my prayers elsewhere, into the ground, toward the trees, but nothing happened. We'd been through this before, and the prayer was used up. It was like a parody now, a sad, belated simulation.

Still, there were many mysteries that I couldn't understand. If God was everywhere, I wondered, and in everything, then why wasn't He in me, too? Or if He was, why didn't I feel Him? And why would He implant me with the illusion of freedom, and offer me a seeming choice, only to make me choose wrongly? Why would He imbue me with these desires only to hunt me down for my mistakes and punish me with such cruel, asymmetric force? What kind of system was that? As I stood on the deck, gripping the railing, the whole rabbit hole of free will opened before me.

And so, within moments of feeling God's power, I was already doubting Him again, and hating Him, too. I hated Him even though I didn't believe in Him. And then, even as the rage and wonder got tangled, and tangled again, I could see I was thinking about the situation all wrong anyway. What kind of egomaniac was I, to put myself at the center of this? I wasn't the origin of these events. They weren't my doing. Sarah and Phil had been in a terrible accident. Sarah had died. They were the victims here. I was barely even a bystander.

I stood on the deck and stared at the sky, the cirrus clouds like marbled fat in the sky's blue flesh. In an oak tree, a robin was staring at me. Up until that moment, I'd been holding Sarah's death at arm's length, thinking about it as an abstraction. But now, at last, it hit me as reality. She was gone. I'd never touch her again. I'd never kiss her lips or feel her fingers in mine. I'd never see her drinking wine or walking in the park in the sunlight. I'd never see her lifting her hips to slide off her underwear, or staring at her computer, or chopping garlic on a wooden block. How was that possible? How was I supposed to live in a world where she wasn't?

Even though I didn't believe in God, I cursed Him. What the fuck is Your problem? I asked the clouds. You could have done anything. You could have moved Sarah to another city, or changed her heart and saved her marriage. Instead, You murdered her in cold blood. The punishment was so out of proportion to the crime. It was the act of some deranged cartel boss, not the wise, loving father or mother we heard so much about. I got no answer from the clouds. How could it be, after all this divine activity, that I still expected a sign?

I staggered back indoors and lay on the couch and spent the next hour trying to stockpile every memory of her I had. I tried to harvest every sense impression from my synapses before they disappeared. I thought about the sound of her voice on the phone, the sound of her peeing in a toilet. I traced the curve of her back, the freckles on her shoulders. I imagined the diameter of her ankle, the funny, splayed arrangement of her toes. It was her body that kept coming back to me, in every light, naked and clothed. I tried to recall her smell, the feel of her hair. I wanted to remember all the clothes she'd worn, like those black galoshes, and the tan shorts that'd ended up crumpled on the floor. I wanted to map all the rooms she'd walked through, the logic of all her arguments. I wanted to imagine how she might have aged.

There were calls coming in but I ignored them. It seemed the news of her death was traveling fast. The librarians knew, and the people from her solstice party, judging by the numbers appearing. Her parents must know by now, too, I thought. How horrible. They'd received the worst news two people could receive, and they were surely pulverized. I wondered if I should call anyone to tell them the news myself, but I didn't move from the couch. All around the world, her memory was lighting in people's minds, connecting us all in a spherical constellation of grief.

Most of all, I began to think about Phil. He was lying in a bed somewhere, broken and afraid. I pictured him being dragged from the smashed car, placed in a gurney, and driven through the pine wastelands to the hospital. Was he awake for any it? I wondered. Was he awake now? He'd been through hell, and he'd awaken in hell. He'd seen his wife die in front of his eyes, and now he had to live with that image for the rest of his life. He was in wracking physical and emotional pain. How thoroughly I'd wronged him.

I thought about going to see him in the hospital, but I wasn't sure if that was a good idea. I doubted he wanted a visit from me at the moment. In other circumstances, I would've gone immediately. If he'd been in an accident alone, Sarah and I both would have been there, waiting in the room. But in this situation, considering everything I'd done, it was more complicated. I doubted Phil wanted to wake up and see his wife's lover hovering over his bed.

Lying on the couch, staring at the wall, I debated what to do. What was I being called upon for? And for that matter, who was doing the calling? I wanted nothing to do with God's calls anymore. But what about my own calls, the calls to myself? If only I knew exactly how much Phil knew about Sarah and me, I would've had a better idea of what the moment demanded. But I didn't know how far the conversation with Sarah had gone. Had they already gotten to the confession when the buck hit, or had they only gotten partway? And if they'd only gotten partway, how far? The specifics mattered, because if Phil knew about the affair, I probably needed to stay away and give him space. But if he didn't know, maybe I was in a position to help.

In the end, I decided to go. It seemed worth the risk. If Phil didn't want to see me, he could always tell me to leave. But if he did want to see me, I wanted to be present and accounted for. I figured we'd blown beyond the point of normal etiquette by now anyway. Whatever betrayals had occurred were over, and the moment had come to be together, human to human. It was time to go offer myself as a friend.

I drove slowly through town, careful to obey every traffic signal and stop sign. I wanted to avoid any more judgments, even the petty kinds. Plus I now saw every car on the road as a possible projectile of God. Every cat, dog, and plant was a possible spy, fabricating their reports, all agents of His cosmic police. They might appear as living creatures, with their own agency and appetites, but in fact they were instruments of God's surveillance. Or maybe they weren't. I had no idea. Maybe He granted us all life and then turned His back on us. Maybe He allowed His machine to operate without any attention. He let His monsters run wild.

I parked in the visitors' garage and proceeded to the front desk, where the nurse guided me to room 312. I walked slowly to the elevator, passing an old man in a wheelchair with an oxygen tank and a young woman holding a bloody rag to her head. In every room, I imagined, there were other patients suffering. There were victims of gunshots, circular saws, roach poisons, and cancers. Had they all made their own bad deals with the Almighty? I didn't think so. Only me.

My stomach was queasy as I rose in the elevator, drawing closer to Phil's room. I knew on a conscious level I hadn't caused the accident with my divine disobedience, but even if that was the case, I could also see how it might be argued I'd caused it by my sneaking around. If not for me, Phil and Sarah never would have been out on that road. Phil would have been home, preparing for classes. Sarah would have been at the library, shelving books. They'd have eaten dinner together, and gone to sleep, and awakened this morning as happy or unhappy as they'd been the day before. I could see how, through Phil's eyes, I might be a vile, guilty person, with or without God's help. I almost pressed the button to go back down but I kept rising.

The elevator opened and I walked the last length to Phil's room. The air was bright and smelled like lemon disinfectant. At the doorway I paused and took a deep breath, and did one last inventory of my intentions. Was I here for the proper reasons? I asked myself. Or was it only out of my own selfish need to feel virtuous? I tried to peer through the contradictory emotions of shock, grief, guilt, and love, and reminded myself again that the love that Sarah and I had shared wasn't any crime. It was a gift we'd been given. Any sane person, including Phil, would understand that. He'd also understand that the accident was unrelated to anything I'd done or failed to do vis-à-vis God. At bottom, I told myself, I was here as an act of kindness. I wanted to serve Phil.

I stepped across the threshold to find a curtain dividing the room. The near bed was empty, which meant Phil was in the far bed, behind the curtain. There was a nurse in the room, checking some charts, and in the corner sat a man I recognized from Phil's department. He had a walrus mustache and reddish, unruly hair. He looked like he'd already been there for hours. He gazed up at me with exhausted eyes and communicated silently that this was a profound moment we were living through. We were meeting in the deepest foundations of existence here. We didn't need to bother with introductions.

"I was hoping to see Phil," I said. "Is he awake?"

"I think so," the man said. He peered over at the bed. "Yeah. He is."

"Is he seeing people now?" I said.

"I'll find out," the man said. "Phil? Are you okay with a visitor?"

"Who is it?" I heard Phil say.

The man looked over at me questioningly.

"Arthur," I said.

The man looked at Phil, and waited, and for a moment my fate seemed to hang in the balance. Which way would the pin fall? One path stretched into the room; another, somewhere else. Maybe the two paths converged up ahead, or maybe they bent off into disparate realities. Maybe the fork itself was an illusion. But maybe, too, the fate of my very soul was spinning at this moment, waiting for the arrow to land on its ultimate number.

The man turned toward me again, nodding me in.

"He's going into surgery soon," he said, "so he probably can't talk long."

"Okay."

I walked beyond the curtain and stood at the foot of Phil's bed. Phil was lying on his back, his hands clasped on his stomach, a brace around his neck. His face was abraded and swollen. On his head was a thick, gauzy helmet. He had two black eyes. His cheeks were marred by yellowish smudges, bruises feathering out from under the bandage. Looking at him, I could feel the last vestiges of doubt about the accident's reality evaporating. The shock of it went through me all over again. Sarah was gone.

Phil looked at me with druggy bewilderment.

"Arthur," he said.

"I'm so sorry," I said.

He sighed and seemed slowly to shake his head. I waited as time elapsed in slow motion to hear the verdict. At last, after twenty years, he spoke.

"I'm glad you're here," he said. His eyes were hazy but filled with what seemed like genuine gratitude. "Thank you for coming. You're a good friend."

We didn't talk long. Phil was still in shock, and muddled by painkillers, but in the time we had I could tell he was pleased I'd come. I'd done the right thing. He didn't seem to hold me responsible for anything. He didn't even seem to know about the affair, which was the best news of all. The relief I felt was almost grotesque. The terrible, awful, liberating relief from the truth. Going forward, I vowed, I'd never bring it up. Whereas the day before, it had seemed evil to keep Phil in darkness, today it seemed evil to cast him into the light. The only thing to do now was be of use.

I talked to the other man in the room for a few minutes and gave him my email address. In an hour, he said, Phil would be getting a piece of metal screwed into his hip and a rod inserted in his leg. The recovery would take three months, at least, with much agony and grueling rehabilitation involved. I told the man I wanted to be on any food tree or help wagon that developed. Then I went home, feeling shaken, but cleaner.

Over the next few days, I fed myself, and bathed, and tended the regular stations of my life. At times, shame rained down on me, and other times, morbid grief filled my bones, but overall, I kept busy. I fed Phil's cats and picked up his mail and volunteered with the group that coalesced to prep his house for his return. I went to the hospital at least twice a day to advocate for him with the physical therapists and went grocery shopping so his refrigerator would be stocked when he got home. I picked up books from his office and arranged a workspace he could use lying down.

At all moments, Sarah was on my mind. Where was she now? I wondered. Her voice, her smell, seemed to float just out of sight. For all the progress of humankind over the millennia, all the new technologies, all the new science, I found it hard not to think about her soul in the most old-fashioned terms. I found myself imagining Sarah as a ghost in the sky, or a watchful presence hovering somewhere behind the colors of the world. I talked to her in my head as if she could hear me and entertained the idea that I'd meet her again someday on a cloud or in a misty alpine meadow. The world conserves its matter, I told myself. Why not its spirit, too? How could anything truly die? It only transformed in some way. So went Phil's compost thinking.

Wherever she existed, though, she was utterly inaccessible. She never answered, as much as I talked to her. It may have seemed like her essence was everywhere—infusing the pillows in her house and the waxy rhododendrons on her street—but it also was definitively not there. It was like she was locked behind some soundproof wall.

It was shocking, I thought, how life never reconciled itself to death. In the entirety of existence, life had never figured it out. How could it? The leaves returned every year, but they weren't the same leaves. The future recurred in a weird way, and resembled the past, but it wasn't the past. New people were born who looked like the old people, and echoed the old peoples' lives, but they didn't have any of the old memories. There was obviously some kind of circle in play, but it was a broken, lopsided circle, kicking dust on every previous cycle, keeping the future always out of reach. The circle of time was a cracked mandala, a rolling, oblong prison without windows.

After the accident, I didn't work on the book at all. I couldn't stand being at home, so I took walks in the hills instead. Traveling under the boughs of the incense cedars and ponderosa pines, over the cold, wet ground shining with slug trails, I thought about what I was going through, and tried to tease out all the theological ramifications. The forest was helpful, as always, in reminding me of life's natural seasons, the ebb and flow of creation and all that, but even the trees couldn't answer all my questions. If Sarah had died in a more commonplace way, without the seeming miracle involved, maybe I could have gotten over it more easily. I might have grieved naturally and accepted our fate as a sad but comprehensible turn of events. But instead the grieving was compromised. I was haunted by something I couldn't grasp.

I walked into town trying to distract myself, but the town was too small and didn't offer anything of interest. And even on the empty streets, the ghosts of Sarah were everywhere. I saw her disappearing around corners, passing in cars. I imagined her shelving periodicals in the library and buying baguettes at the bakery. I stood outside the bakery window for long minutes replaying our first polite conversations together, waiting for our numbers to come up. I visited the offices of the Barn, but that was a mistake. The rooms were so infused with her I almost collapsed.

I stood at the fence of the elementary school and watched the children playing, filled with aching desire. I'd never dreamed of fatherhood before, but now, too late, the dreams poured through me. I thought about the life we might've lived together, the mornings spent making French toast, the afternoons picking up the kids as they climbed off the bus. I thought about the little shoes and little pants our child would've worn. I wondered who their friends would've been. Watching the kids clambering on the play structure, shaking the chains of a giant metal web, I wondered if the embryo had already been growing. Was it a double murder God had done?

I was living inside two realities at once, unsure which was true. I was the one to blame yet I was not the one to blame; in either case, Sarah was gone. There'd been a child; there'd never been a child. Who could say? One thing I knew, standing there at the playground, I hated these fathers. To watch them standing there around the perimeter of the playground, thumbing their phones, was to despise them for all their inattention, their utter ignorance of their gifts. I wanted to walk over and knock the phones out of their hands. Look at your children! I wanted to yell at them. Look at your blessings! Don't you know how lucky you are? Don't you know how soon this will all be gone?

13

When Sarah's parents came to visit, Phil asked me to meet them at the airport and drive them to the hospital. It wasn't exactly how I'd imagined meeting my future in-laws, but once the request came in, I knew I couldn't refuse. It seemed almost fitting somehow, as if it fulfilled some larger pattern. My big test had come, and I'd failed it, but there were still more tests. I didn't want to fail any more of them if I could help it.

When Sarah's parents finally emerged from the terminal, they looked nothing like their reputation had led me to expect. Whatever orgies they'd enjoyed in their youths hadn't left a single mark. They were just two elderly people now, stricken and confused, blinking into the afternoon light. Sarah's father was smallish, roundish, and bald, wearing thick glasses and bright white tennis shoes. Her mother was taller, a bit gristly, with lipstick edging outside the lines of her thin lips. They looked around, almost doddering, and I waved them over. I took their bags and hoisted them into the trunk. I wanted Sarah's parents to feel well taken care of.

We drove across town in silence. I'd composed the lines I'd give them if they asked any questions, but they didn't seem to have any. They didn't care how long I'd known Sarah or how I'd met Phil. They weren't curious to learn I was a writer. They barely noticed me at all, in fact, which was probably for the best. Not that it was a contest, but I knew their grief dwarfed mine.

I drove them directly to the hospital and guided them to Phil's room, where the reunion was somber. Sarah's parents both cried when they saw him, and asked him many questions about his injuries and his projected recovery. Phil was still bedridden but off the pain meds, which meant his energy and personality had returned. He did his best to seem cheerful, but there was no way to make the meeting anything but sad. I brought everyone sparkling water and sliced melon from the cafeteria and repaired to the corner, near the cylinder of Sarah's ashes, where I waited in case they needed anything else.

Sarah's parents mostly wanted to hear about the accident, which made sense, and Phil told them his story in gruesome detail. I'd never heard the full tale myself, and I listened with fascination as he went through the chapters—driving through the desert pines, the slanting afternoon sun, the leaping buck. He talked about the spinout and the river plunge and nodding in and out of consciousness as the car filled with icy water. He talked about awakening in the speeding ambulance, heading west. I listened closely the whole time for any clues as to the conversation leading up to the crash, any notes of strife or hurt feelings, but I didn't catch anything. Mostly, I just kept hoping the story would end differently.

"It all happened so fast," Phil said, summing up. "I saw the buck out of the corner of my eye and before I knew it, it was right there, hitting us. He slammed into the passenger side and then kind of bounced over the windshield. For a second his eye was right in front of me. All the hair pressed against the glass. And then he was gone. Over the other embankment, I guess."

"And then you ran into the other car," Sarah's mom said, although we'd already gone over that part.

"That's right," Phil said. "We clipped it, just barely."

"But they stayed on the road," she said.

"They did," he said. "Thank God. They were the ones who called the ambulance. I mean, I wish they'd been able to call even faster . . . but . . . well . . . "

Sarah's mother had yet more questions to ask. She wanted to hear about the time in the water, how the passenger side nestled on the river's bed, and how the water streamed in the windows. She wanted to understand how Phil could breathe, being up higher, trapped behind the wheel, and how underneath him, Sarah was quickly covered by the water. She wanted to know everything about the horrible event, every angle and degree of torque. And after she'd comprehended the forensics, she wanted to go back and hear another version. She wanted to know about the signage on the road, the moisture, and the ice. She wanted to know about government agencies involved in road maintenance, like the Department of Transportation, and the county road crews. She wanted to squeeze every drop of mystery out of the tragedy and leave only inert objects in her wake.

"I still feel like I could've done something if I'd just been a little quicker," Phil said, almost to placate her with a new variable. "They tell you to turn into a skid but I didn't even know I was skidding. I didn't turn into it. I should have. We might have clipped them differently. I don't know."

"Don't think that way," Sarah's father said, stepping in abruptly. "It does no good to think like that, Phil."

"It's hard not to," Phil said.

"I understand," Sarah's father said, "but you did everything you could do. You must know that. We don't blame you for anything."

Phil bowed his head and closed his eyes. He took a deep breath and raised his eyes to Sarah's father. "Thank you for saying that, Christopher," he said. "I appreciate it very much." And I realized this was the judgment Phil had been waiting for.

The conversation still wasn't over. It had already been exhausting, but the biggest agenda item hadn't been covered, which was the plans for Sarah's remains. It was macabre, but it needed figuring. It turned out Sarah's parents hadn't even known she planned to be cremated until a few days earlier.

"She talked about it," Phil said. "I'm sorry you didn't know. There was no paperwork or anything. I assumed you were okay with the decision."

"It's fine," Sarah's dad said. "If that's what she wanted, then that's what she wanted. But did she say anything about where she wanted to be . . . scattered?"

"We never talked about that," Phil said. "I doubt she'd even thought about it herself."

"To be cremated, but not tell us what to do with the ashes," Sarah's mom said. "It's unfortunate."

"I've been thinking about it a lot the last few days," Phil said. "It's actually given me some comfort. Thinking about the places she loved the most. The places that really meant something to her. It's been good."

"And did you think of some place the ashes should go?" Sarah's father said.

"I have an idea, yes," Phil said. "If you'd like to hear it."

"We do," Sarah's mother said. I was curious to hear, too.

"One thought that keeps coming back," Phil said, from his bed, "is the ocean. Sarah loved the water. She loved the coast in Mendocino especially. I could see a little ceremony in the summer, maybe. Something simple. Scattering the ashes in the waves."

Sarah's parents listened stoically. For some reason, they didn't seem to find the idea very attractive.

"Or do you have a different idea?" Phil said.

They looked at each other. Sarah's mother gave their answer. "We were thinking about the Santa Cruz Mountains," she said. "That's where she went to camp as a child. She loved it there all her life. It should be a warm place, a sun-filled place. Not somewhere cold and ugly."

"I never thought of the ocean as ugly before," Phil said.

"On the bottom, it's ugly," she said. "And cold. Look how hard we worked to get out of the ocean. It took us millions of years. No one wants to go back there."

I almost had to laugh at that. It was such a thing Sarah would have said. I felt a sudden burst of love for her mother.

"Better in the mountains," her father said. "Where we can plant a tree."

Phil took the idea into himself and turned it over a few times. It was clearly something her parents wanted. I could see him negotiating with himself, wondering if he was supposed to hold a line. He was the husband, after all. He had a certain leverage in the matter. It was probably his right to decide. But why push it? he seemed to ask himself. Again, as always, he acquiesced, not out of weakness, but out of strength.

"If that makes you happy," he said, "of course."

The sun fell into the room and for a moment something like peace descended. Sarah's spirit seemed to throb in the air and offer its blessing. Then Sarah's mother began sobbing into her hands. I worried that maybe Phil had said something wrong after all, or maybe I'd done something wrong, but as it turned out, the tears were coming from another place entirely.

"We always hoped she would have children," her mother said, wiping her face with her sleeve. "We never pressured her about it, but we always hoped she would. It was a dream we had . . ."

"It wasn't what she wanted," Phil said gently. "I can tell you that. It really wasn't."

Sarah's mother nodded and continued weeping. "I know," she said. "I know. She said it to me many times. I just always hoped she'd change her mind."

"She knew her own mind," Phil said. "That was one of the beautiful things about Sarah."

"It's true," her mother said, between small gasps. "She knew her mind. And I revered her for that. I never doubted her. It's just that now . . ." She waited through another convulsion, then braced herself, knowing more were on the way. "Now, it's just so awful . . . Now, I'm just so glad there are no children."

She wailed, and shook her head, and her husband sat despondently beside her, patting her hand. I could see for a moment the enormous depths of their pain. Their daughter was dead, and now they were left to wander the world, wondering what might have been. Why had she refused to re-create their lives? Had her childhood been flawed in some way? How was it not a judgment on them, her not wanting a family? The questions would be endless and unanswerable.

In that moment, I saw I had the power to heal them a little. I could have told them that Sarah had indeed changed her mind. She'd wanted a child after all, and she and I had been on the verge of delivering one. She might even have been carrying one at the moment of her death. But I didn't say anything. It would've been too bizarre, too complicated. They barely understood why I was in the room. I didn't see how the news would do anything but confuse them. So I sat there silently, watching them weep, telling myself that if I'd been able to release them from their pain without causing a larger pain, I would have, but that I simply didn't see how.

It was three weeks after the accident that Phil was discharged from the hospital, and I was the one who took him home. A few other caretakers had offered, but I'd won the draw, having emerged as his main caretaker in the wake of the accident. I was the one who'd installed the handrails in the bathroom. I was the one who'd found the cheap hospital bed on Craigslist. I'd earned the right to ferry him from the hospital back into his life.

He didn't have a cast when he got out, only a stiff brace, though the bolts in his femur made him almost immobile. We used a wheelchair to transport him to the car and somehow laid him across the back seat. I folded the wheelchair into the trunk, which I couldn't close all the way, and then, without any particular instructions or guidance, we departed. A nurse would be visiting Phil on a regular schedule, and he'd be going to the hospital for daily physical therapy appointments, but for many hours every day, he'd be alone, sitting in a chair.

I helped him up the stairs of the house and maneuvered him

inside the front door. We'd done our best to prepare the main floor by taking away the throw rugs, putting new, bright lights in the sockets, and rearranging the furniture, but I could tell he barely noticed the improvements. He just stood there in the foyer for a long time, staring into the living room and dining room, unsure where to go. The house fairly vibrated with Sarah's memory. The smell of the wood floor, the arrangement of the fossils on the hearth, practically shouted her name. Most of all, Phil seemed disturbed by the piles of her mail. Her bills were still unpaid.

"I don't know if I was prepared for this," he said.

I helped him into the living room, where he could sit on the recliner we'd borrowed from the university. Once I got him installed, I brought him some water and his computer. I asked him if he wanted any food, but he said no. He seemed to be in shock. The nurse would be visiting in a matter of hours, but it didn't seem right to leave him alone, so I fabricated a chore and started watering the plants. I filled a Mason jar and went around the rooms, plant to plant, talking to Phil as if this were a normal visit. But in this case, the only topic of conversation was our dead lover, Sarah.

"She really had a way with plants, didn't she?" I said, drizzling water onto a wild-looking plant with burgundy leaves rimmed in bright green ruffles. "What's this? I don't know this one."

"That's a coleus," he said. "That was a real stretch for her. Usually, she only liked the simple, cheap plants at the big-box stores. She didn't like going to the fancy nursery. She was cheap that way. But that coleus. She couldn't resist. It's so outrageous. She loved it."

"And she grew vegetables, too, didn't she?" I said, moving on to a philodendron. I knew the answer to the question, but I was serving him easy topics to keep his mind occupied. If we could just talk about Sarah in the most innocuous ways, I thought, it might offer some kind of consolation for both of us.

"She grew a lot of vegetables," he said. "But mostly tomatoes. She loved a tomato. They blew her mind every time. 'Oh my God, what a tomato.' I don't know how many times she said that."

"And eggs," I said.

"She did," he said. "It's true. She loved an egg. A perfect fried egg."

"Is it true she used to not like cilantro?" I said. "She mentioned that once."

"When we first met, she hated cilantro," he said. "But she came around. She became one of the great lovers of cilantro. She couldn't believe she'd been so wrong."

I ended up staying with Phil for hours, listening to his stories about Sarah. I'd heard most of them before, but I pretended they were all new. He told me about her childhood obsession with typewriters, and the time she broke her arm doing gymnastics. He told me about her church youth group and the secret sexual liaisons among all the teens. He told me about the tragic death of her dog, Maria. All classics.

He told me some things I'd never heard, too, like the story of their honeymoon in Puerto Rico. They'd rented scooters and motored all over the island of Vieques, he said, but they'd never been able to get to the far shore because of the naval base in the middle. The amount of ordnance the US had blown up there in the twentieth century was obscene. It was a beautiful vacation, though, he said, wheeling around on those scooters in the humid air, passing all those tropical flowers. I guessed that Sarah had avoided telling me about their early romance out of kindness. But she'd said she liked mopeds, and now I knew why.

"I haven't thought about that trip in a long time," he said. "I've been thinking lately about a lot of things I hadn't thought about in a long time. I thought we had all the time in the world, you know? But no. It turns out we didn't."

"You guys had a lot of good times," I said. "You're lucky for that."

"I am lucky," he said. "I've been thinking that, too. I'm lucky for all the time we had. What else is there? She really liked you, you know."

"It was mutual," I said.

"She'd be glad to know you're helping me out, I think," he said. "That would make her really happy."

"I hope so," I said.

"I know it would," he said.

The nurse came. After dinner, I helped clean the dishes and ended up falling asleep on the couch in the library. I could see that Phil and I had been able to help each other in some way. Maybe we could help each other more if we tried. And that was when I basically started living with Phil.

14

Rumi says, "Welcome the guests, even if they are a crowd of sorrows." I had no idea what Phil thought of Rumi, that thirteenth-century Sufist so amenable to modern readers, but such was the spirit, I thought, when Phil welcomed me into his home. What exactly he was imagining by the invitation, I wasn't sure. I wasn't sure he knew himself, other than his misery seemed to need company.

I had my own sorrows, which were mostly identical to his, but slightly different, too. They included not only the loss of our shared loved one, but my own feelings of culpability in Sarah's death, which continued to nag me. Even if the command I'd disobeyed hadn't been from God, it'd come from somewhere. It might have come from my own mind, some unknown precinct where moral understanding was born, and in that, I still wondered if I'd committed some crime. I'd committed a crime against myself, perhaps, but wasn't that also a crime against creation?

I could see that my sorrows would follow me anywhere and, thus, I might as well entertain them at Phil's. Plus, more and more, I'd come to believe that our fates were bound together in some way, that

I had a karmic debt to repay. I didn't believe in the concept of sin, necessarily, not at all, but I believed in the concept of spiritual labor. Through service to Phil, I thought, I might be able to dig my way out of this hole.

I set up a space for myself in the library. It was a pleasant room even now, with all its books and its bay windows looking onto the side yard with the plum trees. When the sliding door closed it became a private little boudoir. The couch folded out, like the sleeper in the Barn, so every morning and every evening I had that mild rebuke.

I brought over a few bags of clothes, my laptop, and a handful of books. Everything else I left at my mom's house. In the morning, I would get up early and make us coffee. I'd bring Phil his cup in bed and help him to the bathroom, waiting at the door until he was done, at which point I'd help him back to bed. Sometimes we chatted for a few minutes, both of us checking the news on our phones, but overall, we were quiet in the mornings. After breakfast, a van came to take him to physical therapy, and I spent the late morning working in the dining room. I usually worked until sometime after noon, making what fractional headway I could, at which point I fixed us lunch or went into town. I'd try for another round of writing later in the afternoon, after which I cleaned up my mess and put everything back in the library. I found great comfort in work, as always. Phil gave me a key.

Evenings were our main social time. I usually made dinner while Phil rested on the couch. Sometimes we had Manhattans or Negronis, depending on the weather, but more often, a couple of beers. I'd make us a beef stew, or pasta primavera, and then I'd clean everything up afterward. Later, we often watched sports or prestige TV. We went through all of *The Sopranos* and much of *Deadwood* together.

We were drawn to stories of powerful men grappling with shameful secrets, prone to violent outbursts against enemies and loved ones alike. I'd once read a profile about two old widowers in the Midwest who'd pooled their lives much as Phil and I were doing. They'd made their trips to Walmart together, and done their chores together, and generally became each other's wives. We were a little young for that, but our arrangement wasn't so far off.

We talked often about Sarah. It was a form of therapy, I guessed, this constant worrying of our wounds. Sometimes I wondered whether it was more salt than salve, but in any case, we couldn't seem to help ourselves.

"She really hated overhead light," Phil said one night, as I turned on the table lamps around the living room. He was lying on the couch, his usual spot. The windows were almost black.

"Is that so?" I said, taking my normal seat in the wicker rocking chair.

"She actually judged people about that," he said, chuckling. "She just couldn't understand how anyone could sit in a room with an overhead light on."

"I understand that," I said. "I mean, I don't think it's a moral question, like she did. But overhead light can feel kind of clinical."

"She said it was like sitting in an operating room, exactly," he said. "I guess I don't have that feeling. I don't see overhead light as that bad."

"She never drank a single glass of water in her twenties," he said, another night, as we ate our dinner of roasted chicken and root vegetables. "Only Diet Coke. For ten years, at least. She thought diet soda was healthy. Or she convinced herself, anyway."

"I heard she smoked a lot then, too," I said.

"She was a smoker," he said. "It's true. Marlboro Lights."

"How many a day?" I said.

"Hmm. Good question," he said. "I don't remember."

Phil had the advantage on me in these conversations, having logged so much more time with Sarah than I had. He knew all her daily habits, all her quirks. He knew where she'd napped, how she'd folded the laundry. He knew how she'd put the sponge in the microwave to disinfect it. As the conversations became more in depth, with speculations about her birth in the commune and the influence of her parents' ideology on her life and personality, Phil remained the undisputed expert. She became a holy text that we studied and extracted meaning from, with Phil the priest, and I the supplicant. It was as it should have been. I didn't question him, nor did I confess my own intimacies. Quietly, in his shadow, I was working something through, but being the junior, I accepted his authority. I didn't mind. As the weaker one, I also understood more about our situation than he did in a way. It was the nature of the powerful to be ignorant.

"I could tell when she was mad about something by how she walked," he said. "She'd stomp around the house with these very firm footsteps. She wanted everyone to know she was angry."

"Did that happen a lot?" I said.

"All the time," he said. "It was subtle, though. Just a little extra energy in the stomping. And then she was over it. We'd move on."

After dinner and TV, I'd lie in bed in the library, strapped to the turning wheel of my thoughts. They were always the same. I had to explain to myself over and over again how I hadn't done anything wrong. How the events bringing me to this point were all perfectly normal, if tragic, and out of my control. I'd loved a woman, I told myself. And she'd loved me. Our love had unfortunately meant someone would get hurt, but that wasn't so odd. It was something that happened all the time, in fact. The history of love was littered with unfairness. Then the woman had died in a horrible accident. There'd never been any miracle on a mountain.

To see it from outside myself, everything looked all right. Or if not all right, at least bearable, no worse than a lot of people had it. Definitely, no one seemed to judge me in any way, not even Phil. On the contrary, everyone seemed to think of me as an admirable person. They congratulated me for moving in with Phil in his time of need. They thought I was a true Samaritan. But something still felt unsettled in me, especially at night. Some ineradicable intuition of guilt.

I'd always had trouble sleeping, but in Phil's house, the problem became much worse. My body forgot how to shut itself down. I'd lie there on the hide-a-bed for hours, waiting for sleep to come and transport me away from myself, and it never came. The waves barely lapped at the shore. I felt like I had some dam in my skull that repelled sleep's waters, some thick membrane that barred my waking self from any relief.

I remained on the lookout for signs from the universe, seeking meanings in the flight of birds, or a reflection in a glass, any indication at all that someone might still be talking to me. I hadn't given up on the idea that I'd been addressed, much as I wanted to. But had the speaker been God? I wondered. Maybe there was another God, I thought. A God behind the God on the mountain. Maybe there was a God above or below that God. If so, I wanted to talk to that God, the real God. I'd like to find my way to that God's ear.

"For by this name is signified that thing than which nothing greater can be conceived," Aquinas wrote about God. I liked that description: "than which nothing greater can be conceived." It was so ungainly, it stuck in your mouth, and yet it couldn't be phrased much better.

In those early days after Sarah's death, I found myself unable to conceive almost anything, and thus, in a way, I was surrounded by God. God was everywhere, pressed close around me, in every form of ignorance. All I couldn't conceive about Sarah, God lay there. All I couldn't conceive about Phil, God lay there, too. All I couldn't conceive about a tree: that was God. I saw Him flickering at the edges of my vision at all times, a guttering flame just outside my awareness, never speaking, never throwing light.

In turn, I became a mystery for Phil. Outside Phil's comprehension, all the secrets I held were a form of divinity over him, the source of his confusion, his daily bewilderment. As he held a mystery for me, so I held a mystery for him, and in this way, we became each other's Gods. This was possibly why we were bonded in this time. It was our mutual ignorance, our double unknowing, that kept us in orbit. The less we understood, the closer we came to God, and to each other. We were two collapsing stars, circling.

Thankfully, Phil didn't know anything about the afternoon Sarah and I had shared on the floor of his library, those wanton moments in the very room where I now slept. I was glad Phil was spared that vision. But I had it in my memory, and at night, I replayed it over and over, stroking myself, bringing myself to climax. I saw us there on the carpet, making love, as Phil lay in his bed upstairs, basting in his own fading memories, probably coupling with Sarah in his own imagination.

At night, in the library, lying on the hide-a-bed, I felt Sarah's body next to mine. I summoned her completely, catching hints of her scent, the curve of her thigh, the bend of her leg. I could taste her tongue, with its vanishing sulfur flavor. I could feel the weight of her breast in my palm. She was still vivid to me, but I knew she wouldn't be for long. She'd disappear sense by sense, stripped away, until only occasional ghost impressions came through, sparked by a song, an angle of light. In the end, I'd be left only with these wads of toilet paper, these crusted tube socks.

Sometimes during the day when Phil was gone I'd go into Sarah's closet and try to retrieve traces of her. The closet was filled with dresses and sweaters and a lifetime of shoes. It would all go to the Salvation Army eventually but so far Phil didn't have the will to part with it, and so the closet became my chapel. I stood under the naked bulb and touched the cashmere, the denim, the silken pleats of a forgotten skirt. I held a pair of canvas sailor pants she never wore. I pulled her jogging jacket off the hanger. It was so generic, this gray fabric with white piping. It seemed like a weathered, shed skin. The smell of her was almost in the weave but not exactly. I always exited the closet well before Phil came home, careful to leave everything exactly as it was.

"I don't know what to cook anymore," he said one night, staring into the refrigerator. "Everything I eat is something she made."

"What did you like to make before you knew her?" I said.

"Nothing worth eating," he said.

"We can order something," I said.

"I don't know what to order, either," he said. "She never wanted to order food."

And he heavily climbed the stairs back to his room, leaving me alone in the living room, surrounded by photographs of Sarah. There were doilies she'd made, too, and books she'd read. The objects belonged to Phil, but in time, they would have become mine. And so

Phil and I sat in our separate rooms, like two sentries, guarding the doorways to the past and the future, neither of which existed.

Work on my book stalled entirely. I was barely able to keep track of the grammar anymore. I could hold on to one sentence at a time and no more. A whole paragraph was beyond my reach. I was going days without a single minute of sleep, and my head was becoming like a block of wood. At night, lava boiled in my nerves, overflowing my chest. In the day, I lived in a darkened cave, peering out of a stone portal. My teeth started to hurt. My joints were like hardened gum. I was turning into marble.

Everyone had advice for me. They suggested melatonin, magnesium, and Chinese herbs, all of which I tried and none of which helped. I tried acupuncture, which was fine, but also didn't help. I enjoyed lying on the acupuncturist's bed in the quiet room, seeing the hairline needles sprouting out of my hands, my feet, but I never fell asleep like other people did. I could hear them snoring all around and I envied them. I found an old woman online who taught me chi gong. She had a wonderful way about her, shifting mellowly from pose to pose, so happy, so free. She opened new channels in my body. But none of it helped me sleep.

Some nights I felt like I had a succubus on my back, living off my essence. It was like a giant bug, sucking on my spinal column. I tried prying it off in my mind, digging under the lip of the shell and yanking, but there was no shell to rip away. There was no monster at all. Nothing was stuck to me. I was simply afraid to sleep because some part of me believed that sleep meant death, and my whole life had become a form of vigilance against going under.

Increasingly, I came to think my insomnia foretold something even worse. "Hell is training," Suzuki said, in which case the hellish insomnia I was experiencing was practice for more hell, a worse hell. It was my body understanding that whatever had touched my life that day on the mountain was still waiting for me out there. It was a giant wheel turning, a giant clock waiting to strike. My punishment was lurking on the horizon, and as sure as the sun would rise, it would find me.

At night I lay in bed, turning over every minute or two, mashing my pillow into different shapes. Every sound gave me a fright. Every change of perception seemed like a trapdoor into a void. Even a creaking branch or a passing car caused a little splash of adrenaline. I was afraid every second might spin out and explode. I never went to church or temple, but tried in my own way to invite the creator back into my life. I wasn't sure how to address the spirit, or even how to imagine it, but I tried gently asking it questions, politely making it new offers. But the line never opened. The jewel of pure intention never formed. And thus, the divine hand never came back down to take it. I'd been cast out.

One day, to avoid my desk, I drove to the crash site. It was a three-hour drive, through beautiful, rugged terrain, exactly the kind of dull pilgrimage I needed. The landscape unfolded in slow chapters, morphing gradually from savannah to foothills to evergreen forest, the trees gathering snow as they climbed to the pass, and losing the snow as the road descended into the brown, arid countryside of the high plains. The mountains receded and I kept going, farther east.

I finally came to the spot, a blind curve in a wooded flatland. Burnt flares were still scattered on the road and the crumpled guardrail was still unrepaired. I continued on to a turnoff a half-mile up the highway and parked and walked the shoulder back to the bend, the occasional car or truck whooshing by, shaking the air. At the turn, I could follow the skid marks to the broken guardrail and track the mangled path down to the water.

I climbed down the embankment of shale and stood on the rocky shore. All evidence of the crash was gone. The river had cleansed itself of debris, the fast winter waters sweeping everything away. The only litter on the shore were a few beer cans, an abandoned fishing fly. I walked to the river's edge and dipped my fingers into the icy flow. The rocky bed rippled and tore under the current. How incredibly stupid, I thought, to survive a fire only to drown in a river. Who'd authored that story, anyway?

The story could have gone so many other ways. The author could have led me to obey His command. It would've been hard to explain my reasoning to Sarah, but I could have done it. She might have gone on and lived a long, satisfying life somewhere. I might have met another woman. Over time, our love might have receded into memory, and one day we might have bumped into each other in a bookstore in some European city. We might have shown each other pictures of our kids.

Or maybe the story would've been even better than that. Maybe, if only I'd had enough patience, God would have released us from the covenant. He would have returned us to each other's sides, whole, without doubt, and blessed us with healthy babies. They would have grown up and had children of their own, on a planet that somehow survived. We might have gone on and lived long lives in a ranch house in Northern California, still friendly with Phil, who might have found new love himself, and prospered. There were a million ways it could have unfolded, every version better than the draft we'd been given.

The more I thought about the alternate fates, however, the more I realized the whole question was becoming too abstract. It was becoming a mere intellectual premise, without any emotion attached. I was healing, in other words, or maybe moving on. And what did that make me? A person who'd sacrificed my lover for nothing.

I got home after dark, and Phil was in the kitchen. He called out as soon as I walked in the door.

"I was getting worried!" he said.

"Sorry," I said, putting away my keys and wallet. "I should've called, I guess."

"I wasn't that worried," he said. "I could have called you, too."

I went into the kitchen to find Phil sitting at the island, his leg resting on the stool beside him. On the floor was a spill of dry flour. A blue plastic bowl was overturned near the cat door. The light was on, glaring down.

"I couldn't clean it," he said. "Sorry. All the bending and getting up. I was trying to make cookies. The bowl fell."

"No worries," I said, and went to the slot behind the refrigerator where we kept the broom and dustpan. It was funny how Phil could manage to do so many things, and yet not sweep the floor. I didn't mind. I did all the cleaning in the house. It was part of my job.

"So what did you do today?" he said.

"I took a drive," I said, as a little berm of flour formed. There was enough flour on the floor that the sweeping would take a few passes. Thankfully, he hadn't added the eggs or butter yet.

"Where to?" he said.

"Over the mountains," I said.

"Oh?" he said. "How far?"

"I actually went to where you and Sarah had the crash," I said, dropping the first load of dirty flour into the garbage can. "I wanted to see it for myself."

"Why?" he said.

"I don't know," I said. "I was just curious to see it, I guess."

"And how was it?" he said.

"Unremarkable."

"Everything is always changing, isn't it?" he said. "Always becoming something else, constantly on the move. I'm not surprised nothing was out there anymore."

I didn't respond. I found Phil's wisdom irritating. I was getting tired of all his faith and groundedness. It was all so predictable.

"How are you getting through this, anyway, Arthur?" he said, watching me sweep near the baseboard. "I don't feel like we talk about your feelings very much. I know it's hard for you, too. I know you've been dealing with a lot. You have your own share of grief in all this."

"I like being helpful," I said hollowly. "It makes it all a little easier to bear."

"Sarah had a lot of affection for you, you know," he said.

"I know she did," I said.

"You've been a tremendous help to me," he said. "If I haven't said it already, I'm incredibly thankful you're here. Every day."

"I'm glad," I said, without feeling. "And I'm sorry. About everything."

"You have nothing to be sorry about, Arthur," he said.

"I do, actually," I said. "A lot."

"You have nothing to be sorry about," he said firmly, and in that moment, I could tell we had passed into a new region. Something in his tone told me that he was responding to the truth of what I was saying, and that he knew everything. We'd shifted into a realm of openness at last. Openness, at an oblique angle, anyway.

"She told you," I said.

"She told me enough," he said. "Everything she needed to tell me. I didn't need all the details. I'm sure there are things I don't know."

"But you haven't said anything," I said.

"What is there to say?" he said. "I assumed we'd talk about it when we were ready."

"We never meant to hurt you," I said. "I hope she told you that."

"Of course you didn't," he said. "She didn't have to."

"And I'm sorry for all the pain I've caused," I said.

"You didn't cause anything," he said.

"If we hadn't been doing what we were doing, though," I said, standing and emptying the dustpan again, "you never would've been out on that road. She'd still be here now." With me, I didn't add.

"You can't really know that," he said. "The accident might have happened anyway. There's no one to blame. That's all I know for sure."

I hated the way he refused my apologies. By his way of thinking, nothing was ever wrong, and thus nothing could ever be made right again. After all that'd happened, all I'd done, he wouldn't even admit that a sin had occurred.

"It was important for me to go there today," I said, kneeling again to sweep the flour I'd missed. "I know you understand this on some level, but it wasn't a small thing going on between us."

"I don't doubt that," he said.

"She was going to leave you," I said.

"I know that," he said. "She told me as much."

It was intolerable. Phil refused to acknowledge any problem. He didn't believe that true love sometimes demanded a violent cutting away. I ached for his forgiveness, but he wouldn't give it to me because he wouldn't ever accept my guilt. I couldn't stand how he refused to hate me.

"We were planning to have a child together," I said.

"Is that so?" he said.

He hadn't heard that before. I could tell the truth was touching a new place in him. I let it burrow down into his nerves.

"You loved each other very much, I have no question," he said, already incorporating the new fact into his cosmology. "We loved each other, too. It might have been different than yours. It wasn't so . . . torrid. But was it less? I don't know. I don't know."

"I don't know, either," I said, already feeling my taste for blood receding. He seemed so sad and dissolute, sitting in the kitchen with his broken femur. I thought about revealing the whole, flaming contract with the Almighty and confessing how I'd sundered it to all of our great suffering, but what was the point? What could it possibly change?

"I think we had some of that kind of love," he said wistfully. "Back at the start. And then we settled into our lives. We were building our lives on something else, I suppose. I don't know if that can make sense to you."

"I think it does," I said.

"Love is time," he said, almost apologetically, like he'd hoped to avoid this truism. "That's what I've come to think. Love grows very slowly. The movies make you think it's all at the beginning. But that's just sex, as far as I'm concerned. It's great, but it isn't love, not exactly."

I put away the broom and dustpan and started for my room. I had nothing else to say. The floor was clean.

"I'm sorry for all of us," Phil said as I walked down the hall. "We both lost her too soon. What else is there to know?"

That night I couldn't sleep, not for a minute. I lay in bed listening to the sound of a faraway dog barking, the swell of a passing electric car. I heard a train chugging through town, going slowly through the empty intersections. Light from the streetlamp branded the wall. I lay there for hours, getting nowhere.

Had we ever loved each other? Now I had to wonder that, too. Or had it only been lust? Somehow, without trying, Phil had won yet again. He'd shamed me, opened all my wounds. Sarah and I had never had the chance to love, not in the truest, most committed sense. We'd had a juvenile precursor to love, unseasoned by any experience. We'd had nothing, in other words. It turned out not only did I not believe in God, I didn't believe in our love, either.

At last, I got up and went into the bathroom, feeling muddled and bleak. My circuits were shorting out, my connections blinking. I flicked on the light and squinted at the bright toilet bowl and stood there waiting for the stream to come.

I'd just started to pee when out of nowhere Phil entered the room. He had his own bathroom upstairs and almost never came down in the night. I didn't know what to think. He wasn't usually even awake at this hour. I assumed he needed something in the medicine cabinet, but I didn't say anything. I only watched him out of the corner of my eye as he puttered around, searching for whatever he was looking for. I couldn't tell exactly what he was doing, but his presence was incredibly vivid.

Then I noticed he had a baby in his arms. The baby started crying, and he bobbed it up and down. Then the baby started vomiting on the floor. The baby was sick, I saw. Its skin was a nauseous greenish blue. "Are you real?" I tried to utter, but the words wouldn't form in my throat. I couldn't seem to look directly at Phil or the baby, even as the wailing got louder and more tortured. I finished peeing and backed my way out of the room, keeping my eyes on the ground, Phil and the baby just blurs in my peripheral vision.

I crept into my room and sat on the bed, terrified. I wasn't sure what was going on. I wasn't sure if I'd actually left the bedroom and gone to the bathroom, or if I'd been in bed the whole time. I checked my underwear to see if I'd peed in my pants but I hadn't. At what point had I exited reality? And had I returned yet, or not?

I was climbing back into bed when I looked up and saw a figure out in the living room. It was coming my way. It wasn't Phil this time. It was Sarah. I could see her out there in the shadows, shimmying back and forth, with a weird smile on her face. There was something demented in her eyes. She didn't seem to see me, but she was moving closer, her hips swaying. I knew on some level that she was not real, but nothing in my physical senses told me as such. She seemed incredibly real, so much that I couldn't look away. The fear of her had me paralyzed.

Sarah approached the doorway. She was still smiling, still swaying, and then, gracefully, she turned around. As her body revolved, I realized she had another face on the back of her head. It was her own face again, smiling like the other face. She had two faces, and as she kept spinning, each face appeared in a slow rotation, eyes closed in the same delirious state.

I climbed under the covers to hide like a child. I had no idea if minutes or seconds passed, or how much time had gone by during this whole episode. Maybe it was all unfolding in real time, or maybe it had all happened in a fragment of sleep, I couldn't tell. Maybe this was a dream I was having, or maybe the waking hallucination of sleep deprivation. Or maybe I'd fallen into the actual reality underneath my life. Maybe this was what I'd been deserving all along, the nightmare I'd been sentenced to.

When I finally peeked again, the double-faced Sarah was gone. The living room was empty. Beyond the doorway, only the arm of the couch and the frond of a fern waited. I was awake to see the sun rise.

15

Time rolled on. Or flowed. Or rose. Or fell. Or what? Maybe it expanded in globe after globe like the ringing of bells at the center of the universe. Not to sound like an idiot, but what is time, anyway? We see its effects every day all around us. We see it in the mirror, lining our faces and shrinking our bones. We see it desiccating our fruit, jacking up our skylines. But what is it that makes these changes happen? Does time cause the changes? Or does it only bear witness? Who knows?

In any case, over the next months, the Tree Book got done. I don't know exactly how, but one day I called it good and sent the draft in to my editor and my editor was pleased. She said she was pleased, anyway. Editors are experts at making writers feel okay about their work, even special if the case demands it. But the way she said it this time, I believed her. In the end, I always did.

"I think it's an important book," she said.

"You're kind to say that," I said.

"I'm serious," she said. "I wouldn't say it if I didn't think it was true."

"Okay, okay," I said. "It's great, I believe you."

She said she had a few small edits to suggest, which turned out to be quite significant edits, and which were also extremely smart, elegant, helpful edits. She pushed me to simplify the language in certain passages, to extend certain metaphors, to consider some counterexamples. She didn't advise any structural changes, but her notes ended up touching almost every paragraph. I had to climb back into the bramble of the writing, burrow underneath the surface like a mole, but this time, with a guide along, it became easier.

It took about three months of back-and-forth, during which time the days lightened. It became spring and then summer again. The dogwoods turned pink, and then green, and the magnolia blossoms opened and fell. Cherry petals filled the street's gutters like fuchsia snow. There was a certain tree that astounded me, every year an eruption of seedpods. It was a golden rain tree, I discovered.

My sleep was still fragile, but I fell into a pattern of a night on, a night off. I was prescribed an antidepressant, which made even the bad nights more tolerable. In some ways, the passage of time was a curse, I thought, sealing us from the past, but in other ways, it was a blessing, allowing us to forget, which was also to heal. I wasn't the first one to discover this notion, but it was a fact.

The more time that passed, the less I thought about the miracle. I came gradually to classify the crash that followed as a tragic but random event, no more significant than any other accident, which was to say profoundly significant to those involved, but not meaningful in any larger, theological sense. Much as my edits were smoothing my book, time was smoothing the events in my mind, knitting Sarah's death into the larger sequence of my life. The communication on the mountain was a remarkable illusion I'd experienced.

"You slept okay?" Phil said, over coffee one morning.

"Adequately," I said.

"Are you going to the store today?" he said.

"I can," I said. "Do we need anything?"

"We could use milk," he said. "No big deal. I can stop on the way home, too."

Our lives were becoming routine. Our respective griefs still waxed and waned, going in and out of phase, but we were both getting stronger. There were weeks when Phil had trouble climbing out of bed, and days I fell into a stupor, but together we slogged along. Whether we were helpful to each other was hard to tell, but at least we witnessed each other, and that was something. Maybe there was no real helping either one of us, anyway. We simply had to live through it.

"I thought I was a pretty experienced person," Phil said one night, sipping a gin and tonic, watching the *News Hour*. "I thought I had a pretty solid idea of what suffering was like. I've been through some things in my life. But I had no idea what was out there, Arthur. There are oceans that I never understood existed. It makes me realize I don't know anything at all, really. I'm barely starting to map it."

"Better hurry up," I said. "Not much time left."

We both laughed.

The book went to copy editing. The manuscript came back filled with red marks and I made the necessary changes, accepting most, quibbling with a few. Following the next round, I signed off and the final wait began—nine months until the book was printed and bound and entered the world as a commodity. In that window, it lived as an object of pure potential, undefined, and thus redolent with hope.

Traditionally, this was the most enchanted passage of the

publishing process. The hard work was over and all was possibility. No one had read the book yet, and thus, in theory, everyone in the world might love it. But this time around, the floating, optimistic sensation was troubled. The thoughts of Sarah, and all that might have been, still ate at me. And then there was Phil, who still needed to read it.

I'd come to love the Tree Book when I read it to myself. I could open to any page and find the rhythms pleasing, the transitions graceful. The prose had a sinuous, loping quality, at least in my mind, but when I read it through Phil's eyes, something became clouded. Throughout all the revisions, all the reconfigurations, his voice had remained intact. It wasn't everywhere, but it was present in the most important sections—his metaphors, his phrasings—to the point where at least between he and I, the debt was self-evident. The title alone, *A Leaf Is Not Green*, was more than homage. I'd been telling myself I'd fix those passages as I went along, make some alterations to obscure the source, but somehow I'd never gotten around to it. I'd never been able to find better ways of saying anything, and thus, the undigested bits had never been digested. Reading them now, so late in the game, I was haunted by Phil's intelligence. To think of Phil reading the book brought on a vague dread.

The galleys arrived six months before publication. This usually marked the ultimate high point of the experience. To see the sentences typeset on actual paper! To smell the ink sunk into the pulpy fiber. To feel the crisp edges of the perfect binding. It always dignified the writing in ways one didn't expect. It was a physical book now.

But this time, even as I fondled the fresh-cut paper and smelled the glue, the experience was vexed. I knew I couldn't put it off any longer. Phil had to read it.

I left a copy on his bed without any instructions. I didn't want to lead him in any direction. I wanted to allow him his own experience with the text, inasmuch as that was possible. I figured I'd give him a few days. It wasn't a very long read.

The wait became a marathon of self-reflection. As I ate lunch, as I walked the streets, I had to admit to myself, over and over again, that I'd taken everything from Phil. I'd taken not only his wife, but the memory of his wife. When Phil thought of Sarah now, he was forced to relive those final, unhappy hours in the car, learning their life together had been a lie. He had to understand their love had dissolved and she'd chosen to move on. He had to wonder about his own inadequacies. At least I'd wonder if I were him.

And I'd taken his very thoughts. The evidence was in his hands even as I wandered the park or browsed the stationery store. Were he ever to publish a book of his own, he'd be second in line now. My book would forever eclipse his. His theories about tree sentience and photosynthesis now lived under my name.

I could imagine him telling the story to some confidant someday, how I'd arrived in his office as a friend, full of kindness, seeking advice, only to transform into a demon, a vampire who'd come and sucked his life dry. Maybe he'd post insulting revelations on the web about me and ruin my name. He might even threaten to sue me.

Sitting in the park, watching the merry-go-round spin, I turned over my crimes in my head, wondering where they fell in the grand scheme. To steal a wife? I thought. No wife is ever stolen. A wife is a person, with her own agency, her own desire. She chooses when to leave or stay. And to steal an idea? What was an idea? An idea had no mass, no measure. Phil's ideas had simply resonated with me. I'd recognized in them something I'd already known. I'd never claimed them as my property or excluded anyone else from having them. I'd thanked him profusely in the acknowledgments. I barely thought of myself as a person, anyway.

I walked into the bookstore and browsed the season's new titles, seeking consolation in all the other books on the shelves similarly built on stolen goods. Here were novels based on real fathers, real wives, real neighbors. Here were books exploiting the misfortune of entire nations. Here were books clearly drafting on other books' obsessions and structures. Here were covers aping the covers of huge bestsellers. But in the end, the bookstore didn't offer any comfort. If anything it only made me feel worse. Pity the writer in a bookstore, surrounded by all the more successful books than their own. All the covers embossed with gold-foil awards, the anthologies filled with other writers' names. I couldn't enjoy a bookstore anymore. Long ago, I'd become a professional.

I was sitting in the living room after dinner one night, drinking whiskey, when Phil came down the stairs holding the Tree Book. The look on his face was unclear. His leg still made the descent awkward, and his expression was mostly one of physical concentration. Each step demanded both feet on the platform. I envisioned him reaching the bottom of the stairs and walking directly over and punching me in the face, but instead he hobbled to the kitchen and poured himself a whiskey. I could hear the ice crack in the tray. He came back into the living room, smiling peaceably.

"It's wonderful," he said, taking an armchair across the room, placing my book on the coffee table. "You've done something special with this one, Arthur."

"You can be honest," I said. "You don't have to be nice."

"I'm not lying," he said. "I think it might be your best one yet. It's masterful. The section on Merle and Candy especially. They'll be so happy when they read it. I can't wait for that."

"Masterful" was a word reviewers used to mean "competent." But Phil wasn't that cynical. He wasn't offering double meanings or coded insults. Of course he would lie. Everyone would lie, confronted by the author of a book they didn't like. It was the only decent thing to do. But even if I couldn't wholly believe Phil, I was beginning to relax. He wasn't violently angry. Having assumed the worst, and seeing now that the worst wasn't happening, I wanted more. I wanted praise. False or true, it didn't matter.

"You're all over it," I said. "You can see that, I assume."

"I guess so," he said. "In which case, I'm flattered, truly."

"I used a lot of your ideas, your phrasings," I said.

"They aren't my ideas," he said. "I keep telling you that. Ideas all come from somewhere. They came to me from somewhere else, too."

"They seem to come to you pretty easily," I said.

"But they don't come from inside me, that's the thing," he said. "They all come from outside, in the world. They impress themselves on you. We're just like the paper the ideas are written on. We aren't the hand doing the writing. Are we?"

"Well, I guess some people are better paper than others," I said.

"In all seriousness," he said, "I'm honored that you found something in our conversations that inspired you. And thank you for the dedication."

"You're welcome," I said. But something in the transaction seemed wrong. He'd twisted it up again. Somehow, yet again, he'd flipped me into the position of authority, acceptor of gratitude. I'd become the giver, him the receiver of the generosity. He'd made me the opposite of a thief.

"You're not interested in writing your own book about trees?" I said. "Tree dreams? This book might make it a little harder for you."

"There are a lot of books out there about trees," he said. "It's all in the style, anyway. You have a very fluid style, Arthur. I'd read anything you wrote. The world doesn't need more academic books about trees, anyway. I'll leave that to someone else. I have my hands full teaching."

"You have important things to say," I said.

He sat quietly, faintly smiling. "I just don't feel the need," he said.

His maturity was galling. He was so capacious, so deep. Was he telling me the truth? I wondered. I wasn't sure. This might be yet another punishment he'd devised. He was roasting me in the fire of his kindness, branding me with his red-hot poker of forgiveness. Did he see me as such a deluded idiot that I wasn't even worth confronting? I'd stolen his entire life, and yet he carried no grudge. He didn't even seem to notice. I imagined him laughing at me, or even worse, shaking his head in pity. I wanted to talk to Sarah but she was nowhere to be found.

That was the day I started writing this book, the book about Sarah, and Phil, and me, and what happened. Who is it for, exactly? I don't know. I didn't know then and I still don't know, even as I'm coming to the very end. l know who this book isn't for. It isn't for Sarah, that much is obvious. If she could read it, I'd be living in a different world, changing diapers somewhere in the sun. It isn't for Phil, either, as he lived the whole story alongside me. There's nothing in here that he doesn't already know, nothing that would bring him to care any more about the fact I betrayed him, which is not at all.

Maybe it's a book for me, a way to reach a deeper understanding of who I am, and how I should feel about everything I've done. Maybe this book is a method to get myself to sleep. Maybe it's for the children I may or may not ever have.

Or maybe I'll never know who the real audience is. Maybe it isn't for anyone at all. Does a writer ever truly know their readers? I don't think so. The whole idea of a book is predicated precisely on the writer not being there at the end. A book exists wholly to facilitate this absence. As meaning becomes portable, the writer is able to disappear, leaving the book as their surrogate. How strange it would be if I were standing there watching you reading these words. How deeply no one would like that.

The Tree Book was a fall publication, which is traditionally the most prestigious season. Fall was the time when the heavy hitters launched, the Deepak Chopras and James Redfields. The hardcovers were beautiful when they came, chlorophyll green, with embossed golden veins running across the jackets like lace. The book was dedicated to Phil and Sarah, each on their own line.

I had a reading at the local bookstore in Ashland, as I did for every new book. Only three years had passed since the publication of the Light Book, which for me was a short turnaround. I was probably oversaturating the marketplace, sending my book onto shelves already clogged with my own remainders, but what could you do? The timing was never ideal. Here at home, anyway, I could always count on enough people coming out to fill the seats.

I got there early, and helped Jane, the owner, unfold the chairs.

The usual digeridoo music played softly on a boom box near the register. Cars passed quietly outside.

"Sorry about your mom's house," Jane said. "Those people. Such a crime."

My mom had sold the house. The new owners had promised her they wouldn't change anything, said they loved the house exactly as it was, but of course, as soon as they'd taken possession, they'd knocked it down and built themselves a McMansion. It was the kind of thing one expected from people with that kind of money. We should've known.

"They just wanted the view, I guess," I said.

"It's a shame," she said. "That house was so beautiful. I can't even walk on your street anymore. Where did all your mom's work go?"

"Storage," I said. "She's taking offers for her archives now. It'll end up somewhere."

"And what are you working on, Arthur?" she said. "May I ask?"

"Too early to say," I said.

She knew enough not to press any further.

Soon, the regular crowd assembled. There were Barn people, childhood people, my friends Jerry and Lisa and their kids. Phil was there, too, sitting in the back, a fresh copy of the Tree Book in his lap. He was buying a copy even though he had the advance galley at home, which was to say, he understood the ritual. This was a shakedown.

When the time came, Jane rose and did her introduction. She went all out, naming all my regional awards and reciting my most potent blurbs. Here he is, she said. Our prodigal son, who wandered afar and came back home to roost.

I went to the podium. The audience's eyes were soft and warm, their smiles fixed. They were all proud of me for my accomplishments, small as they were. There was nothing I could do that would make them disappointed or angry.

I'd moved out of Phil's house into an apartment downtown, both of us understanding the time had come for me to go. I'd begun looking at listings in other states. I had friends in Seattle and San Diego who thought I should try out their towns. Depending on the teaching gigs I could drum up, my decision could still go in various directions. Regardless, I was ready for new landscapes.

In the afternoons, I walked in the woods and noted the newly fallen snags, the fresh burrows, and the abandoned nests of the paper wasps. I saw the fruiting bodies of the fungi inside the trees, and the many holes and cavities in the bark left by the woodpeckers. I joked with the trees sometimes. I imagined them sending out desperate missives to the solar system, seeking help against humanity. They were trying to contact extraterrestrials to come defend them. Don't blame me, I said. I wrote you a book.

One day, I came to a persimmon tree with some old fruit left on the higher branches. Even deep into the fall, the persimmons seemed to glow from inside, emanating some inner light. On one branch, a robin was eating from a broken persimmon, gorging itself. The persimmon was like a split-open sun, orange bits falling from the robin's beak with each take. I watched the feast until a hunk refused to come clean and the robin lost its balance, flapping off to another branch. The bird sat there, looking around. It had no idea how to find its way back.

The Tree Book ended up doing decently well. The reviews were not rapturous, but not bad, either. It was an adequate outing, a little better than average, leaving the door open for another book, which was all I could ask. Had the book been more successful, I might have drawn some correlation between my sins and my success, but the equation didn't hold. I couldn't say I'd made any great subconscious deal with a devil. Cause and effect remained obscure, as ever.

The anniversary of Sarah's death approached and I thought about driving to the Wy'East Lodge and visiting the scene of the miracle. I also thought about visiting the site of the crash. But both places seemed a little morbid. I preferred instead to commemorate her life by visiting a place we'd been happy together, a time when we'd both felt blessed. I decided to pay a visit to Candy and Merle's meadow.

I drove the highway I'd driven with Phil and Sarah once again, over the Siskiyou Pass, into northernmost California. The trees were covered in snow from an early freeze, and soon the base of Mount Shasta appeared, the peak hidden in a low, hanging belly of clouds. I headed off the highway and began climbing the foothills.

I parked at the edge of the meadow and clambered up onto the airy expanse. The snow was a perfect field of whiteness, the silence immaculate. Again, the clouds were breaking apart in the sky, becoming giant pillows, pregnant with light. I trudged across the blank meadow, leaving a delicate wreckage of footprints.

I found the spot where we'd listened to the trees drinking, or I was pretty sure it was the place. It was hard to tell with all the snow on the ground. I wondered how the meadow was doing under there, how healthy everything looked. I assumed the seeds were kindling, the shoots preparing themselves to stiffen and grow. In spring, the grasses would return, the yarrow and the Scotch broom coming back into bloom. What a system, I thought, so fragile and yet so indomitable.

My thoughts turned to Sarah, as I made an effort to remember her in full. I thought about her voice, her skin, her eyes. I summoned all of her being the best I could, though I was a little chaste in my imagining. For a moment, I felt like she was almost there with me, standing in the meadow, or maybe watching from above. I could detect her ongoing love and forgiveness in the air, or if not forgiveness, her understanding. She possessed a magnanimous understanding of the world now, I assumed, so wide it almost precluded me. I was only one small part of her consciousness anymore, a tiny piece of the ongoing life of the mountain.

For a moment I felt like I became the mountain. I felt the heavy clouds coiling around my flanks, mist rising off my forests. I felt blizzards and long spells of sun and salmon spawning on my back and birds making their nests in my branches. And then, as quickly as it came on, it was over.

When I opened my eyes, the sun was just breaking through the clouds and raining down onto the snow. The world turned into a burning sheet of whiteness. I couldn't see anything as the light ricocheted on the icy ground, into my retinas, pressing fossilized silhouettes of the trees into my mind.

I loved you, I thought. I love you still. I'll never stop loving you, my dear.

And then the world dimmed, leaving only afterimages on my eyes.